COURT OF BLADES

KINGDOM OF CHAINS BOOK TWO

TANYA BIRD

CHAPTER 1

a chill settled in Brock Tatum's bones as he dismounted his horse and looked up at the imposing keep at Dinefwr Castle. The stone walls were washed in orange light cast by burning torches. The dark clouds above seemed to bow in reverence, as if they knew what had occurred inside.

It was a rather cliché setting for a murder.

Handing the reins to the waiting groom, Tatum drew a long breath and headed up the path towards the inner-ward, gravel crunching underfoot. His gaze swung to the English flag flapping angrily above, then to the guard at the chamber rooms' entrance up ahead. The man ran his eyes over the defender's uniform, then nodded once.

Tatum entered the dark corridor, the smell of blood greeting him. Copper and iron. Sweet and sickly.

Familiar.

He headed towards the open door at the end, where soft light and hushed voices drifted out. When he stepped inside the bedchamber, his eyes went to the corpse laid out on the bed. The Earl of Cornwall was dead. Even from that distance, Tatum could see a bloodied slash across his throat. On one side of the bed stood a sombre-looking Lord Wybert and on the other side a priest. Wybert glanced in his direction, and the men exchanged a silent greeting before the duke returned his attention to the priest.

Tatum looked around for his men and found Kelton Alveye and Nixon Hadewaye standing in the corner of the room, brows slightly furrowed and lips pressed tightly together. He walked over to join them.

'Where were you?' Hadewaye whispered when he came to a stop next to them.

He had been naked in a warm bed with his favourite silk-weaver. She was a pretty thing with an infectious laugh. He loved to make her laugh, and the fact that she was easily amused meant he always left with an inflated ego. 'I had business in Llanddeilo.'

Alveye rolled his eyes. 'Was that business a curvaceous blonde with a husband who's currently away on a ship delivering silk?'

Hadewaye frowned. 'She's *married*?'

Tatum quietly cleared his throat. 'This is a very shocking, and brand-new, revelation. I'll be sure to raise the subject with her tonight.'

Alveye shook his head. 'Optimistic. When the warden learns of the earl's death, he's going to call us all back to Chadora and skin us alive.'

Tatum winced. 'What do we know so far?'

Alveye brushed a hand over his cropped rust-coloured hair. 'I guess someone wanted to send a clear message to King Edward about who is and isn't welcome here.'

'A rather personal one,' Hadewaye added. 'This kingdom's going to end up fighting a war they aren't ready for if they keep this up.' His voice was thick with fatigue.

They watched as Father Amlyn brought a hand to his nose, gaining control of his senses before making the sign of the cross. This was known as a *bad death* because the earl had passed away unprepared, with no confession of his sins or last rites. This could earn him a spot in purgatory or even hell, according to his beliefs.

'Four English noblemen dead within twelve months,' Alveye said with a heavy breath.

Hadewaye glanced at him. 'And we may be training the killers.'

'More likely peasantry,' Tatum said. Though he had to admit, it did not paint a very good picture of the work underway in the newly defined kingdom of Carmarthenshire. It had been twelve months since the English were driven out, but the wounds left by them were still painfully raw for some.

'Amen,' Lord Wybert said when the priest concluded his final prayer.

Hadewaye made the sign of the cross, prompting Alveye to flick his ear. 'You're not Catholic.'

Hadewaye threw his elbow into the defender's side. 'I was being respectful.'

A stern-faced Tatum nodded to the door, and the three of them quietly exited the room. They had barely made it out into the corridor when Lord Wybert stopped them.

'Commander.'

Tatum moved away from the door, then waited for the young duke to reach him. He was an imposing sort of man with a calm persona and confident stride. 'I'm sorry for your loss, my lord. I know the two of you were close.'

Wybert bowed his head in a gesture of appreciation. 'He was a good man and loyal friend.' A beat of respectful silence passed. 'I shall be leaving for England in the morning to meet with King Edward. I am certain he will have questions.'

'We're working hard to find out who's behind these attacks,' Alveye said.

Wybert nodded. 'I appreciate that. We must keep Dinefwr Castle open for trade purposes. Many back home are dependent on the grain, and Carmarthenshire still needs iron.'

The kingdom was mostly self-sufficient. Iron was the only thing it needed brought in, while England was reliant on the region for copper, silver, *and* grain. The only reason the Carmarthen Militia had agreed to the deal was for weapon production. Weapons that would be used *against* England if the relationship soured.

'Is that wise given what's happening here?' Tatum asked. 'Perhaps you should consider closing Dinefwr until we can guarantee the safety of its occupants.'

Wybert looked between the three of them, eyebrows raised. 'Dinefwr is the only English-occupied castle in the kingdom. Closing it would halt trade.'

The lord owned one of the largest iron mines in Gloucestershire and therefore had the most to lose.

'Maybe that's not a bad thing.' Hadewaye gestured to

the room where the body was. 'Honestly, I'll be surprised if this news doesn't trigger a war. The king will be—'

'Let me handle the king,' Wybert replied. 'He is not one to put his own grief before the welfare of his people.'

That was a relief to hear, because a war would be disastrous for everyone involved, regardless of the outcome.

'I might have a solution,' Wybert said.

The three defenders waited for him to continue.

Wybert leaned in. 'What if we were to bring in welcomed occupants?'

Tatum crossed his arms. 'Meaning?'

'Meaning, what if Dinefwr Castle were occupied by *Welsh* nobility?'

Tatum glanced at the others to see if they were as confused as he was. 'A sound plan except for the fact that every noble family is either dead or still hiding in the north. The only Welsh people around these parts are the peasantry who were too stubborn to die.'

Wybert clapped his hands together as though deciding something. 'Leave it with me. I think I have a solution that will suit everyone.' His gaze locked on Tatum's once more. 'I need your assistance in keeping Dinefwr Castle secure until I return.'

The entitlement was exhausting. 'Our orders come from Chadora, my lord. We'll continue supporting the Carmarthen Militia until the warden tells us otherwise.'

Wybert appeared unfazed by the gentle rejection. 'Then I shall write to him personally.'

Of course you will.

Wybert clapped him on the shoulder. 'We are all so

fortunate to have Chadora's support through this transition.' He stepped past the defenders and strode away.

The three defenders watched him until he was out of sight.

'So… what did we just agree to?' Hadewaye asked.

Tatum glanced in his direction. 'Anything he wants, apparently.' He released a noisy breath. 'Let's go. We've a killer to find.'

CHAPTER 2

Charlotte stood with a paintbrush in hand and eyes fixed on the grey horizon. Her brother was seated on a wool blanket with the dog beside him, his face turned up to the sky.

'I smell rain,' he announced.

Charlotte touched her brush to the wooden board depicting the scenery before her. 'It is definitely on the way.'

Oliver turned his head in her direction. 'What does it look like today?'

She studied the bleak view. 'It looks like... the sadness one carries in their chest. Heavy and dreary.'

Oliver reached out to pet the oversized brown-and-black dog who was keenly watching their surroundings. Sir Miles took his role as guide and guard dog *very* seriously. 'And yet it tastes clean and invigorating.'

She suppressed a smile. 'Further confirmation that sight is quite overrated.'

Her brother had been born blind a few years before

her own dramatic entrance into the world, which left them both without a mother. Their priest had once told her that Oliver's blindness was atonement for her mother's past sins—it was *always* the mother's fault—and the price for getting a healthy child had been her life. Charlotte's faith in God waned after that conversation. Though coincidentally, it returned when the man dropped dead from heart failure a few months later.

'Are you cold?' Oliver asked.

She was covered in goose bumps but not ready to return inside. 'A little.'

'I have trouble gauging the temperature when Sir Miles is pressed up against me like a heated stone.'

The dog was ideal company in the cold months and suffocating in the summer.

Charlotte looked down at the animal, a string of drool hanging from his mouth. 'He has gained a little weight, which probably is not helping matters.'

Oliver reached up and covered the dog's enormous ears. 'Stop. You know how deeply sensitive he is. His physique is appropriate for the breed.'

'Which breed of elephant is that?'

Her brother tutted and withdrew his hands, and Sir Miles resumed panting. She watched Oliver rake hair back from his eyes. Many men she knew were cutting theirs shorter, and she had been wondering if she should tell him, but he was more concerned with ensuring he kept up with the latest clothing styles. On the rare occasion that they attended a dinner or social event, he always wanted descriptions of what the other men were wearing —so she left the topic of hair alone.

A soft whine from Sir Miles had her whipping her head around and Oliver listening intently.

'Carriage,' he said.

Charlotte looked to the road in the distance, and sure enough, a carriage appeared through the trees a moment later. Her hands became clammy when she recognised it. 'Ready for some uncomfortable family time?'

'I gather from your tone that we are about to be honoured with a visit from our dear father.'

Charlotte was throwing her brushes into the canvas bag. 'I am afraid so. Hopefully it will be a short-and-sweet visit—like always.'

A low growl premised a deep bark that had birds bursting from a nearby tree into the sky. Sir Miles was already on his feet, waiting for Oliver to join him. He would never abandon Oliver in the middle of a field in order to make a scene—he would wait so he had a full audience.

Charlotte took her brother's arm, but he immediately withdrew it.

'I can manage.'

Oliver was always fiercely independent whenever their father came by. He would sooner fall down a flight of fifty stone steps than accept help from anyone. Though he was happy to take hold of Sir Miles's collar in order to navigate the uneven muddy field back to the main path. He walked with his chin up and back straight, as though their father's eyes were already upon him.

Lord Elis usually spent his days at court, advising the king. The recent murder of His Majesty's brother had every lord in the country holding their breath. No one knew whether to brace for food shortages or war—or both.

It was raining by the time they reached the front of the house. The pair did not bother taking cover, instead waiting on the road for the carriage to roll to a stop. They watched the driver climb down and open the carriage door.

Charlotte nearly fell over when Lord Wybert stepped out. It was like someone had thrown a bucket of ice at her face. How many years had it been since she had seen him? Six? Seven?

Wybert looked briefly around before his gaze landed on her. His eyes creased at the corners as he gave a polite bow. 'Lady Charlotte. You are looking well.'

'Oh shit,' Oliver muttered upon registering the voice.

Seven years. That was how long it had been. She had been barely seventeen when he had promised her the world, then subsequently ruined her life.

'What are you doing here?' She tried to hide the surprise but made no effort to hide the disdain.

Before he had a chance to respond, her father stepped down from the carriage, frowning the moment his eyes landed on her. 'Goodness gracious. You look like a drowned kitten.'

Charlotte forced her attention away from Wybert and drew a sudden breath when she realised she had forgotten to breathe. 'Father. Back from court so soon?'

The scowl on his face deepened. 'Do not sound so disappointed.'

She was more disappointed at the company he was keeping.

'To what do we owe the pleasure?' Oliver asked, keeping a firm hold of Sir Miles, whose deadly stare was fixed on Wybert.

Elis gestured to the house. 'Let us take this inside before the pair of us end up looking like the two of you.'

The last person Charlotte wanted in her home was Lord Wybert. The man was a walking reminder of her youthful naivety and still evoked the same shame and anger despite the time that had passed. 'I do not mind the rain. I am sure Lord Wybert is keen to be on his way.'

Ignoring the comment, her father strode towards the house, leaving the three of them standing there. When Wybert went to follow him, Sir Miles lowered his head and bared his teeth in warning. The duke stiffened.

'He was just a pup last time I saw him. Large for his breed, is he not?' He looked between the siblings.

'We have all grown up since you were last here, my lord.' Charlotte glanced down at Sir Miles. 'I would advise a slow walk to the door so he does not give chase.'

The faintest smile came and went on Wybert's face. 'You really have grown up.' He side-eyed Sir Miles as he stepped past, then went into the house.

Charlotte and Oliver remained where they were.

'Please tell me he is balding,' Oliver said once they were alone.

Charlotte stroked Sir Miles's silky head. 'I am afraid not. He has a lot of nerve coming here.'

'Maybe he has changed his mind and wants to marry you after all.'

She looked at the door Wybert had just disappeared

through. 'I would sooner cut off my own head and throw it at him.'

'I am not sure that is even possible.' Oliver clicked his fingers to get the dog's attention. 'Inside.'

Sir Miles led the way.

'Is it weird that he is still unwed?' her brother asked. 'I hope it is not due to that vicious rumour of ongoing gonorrhoea that spread shortly after he broke your heart.'

'You mean the one you started?'

Oliver's mouth curled into a smile. 'I may not be able to defend your honour with a sword, but I can spread misinformation like wildfire.'

Charlotte felt some of the tension drain from her body. 'Let us go find out why he is here.' She hesitated at the door. 'If by some sick turn of events the topic of marriage does come up, I shall need you to grab Father's sword and hold it steady so I can run into it.'

Oliver made a face as he let go of Sir Miles's collar. 'Dark but fair.'

They found their father and Wybert warming themselves by the fire in the main room. Charlotte considered going to change out of her wet clothes, then decided to let the water pool at her feet in hope that Wybert would slip on it on his way out.

Elis waited for Oliver to reach Charlotte, but before he had a chance to speak, the kitchen maid entered the room. 'Welcome home, my lord. Can I bring you some refreshments?'

Elis shook his head. 'No, thank you.'

'You can bring me a tray,' Wybert said.

The maid glanced in Charlotte's direction, as though

seeking her approval. She might have been young, but she was old enough to understand loyalty. Charlotte nodded her approval.

'We were very sorry to hear of the earl's death,' Oliver said. 'He was a good man, by all accounts.'

Wybert's expression turned sombre. 'He certainly was. He will be sorely missed.'

'I am surprised he agreed to go to Dinefwr Castle given its reputation,' Charlotte said.

Her father met her gaze. 'He went for all of us so England would not starve.'

She knew enough to know it was not *only* about the grain. Many Englishmen were making record profits with exports.

'I am guessing no one has volunteered to fill that position,' Oliver said.

Elis and Wybert exchanged a look that made Charlotte's stomach drop. Whatever they were about to say, she knew she was not going to like it.

Her father rocked on his heels. 'It is a privilege to help one's king and country.' He paused. 'Which is why I have agreed to go to Dinefwr and oversee trade alongside Lord Wybert.'

Charlotte looked accusingly at Wybert, who stared back at her with a neutral expression.

'*You* are going to Dinefwr?' Oliver asked, head shaking as he wrestled with this new piece of information.

Elis cleared his throat. 'We are *all* going.'

Charlotte blinked, then blinked again. 'What?'

'Absolutely not,' Oliver said confidently. 'I have zero interest in having my throat sliced open.'

Her father had the decency to appear uncomfortable delivering the news. 'The thing is,' he began, 'your grandfather on your mother's side was born at Dinefwr Castle. Your mother was a descendant of Llywelyn ap Gruffudd, the last native Prince of Wales—'

'We know our family tree, Father,' Charlotte snapped. 'Despite your best effort to erase it.'

'That is not true.'

'It most certainly is. Our Welsh blood has been a constant source of shame for you since Carmarthenshire fell into the hands of rebels.'

Colour rose in Elis's cheeks. He was rarely lost for words, but he was visibly struggling with what to say next. He cleared his throat, not once but twice, before replying. 'Technically, you are both Welsh royalty.'

Oliver laughed, then fell silent when no one else did. 'Father, you cannot be serious. We were both born here in England and have never set foot in the region.'

'Even if we had,' Charlotte said, 'why on earth would you want to drag us into this suicide mission?'

Wybert shook out one sleeve of his tunic before clasping his hands behind his back, always a picture of confidence. It had been a draw in her younger years, but now it made her want to gently push him into the flames of the fire.

'It does not matter what you or I think,' Wybert said. 'It matters what the people of Carmarthenshire think.'

There was a spell of silence before Oliver cracked up laughing again. 'There is a reason why Llywelyn has the words *the last* in his title—because he was *the last* Prince of Wales.'

Wybert was deadly serious now. 'Carmarthenshire is a kingdom of peasants. They have an army that is being handheld by Chadora—and no nobility to lead them. They are lost.'

Oliver crossed his arms. 'Well, this sounds like a job for a half-blood spinster and her blind brother.' To Charlotte, he added, 'No offence, sister. You know your determination to remain unwed is my favourite thing about you.'

She was barely listening, too busy glaring at her father. 'You are overestimating the power of our mother's bloodline.'

'To the contrary,' he replied. 'Perhaps I am even guilty of playing it down. We all agree that, over time, the people of Carmarthenshire will come to accept you as royalty.'

'Or kill us,' Oliver said.

Elis closed his eyes. 'Nobody is dying.'

Oliver tilted his head. 'Can we have that in writing?'

Charlotte was desperately trying to process all the things being said. 'What is it you expect us to do? Ride through villages with a royal wave and pray they do not shoot us with arrows while you run iron and grain in and out of Dinefwr Castle?'

'They have no reason to trust us,' Oliver said.

Elis looked between his two children. 'King Edward has already signed the castle over to me. Dinefwr will go to Oliver when I pass and remain in *Welsh* hands.'

He was assuming their bloodline would continue, but both Charlotte and Oliver were happy to let it die.

'So he is gifting us the castle his predecessors stole from us?' Oliver said. 'How generous.'

Wybert perked up at that. 'I think the use of the word *us* demonstrates a shift in your thinking already.'

Charlotte rolled her eyes. 'Can we address the practicalities for a moment? In case you have forgotten, Oliver cannot see. He is blind and will struggle to navigate an unfamiliar environment.'

'You will be there to assist him, as you always are,' her father responded. 'And you will both have bodyguards with you at all times.'

Oliver stiffened. 'Bodyguards? For how long?'

'Until we are confident that you are safe in your environment' was Elis's reply.

Charlotte glared at Wybert when she asked, 'How did that work out for the previous occupants?'

He was unflustered by the question. 'We will step up the protection. I took it upon myself to write to Chadora's warden, and he has agreed to assist us.'

Of course Chadora decided to help. If there was a war, they would be forced to pick a side. 'Assist us how?'

'What better protection than a defender at your side?' Wybert said. When no one spoke, he added, 'It is only for a short time. I have no doubt the peasants will accept you. They are hardly in a position to be choosy.'

Charlotte angled her head. 'And if they were?'

Wybert closed his mouth.

'So we are to be puppets,' Oliver said. 'Shiny castle ornaments on display to the peasants.'

Elis's mouth flattened into a thin line. 'You will continue to live in complete comfort as you do here.'

Oliver's brow creased. 'I am far from comfortable at this moment.'

'This is happening,' their father said, losing patience. 'If you have further questions, you can ask them on the journey. We will be leaving for Carmarthenshire in the morning.'

Charlotte's mouth fell open. 'So soon? Are we not even permitted a chance to say goodbye to our friends?'

Elis lowered his brows. 'Which friends would they be?'

Charlotte's cheeks heated.

'I will have you know that Charlotte is rather close with the local seamstress in town,' Oliver said.

Ignoring the comment, Elis pointed at the dog. 'I think it best if that thing remains here at Livingston Manor.'

Charlotte was not having it. 'Oliver is reliant on Sir Miles. Of course he has to come.'

'He is aggressive.'

'So is Charlotte,' Oliver said, 'yet you are *insisting* that she goes.'

Charlotte looked tiredly at her brother. 'Thank you for that.'

'Fine,' Elis said, waving the argument away. 'However, he is to be muzzled at all times.'

Charlotte replied before her brother could. 'I swear before God, if you ask if I am to be muzzled too…'

Oliver feigned shock. 'The mere suggestion has me weeping inwardly.'

Wybert clapped his hands together. 'I am pleased that everyone is on board with this idea. I shall leave you to pack and see you all in the morning.'

A thought occurred to Charlotte in that moment. 'Are you to live at Dinefwr Castle with us?'

An amused smile settled on his face. 'Is that a problem?'

'Yes,' she answered plainly.

Elis shook his head and gestured to the front door. 'I shall see you out.'

Wybert's gaze remained fixed on Charlotte as he stepped away, the light in his eyes hinting at laughter. He was thoroughly enjoying the power trip.

The siblings remained silent until the footsteps could no longer be heard.

'Does this mean we will be spending more time together as a family?' Oliver whispered. 'A few months locked in a castle with our father might see us begging to have our throats cut.'

Charlotte's eyes sank shut, and she released a shaky breath. 'Let us pray the wine cellar at Dinefwr Castle is adequately stocked.'

CHAPTER 3

*T*atum jogged up the mossy stone steps and paused atop the wall walk, looking around for Alveye. The defender's gaze was fixed east, and his tense expression had Tatum rushing to the embrasure to see who was approaching. Through the sheets of rain, he made out four horses approaching the gate. His eyes narrowed on the man on the first horse.

'Shit,' he said, pushing off the wall.

Alveye's face slackened. 'Do you see what I see?'

'Yes.' Tatum headed back to the stairs. 'Tell the guard at the gate that the warden is coming. I don't want any delays or questions asked. Let the steward know too. And I want grooms ready to tend the horses.' He looked down at his gold cloak pin, adjusting it as he descended the steps.

Alveye jogged after him. 'No word from the others?'

'Nothing in two days.' Hadewaye had collected Ryder Blackmane from Llanelieu, and the pair had headed north, tracking a grain wagon that had arrived at Dinefwr the same afternoon the king's brother had been murdered. It was their only lead so far.

Alveye was running for the keep the moment his feet hit the ground, and a few minutes later, the inner-ward was abuzz with the news. The defenders reunited on the path as the portcullis went up. Tatum opened and closed his mouth a few times, trying to get his jaw to relax.

'Why do I feel like the earl's death is going to end up being our fault?' Alveye asked in a low voice. 'Despite the fact that we were forty miles away at the time.'

Tatum adjusted his weapon. 'It's our fault until there's someone else to blame. But don't fret. I'm in command, and therefore the blame falls on me.' He looked up at the sky. 'What a miserable day to meet one's end.'

Alveye placed a comforting hand on his back. 'I'll be very sad to replace you.'

Tatum cast a doubtful look at him.

The castle staff settled into their places, and everyone stared at the path that led to the outer-ward, waiting for the infamous warden to appear. It was the longest two minutes of Tatum's life. Finally, Shapur Wright came into view, flanked by three guards. His gaze immediately narrowed on Tatum.

'You're right,' Alveye said out of the corner of his mouth. 'He's coming straight for you.'

Tatum would have shoved the defender away had the eyes of the warden not been fixed on him.

The red silk lining of Shapur's cloak flashed as he walked, his strides long and even.

'Walk with me, Commander,' Shapur said, showing no signs of slowing down.

Tatum glanced at Alveye as the warden passed them. The defender gave him a sympathetic look that translated to 'Good luck'. With a sigh, Tatum hurried after the warden, falling into step beside him.

'Do you know how many times I have left Chadora's walls since I was made warden of the defenders?' Shapur asked, taking in his surroundings.

Tatum tried to think. 'I can't recall, sir.'

'Never,' Shapur said. 'That should give you a sense of how serious this situation is.'

At six feet and three inches, Tatum had always considered himself tall, yet walking beside Shapur, he felt the need to straighten for extra height. 'Sir, we have a lead—'

'Shut up and listen.'

Tatum closed his mouth, trying his best to keep pace with the man.

'King Edward is pointing the finger in our direction.'

Tatum whipped his head to the side. '*What?*'

A warning glance from Shapur had him closing his mouth again.

'My sources report that he believes we are fuelling the flames of this shadow war, pushing independence as we turn the Carmarthen Militia into efficient killers.'

'We train the men to follow orders. They don't even have access to the castle.'

'John of Eltham had a guard with him at the time of his death, did he not?'

'Not a very good one, it turns out.'

Shapur's sharp gaze landed on him. 'He was killed under guard with only a small knife. Only a skilled man could carry out such an act—like a defender. It does not reflect well on us or the work we are doing here.'

Tatum hesitated before saying, 'Perhaps they should be looking at the guards within these walls who had all the access in the world.'

'I would be very careful about pointing fingers at the English right now.' Shapur slowed his pace a little. 'What does General Blackmane say on the matter?'

Tolly had reluctantly taken on command of the new army at the insistence of the soldiers. He had proven to be their greatest asset during their darkest moment.

'He's staying out of it. As far as he's concerned, an English earl was murdered in an English castle—'

'On Carmarthenshire soil.'

'He has no control over what happens in here.' Tatum pointed to the English flag above them. 'If it was outside these walls, it would be a different matter. He's as eager for peace as we are.'

'It has been over a week since the earl died, and all you have is a lead.'

'I'm confident—'

'When I need you to be *competent*. You should have the killer in shackles ready to hand over to King Edward by now.'

Tatum resisted the urge to roll his eyes as they pivoted and began walking adjacent with the stone wall.

'Lord Wybert will be returning to Dinefwr Castle tomorrow,' Shapur announced.

'I hope he's bringing some quality guards with him.'

Shapur stopped walking and turned to him. 'He will be bringing something far more valuable. Does the name Llewelyn ap Gruffudd mean anything to you?'

Tatum thought for a moment. 'Gruffudd… as in the prince?'

Shapur nodded. 'The last Prince of Wales. This castle belonged to his family before falling into English hands.'

Falling was a polite term.

'He has two living descendants—Lord Oliver and Lady Charlotte of Livingston Manor.'

'As in Lord Elis Livingston? I thought he was English.'

'He is. The mother, now deceased, was Welsh.'

Tatum waited for him to continue.

'The siblings were born and raised in England. Their mother died during childbirth.'

Tatum shifted his weight. 'And how is all this connected to Lord Wybert?'

Shapur let out an impatient breath. 'The Livingston family is coming to Dinefwr Castle to live. King Edward has given the castle to Lord Elis on the condition that his children occupy it.'

'I'm confused—'

'A common occurrence with you, it seems.' The warden crossed his arms. 'The king wants an advocate here who the people will accept and eventually trust, someone to help mend and build the relationship between Carmarthenshire and England.'

'If the siblings spent the entirety of the famine in England, then they have no shared history with the people living here. They will likely be rejected.'

Shapur looked away. 'While I tend to agree with you, we are all trying to avoid a war between England and

Carmarthenshire. It would be disastrous for everyone involved.'

Tatum drew a deep breath, preparing himself for what was coming next. 'What do you need us to do?'

Shapur sniffed. 'I am putting you in charge of the family's protection during the transition period.'

He had been afraid of that.

'All training activities with the Carmarthen Militia will cease, and the four of you will relocate here.'

Again, no surprises. 'Blackmane's expecting his first child in a few months. Dinefwr Castle's a long way from Llanelieu.'

'The defender is free to hand in his uniform if the inconvenience of coming here is too great.' The warden paused to ensure his point stuck. 'It will be your job to work with Lord Wybert and General Blackmane to monitor public response and keep the family safe while they perform their duties.'

Tatum replied with the only words that were acceptable. 'We will protect them with our lives, sir.'

Shapur looked up at the wall. 'I will be doing a thorough safety assessment of the castle before I depart. Before I do, there is one more thing you need to know.'

Tatum waited.

'Lord Oliver was born without sight.'

Tatum might have thought it a joke coming from anyone else. 'He's... blind?'

'That is what "born without sight" means, yes.'

Perfect. He was expected to keep a blind man alive in a kingdom with a long history of consuming the weak. 'I'll brief the others. It won't be a problem.' He delivered the lie with confidence.

'If you fail to protect these people,' Shapur said, features hardening, 'I will take your title, your uniform, and possibly your head. Do you understand me?'

'Yes, sir.'

The warden strode away without saying another word.

A few moments later, Alveye appeared, walking over to him with a concerned expression. 'Well? What did he say?'

Tatum exhaled slowly, gathering his thoughts. 'Send word to Blackmane and Hadewaye. Tell them that all training is now halted. They're to report to Dinefwr Castle immediately.'

Alveye's eyes widened. 'What's going on?'

'Dinefwr is about to welcome some new occupants— and we're responsible for keeping them alive.'

Alveye nodded slowly. 'I'll send word to them immediately.'

'And send for Tolly and Ita.' He rubbed his pounding forehead. 'We're going to need all the help we can get.'

CHAPTER 4

Charlotte paused as she exited the house, taking in her surroundings a final time. Livingston Manor had been her only home since birth, and leaving it behind had her stomach in knots. The carriage was loaded with her belongings, including plenty of paint supplies, and her father was already inside. Oliver and Sir Miles were standing by the door, waiting for her. To her relief, Wybert was on horseback.

'I sense your overthinking presence, sister,' Oliver called to her. 'Do hurry up.'

She made her way over to him. 'Remind me again why we agreed to this.'

'Because we had no choice.' He offered her his hand. 'Ready to venture into a kingdom that despises the English?'

Smirking, she took his hand and stepped up, eyes meeting her father's as she settled herself in the seat opposite him. 'Good morning.'

He nodded a greeting.

'In you get,' Oliver said to Sir Miles, prompting the dog to jump up ahead of him.

Elis pushed him away with his boot. 'Must that thing come *inside* the carriage?'

'Yes,' Charlotte and Oliver replied in unison.

Oliver settled himself beside Charlotte, and a moment later, the carriage rolled into action. Charlotte leaned forwards for a final glimpse of home.

'It is not going anywhere,' her father said. He was so uncomfortable with emotion. He had been that way her whole life. Charlotte had no idea if he had been that way before her mother's death, and Oliver had been too young to remember.

Rain began to fall as the house disappeared behind a wall of trees, splattering the windows and streaming down the sides of the carriage. The damp air clung to their clothes, mixing with the smell of waterlogged soil. The slosh of hooves on the muddy road was a soothing sound as they headed into the desolate countryside. Charlotte rested her forehead on the window, taking in every unfamiliar sight.

Oliver leaned closer to her. 'What do you see?'

She reached for his hand and squeezed. 'I see grass drowned by heavy rain and meadows possessed by an unearthly stillness.'

Her father gave her a tired look. 'Why not simply say farmland?'

'Because a person without sight cannot conjure that image,' Charlotte replied flatly. 'Your son has never seen a farm.'

Colour rose in Elis's cheeks. He went to speak, but

with godlike timing, the carriage hit a pothole, and he bounced a foot off his seat. Charlotte suppressed a smile as she dropped her head to the damp wood, eyes on the scenery once more. Wybert came into view, his flaxen hair dripping and his face covered in red splotches from the cold.

'Perhaps we should see if he wants to travel in the carriage,' her father suggested. 'He can tether his horse to the back.'

Charlotte rolled her eyes. 'Riding in this weather will do wonders for his immunity. I would hate to rob him of that.'

Oliver coughed into his hand, and then the carriage fell silent once more.

Charlotte startled awake to shouting outside. She sat up straight as they rolled to a stop, peering out the window to see a group of horses blocking their path. Sir Miles began barking, causing her father to jump.

'Shut that thing up,' Elis said. 'He is going to get us killed.'

Oliver placed a hand on the dog, and the barks reduced to whining.

'Are we being robbed?' Charlotte asked.

'No.' Elis listened to the conversation taking place outside. 'We have reached the border.'

Charlotte leaned forwards to get a better look at the soldiers. '*They* are part of the Carmarthen Militia?'

Her father nodded.

'Where are their uniforms?' she asked.

Oliver patted her leg. 'Dearest sister. The weapons they carry were taken from English corpses. They rely on donations from the church to feed their families. Where do you think they are going to get the funds for fancy uniforms?'

Fair point.

A cloaked figure emerged from the trees on horseback. She knew it was someone with authority because the other guards fell silent and made room for him. The man exchanged a few words with Wybert, and then the rider trotted past him, heading straight for the carriage. Sir Miles lurched at the window with a ferocious bark before anyone could stop him. The rider stared down the dog as he lowered his hood, and then his dark eyes shifted from person to person, sizing everyone up before settling on her father.

'Lord Elis?'

The lord waited until Oliver had control of the dog, then opened the wooden shutter the whole way. 'I am he. And you are?'

'General Tolly Blackmane, chief commander of the Carmarthen Militia.' He glanced at Charlotte and Oliver. 'You're about to cross the border in one of the most English-looking carriages I've ever laid eyes on. That makes you a bit of a target in these parts.'

'Perhaps you would prefer if we arrived on the back of a wagon, dressed in rags,' Elis said, agitation clear in his voice.

'That would have certainly made my job easier.' Tolly's gaze went to Charlotte. 'Last chance to relieve yourselves.

There won't be any stops between here and Dinefwr Castle.'

Her father gestured to Charlotte. 'We have a lady on board.'

One corner of Tolly's mouth lifted. 'I'll be sure to look away.'

Wybert rode up beside the general. 'Once you are inside the walls of Dinefwr Castle, you will believe yourself to be back in England.'

Elis muttered a complaint as the three of them exited the carriage, with a restrained Sir Miles, to do their business. A few minutes later, they were back in the carriage and on their way once more.

As they continued through the foreign countryside, Charlotte watched the scenery change from rolling hills to thick forests, then to a patchwork of small villages where tiny houses with thatched roofs lined the roads and sheep grazed in surrounding fields. The cool air tasted of smoke.

'Should I be worried about the smell?' Oliver asked, sniffing the air.

Charlotte's gaze remained on the window. 'It is from the burning hearths inside the houses.'

'Cottages at best,' her father corrected.

She rolled her eyes inwardly at his snobbery.

The second leg of the journey was the longest. They stopped once to change over the horses but were told to remain inside the carriage. Tolly and a few of his men watched the trees around them the whole time, prepared for goodness knew what.

Six hours after crossing the border, they reached their

destination.

'I see it,' Charlotte said when Dinefwr Castle finally appeared on the horizon, English flags blowing in the wet breeze.

'Finally,' her father muttered, shifting uncomfortably in his seat.

Oliver turned his head to her. 'How does it look?'

Charlotte drank in the sight. 'Formidable. A fortress perched on the highest point of the hill. Its walls are so high that one could be fooled into believing they are impenetrable.'

Oliver's mouth twisted into a smile. 'The previous four residents might have something to say on that particular subject—if they were still alive to speak.'

Elis tutted. 'I pray these *defenders* tasked with our protection are up to the job.'

'And I pray for a full cellar and some good cheese,' Oliver added.

A smile spread across Charlotte's face, dissipating at the sound of a portcullis going up in the distance. Sir Miles sprang to his feet and pressed his nose to the window, ears twitching in all directions.

'Easy,' Charlotte said, stroking his back.

A few minutes later, the carriage crossed a dry moat that was not particularly dry that day, then came to a stop inside what appeared to be an outer-ward. Charlotte spotted some heavily armed soldiers in black uniforms standing in front of the stables.

'There they are,' her father said. 'Chadorian defenders.'

Oliver turned his head towards the window. 'I heard

they consume the dying tears of their enemies for muscle growth.'

Another disapproving tut from their father. 'Whoever told you that assumed you were stupid as well as blind.'

Charlotte studied their serious faces. 'They are made of the same flesh and bone as we are. They just have a little more muscle.'

Tolly dismounted and walked over to join them, conversing with them in a familiar and friendly manner.

One of the men chose that moment to look in the direction of the carriage, eyes meeting Charlotte's through the open window. He was tall with heavy shoulders and a brawny chest, arms and legs made from hard work. His fair hair was cut close to the scalp.

'Violent heathens,' her father commented, drawing her attention from the man. 'Humanity wrung from their soulless bodies via ruthless training.'

Charlotte looked back at the window, startled by Wybert, who was now waiting at the carriage door. Sir Miles emitted a warning growl that had the duke taking a tentative step back.

'Quiet,' her father commanded, shoving the dog towards Oliver.

Oliver took hold of Sir Miles's collar and said to his sister, 'Are you ready for this?'

Charlotte gathered her skirts as the door swung open. 'Absolutely not.'

With her heart racing, she exited the carriage and stepped down onto Welsh soil for the first time.

CHAPTER 5

Whatever image Tatum had conjured in his mind of Lord Elis's spinster daughter, the reality was quite different. He had been expecting some socially awkward, unsightly woman, but Lady Charlotte was a picture of confidence—even in the presence of the duke, who was rumoured to have been romantically involved with her in his younger years.

Tatum guessed her to be in her early to midtwenties. She was average height and attractive enough to hold any man's attention. Her swarthy hair was pulled back at the sides and streaked with golden highlights. Her eyes were as dark as the look she threw Wybert as she exited the carriage, confirming the rumours he had heard. She wore an elegant silk gown beneath a steel-blue cloak that complemented the warm tones of her skin.

Blackmane threw an elbow into Tatum's side. 'Stay focused.'

He looked at the defender. 'I *am* focused.'

'I meant on the job.'

Tatum gave him a tired look before heading for the carriage. He was a couple of yards away when a horse-sized dog leapt from the open door with a ferocious bark, its teeth bared. Tatum drew his weapon, and the dog pulled up an inch from the tip of his blade. The animal snarled in protest, its glazed eyes fixed on the commander.

Charlotte's gaze fell to the blade pointed at the dog's neck. 'Lower your sword, defender. Sir Miles does not respond well to threats.'

Tatum looked up at her. Her eyes were as wild as the animal's in that moment. 'Sir Miles?'

She lifted her chin. 'That is the dog's name, yes.'

He glanced over his shoulder at the other defenders, who all watched with interest. 'They certainly breed them different in England,' he said, turning back to her.

'The women or the dogs?' she asked.

She had arrived like wildfire, ready to set the place ablaze.

'Both.'

'Charlotte,' her father said in a warning tone.

She held Tatum's gaze for an uncomfortable few moments before clicking her fingers and saying, 'To Oliver.'

The dog immediately retreated to the carriage, where it waited for Oliver to climb down. While the training was impressive, Tatum was a little disturbed by the fact that she had waited until she was prompted before using it.

Wybert looked around at the group, waiting for Oliver to join them before speaking. 'This is Commander Tatum,' Wybert said, gesturing to the defender. 'His unit will be responsible for your safety while you are settling in at Dinefwr Castle.' Then, gesturing to the Livingston family, he said, 'May I introduce Lord Elis, Lady Charlotte, and Lord Oliver.' He withdrew his hand from the space when the dog growled. 'Sir Miles you have met.'

'The dog will be muzzled at all times,' Elis said. 'Perhaps you can see to that, Commander.'

Tatum could have sworn he heard Alveye laugh behind him. 'Dog wrangling *is* our specialty, my lord.'

Oliver chuckled. 'I am sure the guards have better things to do, Father. We can take care of it ourselves.'

At least one of them seemed normal.

Wybert was about to continue when a young guard marched up to him. 'Grain wagon approaching, my lord.'

Wybert nodded, then gave Tatum an apologetic look. 'Forgive me, but I have business to tend to. Perhaps you could finish the briefing for me.'

'Briefing?' Oliver asked coyly. 'Are we being given an assignment?'

'Our assignment is to not die,' Charlotte replied flatly.

Wybert offered a small bow before striding away, his guards following him.

Elis cleared his throat before saying, 'I want to take this opportunity to point out that Oliver here is blind.'

The youngest lord's eyebrows rose in surprise. 'Safe to assume the defenders are aware of the fact, Father.'

Blackmane, Alveye, and Hadewaye wandered closer, stopping a few feet behind Tatum. Charlotte eyed each of them with blatant suspicion.

'This is Ryder Blackmane,' Tatum said, gesturing to the defender, who responded with a nod. 'He can take some time to warm up to people, but he's one of the most intuitive fighters I've ever encountered. He's good at what he does.'

Charlotte made a face. 'And what is that exactly?'

'In this instance, he'll assist with general security around the castle and travel with you when outside the walls.'

Blackmane could not have looked more bored if he tried. Tatum moved on.

'This is Kelton Alveye, an excellent swordsman and one of the fittest men you'll come across.' Then to Elis, he said, 'He'll be your bodyguard, my lord.'

Oliver perked up at this. 'A *personal* bodyguard? We each get one?'

'You do,' Tatum replied. 'Yours happens to be one of the greatest archers of our era, Nixon Hadewaye. I thought him a good match because you can't see how short he is.'

Hadewaye sighed. 'For clarity, I'm an inch shorter than our respected commander, who's well over six feet.'

'They might breed them different in England,' Oliver whispered to his sister, 'but they breed them *big* in Chadora.'

Charlotte looked around. 'Are you to be my bodyguard, then, Commander?'

He feigned a smile. 'No. You'll be relieved to hear that I have hand selected a highly trained member of the Carmarthen Militia for you, my lady.'

'I'm here!' came a woman's voice from the path.

They all turned to watch Ita Chapman jog towards them.

'Sorry,' she said, coming to a breathless stop beside Hadewaye. 'I got stuck chatting with Beth in the kitchen. Next thing I knew I was sampling pâté.' She glanced around at the Livingston family. 'What did I miss?'

Elis looked down at Ita's sheathed sword with a thoroughly disapproving expression. 'And who is this?'

'Ita Chapman. She's been training with us for the past twelve months. Before that she was an active member of the St Clare group.'

Elis's face fell. 'You must be joking.'

'A defender never jokes about training,' Tatum replied.

Elis looked between the men. 'The woman was part of a rebel group. She is a wastelander.'

Charlotte's gaze snapped to her father. 'Careful. Every survivor outside these walls came from such a group. To insult Ita is to insult an entire kingdom.'

Tatum and Hadewaye exchanged a look of surprise. Perhaps there was a heart buried beneath all that hostility after all.

'I assure you she's up to the job,' Tatum told Elis. Looking at Charlotte, he said, 'She'll also be a useful resource for you. Ita knows half of Carmarthenshire and can guide you on how best to win them over.'

Charlotte tilted her head. 'I imagine these people have faced enough deception to last a lifetime. My plan is to simply be myself.'

'Terrible idea,' Oliver said. 'We need people to *like* you.'

Tatum pressed his lips together to stop from smiling.

Charlotte must have noticed because she glared in his direction.

Elis crossed his arms. 'What if we come up against hostile men? Will you be able to protect her?'

A hint of a smirk settled on Ita's face. 'Of course. I shall force them back with perfumed oils and emotional displays.'

Colour rose in Elis's cheeks. 'All while dressed in men's clothing?'

Ita looked down at her peasant trousers, altered to fit. 'It's genius, actually. They'll be thoroughly confused.'

Charlotte rolled her eyes in her father's direction. 'Do not fret, Father. If she dies, you will have the opportunity to tell everyone "I told you so". Let us move on.'

Ita straightened her tunic with a tug. 'Cold but fair.'

Charlotte narrowed her gaze at Blackmane. 'Are you related to General Blackmane?'

'We're brothers,' Blackmane answered—always with as few words as possible.

She looked over at Tolly, who was tending to his horse. 'One brother from Chadora and one from Carmarthenshire?'

'Both originally from Ireland,' Ita said. 'It's a long story.'

'I imagine you're all tired from your journey,' Tatum cut in before Blackmane could say anything that might get them into trouble. 'Perhaps a rest is in order.'

Elis nodded. 'Yes. Good idea.'

Alveye stepped forwards. 'I'll escort you to your quarters.'

Elis eyed the defender warily before looking back at his children. 'I shall see you both at dinner.'

Oliver clapped his hands together. 'Wonderful idea. A

family dinner is just what we need after spending many uncomfortable hours locked in a carriage together.'

'I will be eating in my room tonight,' Charlotte said.

Elis shook his head. 'Normally, I would be the first to suggest separate dining arrangements. However, there are things we need to discuss.' He looked between Charlotte and Oliver. 'I will see you *both* at dinner.'

Without waiting for a reply, he marched off in the direction of the castle.

Alveye gave Tatum a 'this should be fun' look before following after him.

Tatum was starting to get a good sense of the family dynamic already.

Walking over to Oliver, and ignoring the warning growl from Sir Miles, Hadewaye said, 'Shall I take you to your bedchamber, my lord?'

Charlotte straightened. 'You do understand that escorting a blind man through an unfamiliar environment requires verbal cues, defender?'

Tatum was also getting a good sense of Charlotte's role within the family—which included being a second guard dog for her brother. 'He knows.' Tatum waited for her to look at him. 'And *you* understand that defenders undergo blindfolded training in order to reduce distractions and develop their other senses? And that we're taught to guide a sightless defender through a disaster site or battle zone using *only* verbal cues?'

Nothing changed on Charlotte's face. 'No, I was not aware of that.'

'Your brother will be in safe hands,' Hadewaye said, reassuring her.

Her eyes went to him, her expression softening.

'She sounds like a protective sister, but she is always first to laugh when I do fall,' Oliver said to Hadewaye as he reached for the dog's collar. 'Sir Miles here has been my guide in this world for nearly seven years. I will be just fine.'

Hadewaye went to pet the dog, but a sharp growl changed his mind.

'He will warm to you,' Oliver said before waving a hand in his sister's general direction. 'See you at dinner.'

'I cannot wait,' Charlotte replied drily as she watched her brother walk away.

Tatum and Ita exchanged an amused glance as the bodyguard ventured closer to her charge.

'I'll be your permanent shadow moving forwards,' Ita told her. 'Lucky for you, I'm excellent company.'

Charlotte's face remained neutral. 'My definition of good company is the quiet kind.'

'I can be quiet if that's what you want. Just remember that I will be your only friend here until we've established that it's safe for you to mingle.'

Charlotte blinked. 'And how will you gauge such a thing?'

'If you're still alive at the end of the month, that will be a good indicator,' Tatum answered.

Ita cleared her throat. 'You know, there are some who are quite excited that you're here.'

'And some who wish me dead?' Charlotte asked.

Ita was momentarily taken aback. 'You'll win them over soon enough.'

'If I can remain alive.' She looked at Tatum. 'Is that not right, Commander?'

She was going to be an absolute pain in the arse. He could sense it already. 'That's where we come in, my lady.'

Charlotte watched him for a long moment.

'Come along,' Ita said. 'I'll share all my best survival tips on the way.'

Tatum bowed his head—barely—as Charlotte passed by him.

When the women were out of earshot, he turned to Blackmane. 'She's going to be a handful.'

Blackmane sighed. 'You're attracted to her.'

'Ah, were you paying attention throughout that introduction? The lady is a few cheeses short of a picnic hamper.'

'You definitely have a type.'

Tatum shook his head. 'Don't you have a perimeter check to do?'

'Promise me you won't sleep with her.'

Tatum pointed at the wall. 'You should wash your mouth out on the way.'

The defender stepped past him, muttering, 'This is going to end badly.'

'I'd sooner sleep with Alveye,' Tatum said to Blackmane's back.

'I'll tell him you said that.'

The commander swore under his breath. 'I don't bed every woman I find attractive, you know.'

Blackmane headed for the wall without saying another word.

CHAPTER 6

*C*harlotte hated everything about the room, from its oversized bed to the bland wool rug. It was as though colour and light were forbidden in that part of the castle. She looked at the trunk in the corner containing her belongings, wondering if perhaps the bedchamber would feel more homely once she unpacked.

Heading over to the trunk, she fought with the latch before finally tugging it up, wincing as it hit the wall. A breath later, the door to the bedchamber flew open and Ita stepped inside, looking around.

'Everything all right?' she asked.

Before Charlotte could reply, Tatum appeared behind her. 'I heard a bang.'

'I was simply opening my trunk,' she said, crossing her arms. 'You cannot be wandering in here at every noise. What if I had been changing for dinner?'

He appeared offended. 'Are you seriously asking a commander in the Chadorian army that question? Obviously, I would have found an excuse to stay and leer at you.'

Ita ushered Tatum from the room while Charlotte was still processing the joke, closing the door behind him.

'Ignore him,' Ita said, turning back to Charlotte. 'He's all bark and no bite—a bit like your dog, I hear.'

'Sir Miles definitely bites.'

Ita's eyebrows rose. 'Oh. Good to know. Have you had a chance to rest?'

Charlotte looked her new guard over. Even in muted tones with a sword belted to her waist, she was effortlessly beautiful with her pretty round face and braided hair. 'Not really. I am tempted to skip dinner.'

Ita gave her a sympathetic look. 'You're not avoiding Lord Wybert by any chance? I heard the two of you were to be married some time back, but he ended things at the last minute.'

Every muscle in Charlotte's body tensed. The fact that this stranger knew intimate details of her life was beyond uncomfortable. 'Who told you that?'

'It's my job to know everything about you.' Lowering her voice, she added, 'Between us, I think you dodged an arrow with that one. He's all work and no fun at all.'

Charlotte barely knew how to respond. She was not accustomed to such brazen conversation. 'You may wait outside now. I need to change.'

Ita suppressed a smile. 'Fair enough. I noticed you didn't bring a lady's maid with you, so just shout out if you need a hand.'

'I am very capable of dressing myself, thank you.'

Ita left without another word.

Walking over to the bed, Charlotte sank onto it, swallowing down the nerves and shame that were magnified by her foreign environment and Wybert's presence in the castle. She was so angry at her father for prioritising the wishes of the king over his family —like always. Not once had he asked her if she was comfortable coexisting with the man who had humiliated her. Because he did not care. Even his own humiliation could be buried for the good of his country.

Charlotte forced herself up. She changed, painted her lips, pinned her hair. After a long stare in the mirror, she headed for the door.

Ita turned to her with a smile when it opened. 'Forget the murderers. It's the admirers I'll have to keep away from you looking like that.' She gestured for Charlotte to walk ahead.

'I would like to collect Oliver on the way.'

'He's already in the hall.'

Charlotte's feet slowed. 'Oh.'

'He's done a tour of the castle and everything.'

'A *tour*?' She was thrown by that, used to being his main guide through life.

'He's seen all the sights.' Ita came up beside her. 'Hadewaye's a fabulous guard and a good man. Your brother's in safe hands. You can relax.'

Charlotte gave her a sideways glance. 'He has been assigned a bodyguard because we are targets, and you tell me to relax.'

Ita was silent a moment. 'Not everyone wishes you dead. Many are excited that you're here.' She gave a royal wave. 'Why, you are Princess Charlotte, descendant of the last true Prince of Wales.'

'Stop.'

'What?'

Charlotte pinched the bridge of her nose. 'The title is ludicrous.'

'You must *own* that title.' Ita leaned forwards to catch Charlotte's gaze. 'If you don't embrace it, then why should the rest of the kingdom?'

Normally, Charlotte would dismiss the advice of someone she had only known for five minutes, but she found herself filing it away for later consideration.

When they arrived at the hall, Oliver, her father, and Wybert were already seated and waiting for her. Her gaze flicked to the defenders lined along the wall.

'Goodness,' Ita whispered to her. 'The tension. One would think someone's died already.'

Tatum glanced at Charlotte, and she immediately looked ahead, forcing her feet forwards.

'Is that you, sister?' Oliver asked, turning his head in her direction.

'Yes.'

Wybert and her father watched her approach.

'You look very nice this evening,' Wybert said as she took her seat.

Charlotte looked at her brother, whose nostrils flared with laughter. He had never liked Wybert, but Charlotte had dismissed his opinion, believing the criticism was coming from his fear of being alone.

'And *you* look tired,' she told the lord. 'Likely due to riding in the rain all day. It really is a shame there was no room for you in the carriage.' She reached for the wine and filled her cup, then Oliver's.

'Wine,' she said quietly, sliding the cup towards her brother's hand.

He picked it up and tapped it to hers before drinking.

Charlotte's gaze wandered to Tatum as she set her empty cup back on the table. She found him watching her with a curious, and slightly judgemental, expression. She refilled her cup to make a point—she did not care what others thought of her.

'So,' Oliver said after a long silence, 'what do people do for fun around here? How is the hunting around these parts?'

Wybert, who was reaching for the tray of roasted meats at the time, stilled. 'Hunting?'

'It is a joke,' Charlotte said tiredly.

Wybert picked up the tray. 'I see. Well, guests are sparse here—and dangerous. You will need to get creative so far as entertainment is concerned.' He looked at Charlotte. 'Do you still paint? I recall you were rather good.'

She took a long drink before looking at him. 'And I recall giving you a painting some time ago and you telling me you adored it—before shoving it into a cupboard.'

The duke touched his napkin to his mouth despite having not eaten any food yet. 'How do you know I did not hang it after you left?'

The man had more audacity than sense.

'And how do *I* know you did not gift it to the young lady you were suddenly engaged to mere weeks after I gave it to you?' She feigned a smile. 'Whatever happened to her?'

Oliver almost spat his drink across the table.

'Charlotte,' her father said in a firm voice.

'There was another young lady after that one, was there not?' Charlotte continued, ignoring the warning. 'I recall your mother approving of that one.' She took another drink. 'She described her to Lady Margaret as coming from a lineage of "strong birthers" and with no history of "sensory birth defects".'

'Enough,' her father snapped.

Oliver was smiling into his drink. 'Sensory birth defects? Oddly specific. Something to do with Charlotte's poor hearing, perhaps.'

Out of the corner of her eye, Charlotte saw Tatum suppress a smile before looking in the other direction.

Wybert watched her carefully across the table as he considered his next words. 'I thought the two of you could ride to Llanddeilo tomorrow, visit the market. It might be helpful to test the peasants' reaction.'

His referring to the people as peasants annoyed Charlotte, despite being an accurate description.

'Will you not be joining us?' Oliver asked.

He shook his head. 'I have a business to run. Plus, I am not a favourite around these parts at present. The less association you have with me right now the better.'

Charlotte raised her drink. 'Hear, hear.' She felt the heat of her father's glare upon her.

'Is this a "let us venture out and see if we are still alive at the end" experiment?' Oliver asked.

Elis swallowed his mouthful before saying, 'You cannot win people over by hiding away. You need to be seen supporting locals, buying their goods at the market and so forth.'

Charlotte angled her head. 'That feels a little performative. I thought we could travel to the eastern camp, get a better understanding of the horrors that took place there before the uprising.'

The silence that rang out was the loudest thing she had ever heard.

'Charlotte,' Wybert said, placing his fork down, 'we are trying to move Carmarthenshire forwards. Dwelling on past grievances helps no one.'

She set her cup down. 'One must heal in order to move forwards. Burying past mistakes helps no one.'

For once, her father did not argue with her.

Tatum walked right up to the table. 'I agree with Lady Charlotte. I think a visit to the camp, or what remains of it, is smart. It demonstrates a desire to understand. Let people tell their stories and feel heard. They've earned it.'

He was the last person she had expected to support the idea. It was clear he cared about the people living here.

Wybert nodded slowly. 'All right. Some empathy never goes astray.' He looked up at Tatum. 'You will need to be careful. Conversations about the camp can get some riled up.'

'As it should,' Charlotte said, picking up her drink again. 'It was a shameful situation.'

Tatum spoke before Wybert could. 'While we're on the topic of safety, now might be a good time to go over the rules.'

'Rules?' Charlotte asked, leaning back.

Tatum met her gaze. 'Yes, rules. Rules are how we keep you all alive.'

'Will there be a test at the end?' Oliver asked. 'If so, I shall slow down on the wine.'

Elis spoke up at that. 'Perhaps your sister should slow down also.'

Begrudgingly, Charlotte placed her drink on the table and folded her hands in her lap. 'Fine. Go ahead, Commander.'

'Ensure you have an escort with you whenever you're outside your bedchamber. Your bodyguard, another defender, or one of the night guards if you must leave your bedchamber overnight. Though I'd prefer you didn't wander about during the night while we're sleeping or during early morning training hours.'

Charlotte rolled her eyes inwardly. 'You train while the rest of Wales sleeps?'

Tatum narrowed his eyes. 'Yes. We train while you sleep to minimise the time you're without proper protection.' He looked at Wybert. 'No offence to your men.'

The duke waved a dismissive hand.

'All doors are to be locked from the inside every evening. Understood?'

Oliver shrugged. 'Sounds simple enough—'

'I'm not finished,' Tatum said, looking around the table. 'As for when you're *outside* these walls, your job is to listen to us and do exactly what we say. You don't hesitate. You don't ask questions. You listen and do.' He paused for emphasis. 'If one of us says "don't move," you stop immediately and *don't move.*'

Charlotte placed a hand on the table, one finger

tapping. 'Thank goodness you explained that to us like we are five-year-olds. I would definitely have moved.'

Tatum's expression did not change. 'People behave in irrational ways when they're afraid.'

'We need you to follow instructions in order to do our jobs properly,' Blackmane said, joining the conversation. 'If we tell you to stay, then don't move even one inch. It could mean the difference between life and death.'

She met the defender's black eyes, then looked away.

'The castle has a range of security measures in place,' Tatum went on. 'There will be multiple checkpoints for all visitors moving forwards. They must receive clearance before entering, and all weapons must be left at the gate-house. Every guard here at Dinefwr has been given specific instructions. Deviations won't be tolerated.' He looked at Wybert again.

'I have said all along that I will support you and your men in whatever way I can.' The duke looked at Elis. 'Your family's safety is paramount.'

Nodding, Tatum looked around the table. 'Any questions?'

Charlotte had one. 'If this all goes wrong, and the people of Carmarthenshire figure out this whole thing is a charade, which then bubbles over into war'—she gestured to Tatum—'whose side will you be on?'

Tatum's eyebrows rose half an inch. 'Whose *side*?'

'Carmarthenshire or England?'

Elis closed his eyes. 'Charlotte—'

'I suppose what I am asking is will you continue to protect us or hang us in the courtyard?'

Elis's fork landed on his plate with a clatter. 'Enough. It is time for you to retire.'

'But I am not done eating,' she objected.

Picking up on the tension, Sir Miles rose to his feet.

'If that thing starts barking…' Elis warned.

Oliver placed a hand on Sir Miles to settle him. 'He is sensitive to tone.'

'Then get him out of here.'

Oliver laughed. 'Am I to be expelled from dinner also?'

Charlotte rose from her chair. 'Come, brother. Let us not inconvenience our father past the allotted fifteen minutes we normally get.'

Elis pushed his plate away.

'Can we at least take some pudding with us?' Oliver asked as he got to his feet. 'It smells amazing.'

Charlotte walked around the table to where the plum pudding sat in front of Wybert. 'Excuse me.' She plucked it off the table and tucked it under one arm before reaching for the jar of wine. 'Thank you for the tantalising company.' Looking at Tatum, she added, 'And for painting such a vivid picture of prison life here at Dinefwr.'

Oliver took hold of Sir Miles's collar. 'Oh dear.'

Charlotte snapped her fingers in Sir Miles's direction, and the dog led Oliver out of the hall. Hadewaye and Ita followed soon after.

The last thing Charlotte heard as she exited was her father apologising to the men for her behaviour.

CHAPTER 7

*E*veryone was settled in their quarters for the evening—except for Charlotte, who had barricaded herself in Oliver's room with an entire pudding and a full jar of wine.

It was nearing midnight when Tatum passed Ita standing at the door with Oliver's night guard.

'What are you still doing here?' he asked her. 'Where's your replacement?'

Ita stifled a yawn. 'He told me, "There's no need for two of us to hang about the same door all evening," and then he left.'

This was the problem with only having a handful of men—they required sleep, and he had to rely on English guards to fill in the gaps. And despite instructions from Lord Wybert to cooperate, they took orders from outsiders about as well as one would expect.

'Go,' he told Ita. 'I'll make sure she gets back to her bedchamber.' He gave a pointed stare at the other guard, who was leaning against the wall looking bored. 'And our friend here can go find his comrade.'

The man drew a long breath before sauntering off.

'Thank you,' Ita said before leaving.

He was grateful to her for stepping into the role when she had no obligation to do so. After training with the Carmarthen Militia for the past year, she was proving to be more competent than some of her male counterparts.

A few minutes after Ita's departure, the door swung open, and Charlotte stepped outside. She stopped when she spotted Tatum. 'What are you doing here?'

He turned to face her. 'Waiting for you to go to bed. I thought it a fun way to fill the time.'

She blinked sleepily—or drunkenly. 'Where is my night guard?'

'On his way.' Tatum threw an angry look over his shoulder. 'I can't leave your brother unattended, so you'll just have to wait a moment.'

Sir Miles appeared behind Charlotte, snarling at Tatum, who instinctively drew his dagger.

Charlotte rested a hand on the dog's head. 'That is quite enough, dear sir. People are trying to sleep.'

'Everything all right?' Oliver called behind her.

'Fine. Good night.'

Charlotte directed the dog back, then pulled the door closed. Their gazes met briefly before they fell into an awkward silence. It was a relief when Oliver's night guard finally reappeared, until Tatum realised he was alone.

'*Where is he?*' he asked through gritted teeth.

The man pointed down the corridor. 'On his way to the lady's bedchamber, like you wanted.'

Tatum pressed his eyes closed. 'That would be very helpful—if she were actually in there.' He pointed to the floor. 'You don't leave this spot until you're relieved in the morning. Understand?'

The guard nodded.

Tatum gestured for Charlotte to start moving. 'Let's go.'

She began walking at a painfully slow pace, and Tatum soon realised just how intoxicated she was.

'On a scale of one to ten, how drunk are you?' he asked.

She reached for the wall, steadying herself. 'Five at most.'

One corner of his mouth twitched. 'I didn't ask how many cups you drank in the first five minutes of dinner…'

She side-eyed him. 'Defender humour. Funny.'

'That's just regular humour. Defender humour is much darker.'

'Example?'

He thought for a moment. 'You know, one time I was captured and tortured by a mime. He did unspeakable things to me.'

She bit her top lip to stop from smiling. 'Terrible.'

He liked that he *almost* made her smile. 'So what's the story with your father? Did you two quarrel on the way here?'

'Yes, we quarrelled on the way here.' She concentrated on walking for a moment. 'And before we left, last week, the month prior, and every year from around the age of five.' Her throat bobbed.

They rounded the corner, and Tatum was relieved to

find the night guard waiting outside Charlotte's bedchamber.

'She is painfully chatty,' Charlotte said as she almost bumped into him.

He gave her some extra space. 'Who?'

'Ita.'

A smile played on his lips. 'You can be a little chatty yourself—when drinking.' Her shoe caught an invisible crevice, and Tatum caught her arm. 'Are we still at a five?'

'Nudging towards a six.'

'Thought so.' He kept hold of her arm, giving the guard a look that very clearly said 'I'll deal with you in a minute' as they came to a stop at the door. He turned to Charlotte. 'Can I trust you to get yourself into bed and stay there?'

She dismissed the question with a wave. 'You will soon discover that I am quite self-sufficient.'

'Is that right?' He reached past her and pushed the door open, getting a lungful of her scent, which coincidentally matched the spices used in the plum pudding she had stolen. 'In you go. I'll see you bright and early.'

She held the doorframe, looking up at him for a moment. 'Will I be shocked by what I see tomorrow at the camp?'

He was aware of the guard listening. 'That depends on what you've been told.'

'Father would not speak of it.' She swallowed. 'I heard only whispers of misery.'

He nodded. 'You might be shocked, but at least your eyes will be open.'

Charlotte pushed off the frame and regained her balance. 'See you in the morning, Commander.'

She entered the bedchamber, and the door clicked shut between them.

~

'Are you sure an excursion is a good idea?' Hadewaye asked Tatum as they left the kitchen the following morning.

Tatum shook his head. 'No, but it's not our job to dictate their agenda, only to keep them safe in the process.'

The sun was yet to rise, but they could make out Blackmane's and Alveye's silhouettes framed by grey light as they stepped outside.

'How are we going to do this?' Blackmane asked in place of a greeting when they reached him.

Tatum looked around. 'Where's Ita?'

'Here!' she called, appearing at a run. She brushed her hair back from her face and looked between the men. 'What did I miss?'

'We were discussing the plan for today,' Hadewaye said.

Ita nodded. 'It's lucky Lady Charlotte is made of tough fabric. I think she's in for a rude awakening.'

'At least she *appears* to be,' Hadewaye said. 'Beneath that little display of hers last night, I sensed a deeply hurt child who's been left to fend for herself and her brother.'

Everyone stared at him.

'You got all that from one drunken tantrum at dinner?' Alveye asked.

Blackmane rubbed his forehead. 'Can we go back to the plan for today?'

Tatum cleared his throat. 'Yes. Now, we know from Ita and others that locals are divided about the arrival of the Livingston family. Our challenge is to encourage interaction with welcoming people while preventing those who don't want them here from stabbing or shooting them.'

Alveye made a face. 'Seems straightforward. So, be invisible while keeping them in arm's reach at all times.'

'Exactly,' Tatum said. 'Hover, but don't *hover*.'

Ita crinkled her nose. 'Speaking of keeping them within arm's reach... do any of you happen to know where Lady Charlotte is at this particular moment?'

Tatum blinked. 'She drank enough wine last night to euthanise a goat. Surely she's still asleep.'

Ita shook her head. 'She wasn't when I went to her bedchamber a few moments ago. The night guard was, however. He's currently looking for her.'

'She's likely with her brother,' Alveye suggested.

'Already checked with him,' Ita replied. 'He said she's an early riser and will show up when she's hungry.'

Tatum pressed his eyes closed. 'Let's split up and find her. Ita, check her bedchamber again in case she's returned.'

The group dispersed without another word, and Tatum headed for the keep. Wybert's guards had so far proven to be useless.

He climbed the steps and asked the men atop the wall if they had seen Charlotte. One of them pointed east, and Tatum headed in that direction. He walked for some time until he finally spotted Charlotte standing in front of an easel, holding a paint palette in one hand and a brush in the other, a blanket hanging from her shoulders. The sun had now reached the horizon, splashing pink light over her.

'Good morning, Commander,' she said without looking at him.

He drew a long breath before making his way over to her. 'What are you doing?'

'Darning stockings.' Her focus never shifted.

'I see you left your quarters without an escort.' He tried very hard to keep his annoyance contained. 'Perhaps you missed the part last night when I very clearly went over the rules.'

She applied a few brushstrokes before replying. 'My guard was snoring so loudly that it seemed a shame to wake him.'

'I'll be sure to tell people that when I'm explaining your death.'

Her eyes creased at the corners. 'I was thinking about that and concluded that I am not important enough to kill.'

'How do you figure?'

She stepped back to inspect her work. 'They will target my father. He is English and has possession of the castle. Then, depending on whether they accept my brother as one of them, they will target him next.'

'But not you?'

She finally glanced in his direction. 'He is to inherit this place. I am just a woman.'

He decided not to join her pity party. 'You can cry

about that later. Did you remember that we're travelling to the old campsite today?'

'Yes.'

He tapped his foot impatiently. 'Then perhaps your focus should be on getting ready.'

'Oh stop. You sound like my father.'

His foot stilled. He looked around, then, with a resigned sigh, wandered over to her. 'What are you painting?'

'I promised Oliver a sunrise to brighten his dreary bedchamber.'

Tatum's eyebrows pinched together. 'Is that a joke?'

'Yes.' She looked at him. 'It is funny because he is blind.'

He ventured closer so he could see the painting. It was only half done, but already he could tell she had talent. 'How long have you been painting for?'

'Since I could hold a brush.' She drew the blanket tighter around her. 'We all need something to escape to.'

His gaze shifted from the painting to her. 'And what are you escaping *from*?'

One corner of her mouth lifted in a smirk. 'Are you trying to figure me out, Commander?'

'It would be helpful if I could.'

She stopped and turned to him. 'It is your job to protect me, not understand me.'

He moved closer. 'The two go hand in hand. In order to protect you, I need to be able to predict your behaviour. That requires some understanding.'

She stepped into his personal space. 'And what have you figured out so far?'

He held his ground. 'That I don't trust you this close with a sharp object in your hand.'

She looked down at the brush she was holding. 'This brush was imported from India and is made from the finest camel hair. I would never risk breaking it, no matter how strong the urge.' Her gaze returned to him. 'You are quite safe.'

He frowned and gestured to the supplies behind her. 'Do you have any cheap brushes in that collection that I should be worried about?'

Another almost-smile as she turned away. 'Let me pack up, and then let us go see this camp.'

CHAPTER 8

'Will you all be comfortable on horseback?' Ita asked as she and Charlotte made their way down to the stables. 'Some parts of the road are impossible to navigate with a carriage.'

Charlotte blinked against the glare, regretting that last cup of wine she had consumed before retiring. And the three before that. 'We are all competent riders, though I have no doubt my father will complain.'

Ahead, she could see Oliver, Elis, and the defenders preparing to depart. And sure enough, her father was ranting about the quality of the roads in this 'godforsaken kingdom'.

'It is one day on a horse, Father,' Charlotte said when she was close enough to be heard. 'Let us not behave like the sky is falling.'

Her eyes met Tatum's, and he nodded once, which she took to mean 'Thanks for shutting him up'.

'You are going to love this horse,' Hadewaye was saying to Oliver as he guided him over to a tall grey mare.

'Battle proof. Nothing scares her, and she has the most comfortable gait.'

The defender had a friendliness about him that enormously contrasted his comrades, who always looked like they were ready to cut someone's eyeballs out. She appreciated the pairing. Her brother deserved good company, and she was not always up to that particular job.

Charlotte looked over to where Blackmane was intensely watching his surroundings. 'Why so serious, defender? Are we expecting trouble in the stables this morning?'

His gaze drifted lazily in her direction. 'I assume you're aware that all your predecessors are *dead*, my lady?'

She offered him a pleasant smile. 'Yes. That is the reason I was dragged here like a sacrificial lamb.'

'Let the poor man do his job,' her father said.

Hadewaye helped Oliver onto his horse, and Sir Miles began to whine, pausing once to scratch at his newly acquired muzzle.

Charlotte walked over to the dog and crouched down. 'You poor darling.' She rubbed his enormous head, and he leaned into it. 'It is such a long journey. I think it best you stay here.' Looking up at the groom, she asked, 'Is there a stall we can use? He will not like it when we leave without him.'

The groom nodded, then reached for the dog. Naturally, Sir Miles lunged at him, barking madly. All of the horses stirred—except for Oliver's.

'See?' Hadewaye said. '*Battle proof.*'

Tatum stepped up and grabbed the dog by the collar. To Charlotte's absolute surprise, Sir Miles trotted off to the stables with the defender. She rose to her feet, watching the pair until they were out of sight.

'They're pack animals,' Hadewaye said, as though reading her mind. 'Sir Miles will accept us if you do.'

She tore her gaze from the stables. 'Your theory is flawed, defender, as I am still undecided about that particular pack member.'

Hadewaye chuckled all the way to his mount.

'Your horse, my lady,' the groom said behind her.

She turned to find a medium-sized chestnut mare with four white stockings and a blaze down her face.

'Best to not have your back turned to this one.' The groom gave her a pat. 'She's known to bite.'

Tatum returned to the group. 'Another good pairing, I see.'

Charlotte gave him a tired look.

Undeterred, he walked right up to her, taking hold of her waist and lifting her into the saddle. The speed and ease with which it all happened caught her off-guard.

Her eyes followed him all the way to his horse. She was grateful that her brother was blind and could not see the flush of colour on her face. But Ita did. When Charlotte glanced in her bodyguard's direction, she found her holding back a smile.

Tatum climbed into the saddle and swung his horse around. 'Time to move out.'

The group headed for the portcullis.

The moment they were outside the castle walls, the defenders moved into a circular formation around the three of them. What was most impressive to Charlotte was that not one word or look was exchanged in the process. It was all training and instinct.

The sun was well above the hills now, though difficult to make out through the thick cloud cover.

Her father turned to her. 'Be sure to smile and wave as we pass by people today. You have a tendency to always appear offended or angry.'

'Because in your company, I usually am offended or angry. Rest assured, I am not like that all the time.'

'Is that open for debate?' Oliver asked.

'No,' she immediately replied.

They exited the forest, and Charlotte was able to soak up the sight of the lush fields that made up the country-side. The wind ruffled their hair and clothes, bringing with it the crisp scent of grass and damp earth.

When they passed the occasional house or farm, people came outside or stopped working to stare at them. Charlotte felt ridiculous waving, as she was certain that no one knew who they were. She waved anyway. Some waved back, while others scowled and held their children close.

'Smile,' her father whispered, as though that was the problem.

They rode for a few hours before coming upon large, neat fields with varied crops.

Tatum moved to the front of the group, pointing, and Blackmane immediately replaced him.

'The crops you see before you were once part of the camp,' Tatum said. 'Wheat, barley, cabbages, carrots, turnips. They grew it all.'

'The problem was none of it went to the people living in the camp,' Ita said.

'Where does it go now?' Oliver asked.

Hadewaye looked out at the fields. 'Much of it stays here in Carmarthenshire, but they do export whatever they can spare.'

'And they are well compensated for it, I might add,' her father said.

Charlotte ignored the comment.

She had met Lord Hodge once, the man responsible for the running of the camp, and thought him a predator. Her gut feeling had been correct.

'Ahead you'll see what's left of the camp wall,' Tatum continued. 'Much of it has been torn down and reused for other projects. Housing, mostly.'

They all fell silent as they approached the entrance. The gate was missing, torn from its hinges. Charlotte felt a sense of dread as they entered. The group dismounted and secured the horses. Blackmane tended them while the others began their walk-through.

Everywhere Charlotte looked there was destruction. A broken chair here, a shattered jug there—all seemingly frozen in time. Charred wood and stone sat in piles on the ground where fires had once burned, long ago extinguished.

A shudder ran through Charlotte as they reached the centre of the camp. She looked around at the destroyed tents and what appeared to be storage barns.

'They're not storage barns,' Ita informed her. 'That's where they housed the prisoners.'

'They must have really packed them in.' Charlotte

looked back at Ita, who was shiny-eyed. 'Were you ever in here?' The possibility had only just occurred to her.

Ita shook her head. 'No. My mother was.' She swallowed as she looked away.

Charlotte's stomach dropped a little. 'Oh.'

Her father pointed to a fenced area ten yards away. 'Is that where the livestock were kept?'

Hadewaye and Alveye exchanged a look that filled Charlotte with trepidation. She went over to inspect the enclosure, and the others followed.

'What is in there?' Oliver asked. He was holding on to Hadewaye's arm, using him as a guide in the absence of Sir Miles.

Charlotte looked around at the tiny blankets and discarded toys strewn about the yard. 'Is this—' Her throat closed, so she tried again. 'Is this where the children were kept?'

Ita stepped up beside her, pointing to the hole a few feet away. 'That's how we got many of them out.'

'The army?'

Ita laughed. 'It wasn't much of an army back then. Two rebel groups and a handful of defenders.'

Charlotte turned, eyes meeting the commander's. 'I had no idea you had any part in this.'

'From all accounts, neither did the warden,' her father muttered.

Tatum looked back at the hole. 'That's a rather long story.'

'It started as a love story,' Hadewaye said, 'which grew into something bigger.'

'What do you see?' Oliver asked his sister.

She went to him, snaking her arm through his. 'I see children taken from their parents too young, confined, with no way to escape.' Her voice came out despondent. 'I see the kind of grief that drowns a person.'

The group stood in silence for a few moments, and then Elis discreetly exited the yard, Alveye trailing after him.

Oliver patted his sister's hand. 'Careful. These people might figure out that you have a beating heart beneath that icy exterior.'

Her eyes went to the drawn wire atop the fence, and she could bear it no longer. She released her brother's arm and headed for the exit, clasping her hands together when she realised they were trembling.

'Lady Charlotte,' Tatum called after her.

She did not stop until she was outside and well away from the cruelty. Then, drawing a breath, she turned with a questioning look to the commander. 'Yes?'

He approached slowly, looking her over carefully. 'Are you all right?'

She nodded. 'Yes. Why?'

He reached for her face, and she drew back from his hand. He immediately lowered it.

'What are you doing?' she asked.

He gestured to her cheek. 'Your eye is leaking.'

She brushed the rogue tear away, mortified that it had escaped. 'It is this damn wind.'

He dropped his gaze. 'Can I say something?'

She nodded.

He considered his words before speaking. 'You might

have been sent here to play a role for England, but that doesn't mean everything has to be an act.'

'Meaning?'

'Your reaction to what you saw is real. This opportunity you've been handed can be as real as you like. Llywelyn ap Gruffudd *is* your great-grandfather. You *are* technically Welsh royalty—even if that idea seems laughable to some.'

She frowned. 'Are you nearing your point?'

He looked around before continuing. 'You've seen a pinch of the injustice and oppression these people have faced, and you're in this privileged position where you get a say over their future.'

She shook her head. 'You are wrong, Commander. My father may get a say. Lord Wybert definitely gets a say. I am simply—'

'These people don't care what your father or Wybert have to say. Most wish them dead, and the rest tolerate them so they can access England's iron supply.' He exhaled. 'You'll return home when the opportunity arises. You may as well have something to show for your time here.'

She searched his eyes. 'More smiling and waving?'

'You're smart. You can do better than smiling and waving.' Before she could object, he added, 'You came from two parents. Maybe it's time to consider what your mother would do?' He landed that question on her before walking away.

She stood there, a little cold and a little numb, until Ita appeared in front of her.

'I think your father is out of his comfort zone,' Ita said quietly. 'He wants to leave.'

Charlotte looked over at him, standing there with his eyes heavenward to avoid having to look at his surroundings.

'Of course he wants to leave. This place is England's shame, and England's shame is his shame.'

She left to find Oliver.

CHAPTER 9

*C*harlotte was about to step out into the courtyard when she heard Wybert and her father speaking outside. Ita pulled up abruptly to avoid running into her, and Charlotte raised a finger to her lips before she had a chance to ask what was going on.

'Charlotte is not the problem,' Wybert was saying. 'It is your son they are wary of. Not because he is English but because he is blind.'

'They think him cursed,' Elis replied in a defeated tone. 'I would have thought these godless people would be beyond senseless superstitions.'

'They are not godless, I assure you. But they are cautious, and understandably so.' Wybert paused. 'You may want to consider sending him back to Livingston Manor. You have plenty of staff to take care of him.'

Charlotte held her breath as she waited for her father's reply.

'Coming here was a big ask of them. To then separate

them… I cannot do it.' He cleared his throat. 'The people will grow to like him when they get to know him. He is quite charismatic, as you know.'

Charlotte's lungs relaxed. There were only a handful of moments that she could recall Elis behaving as a father should—and this was one of them.

She looked at Ita, who gave her an encouraging smile, and then she stepped out into the courtyard.

When Wybert saw her, he clasped his hands behind his back and offered a small bow. 'Good morning, Charlotte.'

'*Lady* Charlotte,' she corrected before looking at her father. 'Good morning, Father.' Her gaze flicked to Alveye, who was waiting a few yards away.

'Is that what you are wearing into the village today?' Elis asked, disapproval clear in his tone.

Her gaze fell to the midnight-blue taffeta gown with its high collar. 'Yes. Why?'

'It is quite plain for a princess.' His eyes moved over her. 'And not a jewel in sight.'

'I am going for *approachable*, not showy.'

He responded with a scowl.

'Your father is right,' Wybert said. 'You may want to consider dressing the part.'

She dragged her gaze, kicking and screaming, to his. 'If I want fashion advice from you, my lord, I will be sure to ask.'

A discreet smile played on his face. 'Very well. I shall leave you to your day.' He bowed again before striding away.

She frowned when she saw her father's face. 'What?'

'You need to let go of this ridiculous grudge. The match soured. His family did not approve'—he held up his hands—'for reasons that cut you deeply, I know.' He shook his head. 'All this hostility has well and truly run its course.'

'I politely disagree. I think you moved on far too easily —especially for a man who places his pride above all else.'

Elis pinched the bridge of his nose. 'Oliver is waiting in the carriage. Go.'

The family were heading to Llanddeilo to visit the market. It had been Wybert's suggestion to support locals by buying directly from merchants, and Charlotte had to agree that it was a good idea.

Sir Miles poked his head out of the carriage when he heard them approaching.

'Only us,' she said before he had a chance to bark. Her gaze drifted to the stables, where Tatum and Blackmane were deep in conversation. Tatum glanced in her direction, nodding once. She returned the gesture.

'You look positively breathtaking,' Oliver said when she climbed into the carriage. 'If the entire village is not in love with you by the end of our visit, then I am no judge of beauty.'

Charlotte suppressed a smile as she took her seat. 'You know I trust your opinion above all others.'

Elis climbed in after her, looking between his children. 'You might retract that statement if you could *see* her. She looks as though she is dressed for a day of reading in the library.'

'Perfect' was Oliver's reply. 'This is definitely an understated sort of crowd.'

Charlotte gave her father a smug look. 'I could not agree more.'

Tatum appeared at the window, reaching inside to pet Sir Miles. The dog chose to lap up the attention in place of growling, which annoyed Charlotte to no end.

'We'll be nearby on horseback,' Tatum said. 'Remember the rules when we get there. Follow our instructions at all times.' He looked between the three of them. 'Any questions?'

They all shook their heads.

'Good. Then let's move out.' Tatum disappeared, and a moment later, the carriage rolled forwards. They were on their way to Llanddeilo.

The journey there was uneventful. They travelled through the same tranquil forest they had the day prior, then veered east to the village. The carriage drew attention along the way. By the time they neared the town square, people were lining the street in order to get a glimpse of them, some shouting in an older dialect she struggled to understand. She would have preferred they shout in French or Spanish.

When the carriage finally rolled to a stop, a handful of merchants came forwards to welcome them, offering up small gifts, such as apples and hand-woven blankets, that the defenders collected on their behalf. Others were more cautious.

The square smelled of roasted meat and baked bread, which had Sir Miles sniffing the air. Chatter and laughter sounded around them, contrasting the imagery Charlotte had formed in her mind. Carmarthenshire had been depicted by her father as a depressed kingdom incapable of joy, but that was not the case.

'Go back to England,' called the man who was butchering a carcass out front of his shop.

Oliver scrunched his nose at the smell. 'Please tell me that is animal blood.' He kept his voice low so only Charlotte would hear him.

'It is,' she whispered back. 'For now.'

The defenders subtly ushered them away from the man, along the muddy cobbled stones, past the beggars, to a stone fountain in the centre. Charlotte noticed various handmade flags hanging from rooflines, stitched with an emblem of a lion. She leaned closer to Ita and asked, 'What is that flag? I do not recognise it.'

Ita followed her line of sight. 'Surprising, given it is *your* family's emblem.'

Charlotte felt a rush of embarrassment. She should have known that.

'It's based on the arms of the last native Prince of Wales,' Ita explained. 'Your great-grandfather.'

Charlotte was distracted by a young girl who approached with a gift in hand. Ita stepped between them, then looked to Tatum, who nodded. She stepped aside.

The girl was around ten years old. She beamed up at Charlotte as she said, 'I'm so happy we have our own princess.' She held out the cloth-covered package tied with cheap string.

It was the first time someone outside the family had referred to her as a princess. Charlotte crouched in front of the girl to accept the gift.

'Smell it,' the girl prompted.

Charlotte took it, but when she went to bring it to her face, Tatum stepped forwards and knocked it from her hand.

'What are you doing?' Charlotte asked, turning to glare at him.

Tatum gestured to Ita. 'Check it.'

Charlotte rose to her full height. 'For *what*?'

'Poisons.'

The young girl's face fell. 'It's flower petals soaked in fragrant oil, sir.'

Ita took the cloth package and drew her knife.

Charlotte snatched it from her. 'It has a *string*.'

With a sigh, Tatum grabbed it, untied it, then inspected the contents before cautiously sniffing it. 'It's safe.' He handed it back to Charlotte as he looked down at the young girl. 'We're just keeping your princess safe.'

The girl curtsied before Charlotte—*curtsied*—then retreated.

'Well, that was awkward,' Oliver said.

Charlotte turned to face Tatum so he could receive the full heat of her glare. 'Have you lost your mind? She was just a young girl.'

He was unmoved by that fact. 'With two parents whose political beliefs we know nothing about. Maybe that butcher over there is her father. Would you accept a package from him and sniff it if he told you to?'

'He has a point,' Elis said, joining the conversation.

Charlotte's gaze went to him. 'On the subject of knowing nothing about people'—she pointed to a nearby flag—'why have you never shown me this emblem? *Our* family emblem? You must have seen it before. Our mother grew up here.'

Oliver appeared perplexed. 'We have a family emblem?'

'Yes.' She looked back at the flag. 'A lion, with a blue tongue... standing up.'

'Can lions do that?'

Charlotte pressed a hand to her brow.

'Am I expected to hold on to every keepsake *twenty-four years* after your mother's death?' Elis hissed.

Charlotte took a step towards him. 'You erased everything that connected us to this place. Then you have the audacity to bring us here and parade me around, complaining that I do not dress like a Welsh princess.'

Oliver winced. 'Perhaps this is a conversation for later?'

'Incoming,' Blackmane said, reaching for the hilt of his sword.

They all looked in the direction of a group of women approaching with flowers in their hands. The defenders moved to form a protective circle around the family.

'There she is,' said one, pointing. 'Our very own Princess Charlotte.'

Ita moved forwards. 'Morning, ladies. Can I ask that you approach one at a time?'

They peered around Ita, large smiles on their faces.

'A spitting image of her mother,' another said.

A third nodded emphatically. 'A true Welsh beauty.'

The butcher from earlier must have been watching because he shouted from the other side of the square, 'She's no princess of ours. A true princess knows the pain of her people. She suffers through our losses alongside us, not from the comfort of some English manor.' He speared the air with his finger. 'What do you know of our suffering? Go home—the lot of you. Back to England, where you belong.'

Tatum moved closer to Charlotte, gaze darting about the crowd. 'I think it's time to leave.'

Alveye signalled to another man marching towards them, spewing profanities.

'I second that,' Blackmane said.

The skin on Charlotte's arms began to crawl, as though sensing something bad was about to happen.

Ita took Charlotte by the arm and led her away from the man. 'I need you to keep pace with me.'

Charlotte flinched at the sound of Ita's sword leaving its sheath. When she looked back at her brother, she saw him gripping Sir Miles's collar tightly. The dog was on high alert.

'Oliver—'

'He's right behind us.'

Sir Miles barked, and Charlotte jumped.

'Easy, boy,' Oliver said.

A woman came at them from the other side.

'Back!' Blackmane warned.

'Do you have any idea what we went through at the hands of *your king*?' the woman shouted at them. 'While you were living in comfort, we were birthing babies in a slave camp!'

Tatum came up beside Charlotte. 'Head straight for the carriage.'

'Leave the princess alone!' someone else shouted. 'None of that was her doing.'

Tatum gestured to Blackmane. 'Clear a path.'

The defender dashed ahead, forcing people back and out of the way. Sir Miles managed to trip Oliver amid the chaos. Hadewaye pulled him upright at the same time Elis ran into him.

'Stupid animal,' Elis said, swinging his foot at the dog.

Before Alveye could move him on, an arrow struck Elis in the back. Screams erupted from nearby spectators.

'Shooter!' Alveye said. 'I need cover.'

Charlotte's eyes widened as her father began to sink to the ground. Somehow, Alveye managed to pick him up, charging forwards as though he were holding a small child instead of a fully grown, well-fed man.

Tatum retrieved his bow, loaded it, and moved to the back of the group. 'Talk to me.'

'Rooftop, maybe,' Alveye said over his shoulder.

Charlotte could not tear her eyes away from her father, whose face was twisted in pain.

'Who got shot?' Oliver asked.

'Father.' Her voice was a strained whisper.

Tatum glanced in their direction. 'Keep moving.'

Hearing the commotion, Blackmane returned at a jog, eyes going straight to Elis. 'Do we have eyes on the shooter?'

'Not yet,' Tatum muttered.

Charlotte flinched when she saw an arrow whistle past her brother's head, missing by an inch. She whipped her head around when she heard the sickening thud of it hitting flesh. Her feet faltered when she spotted the arrow protruding from Ita's shoulder.

'I'm hit,' Ita said through gritted teeth.

Panic filled Oliver's face. 'What is going on?'

Charlotte could not find words to reply. She reached for Ita, holding her steady as she somehow continued to walk, or rather stagger, forwards.

'Southeast, fourth roof from the left,' Tatum said to Blackmane.

The defender looked over at Ita.

'I've got her,' Tatum said. 'Go.'

Blackmane took off at a run towards the shops, sword already in hand.

'Charlotte, do not stop until you reach the carriage,' Tatum ordered, watching his surroundings down his arrow. 'Nearly there.'

'Charlotte?' Oliver said.

Hadewaye kept him moving. 'Your sister's fine.'

'Out of the way!' Alveye shouted when a woman stepped into their path.

'Is the princess all right?' she called as they charged past.

The carriage was only a few yards away now.

'Charlotte, climb in first,' Tatum instructed. 'Oliver next. I need pressure on the wounds. Hadewaye, ride ahead and have the physician meet us when we pull up.'

Hadewaye took Ita from Charlotte so she could get in the carriage. She climbed in, shaking all over. A moment later, Oliver and Sir Miles scrambled in after her.

'Clear the seats,' Alveye said as he hoisted Elis inside.

Charlotte helped him, then made room for Ita. Oliver

sank to the floor of the carriage, visibly terrified. She guided his hands to their father's back. 'Press firmly either side.'

Oliver felt around the arrow. 'Is he alive?'

A groan from Elis confirmed he was.

'Get back from the carriage!' Tatum shouted outside, making everyone flinch.

Hadewaye's horse galloped by, the curtain lifting slightly in his wake.

'Can you tell if the arrow is barbed?' Ita asked her, trying to sound brave.

Charlotte tore the fabric to get a better look, then realised she had no idea what a barbed arrow looked like. She knew nothing about weapons because she had never been forced to learn in order to survive. 'I… I do not know.'

'I'm conscious,' Ita murmured, 'so that's a good sign.'

Charlotte took hold of her hand and squeezed it. 'We will be back at the castle before you know it, and the physician will see to you.'

Tatum's fist pounded the carriage twice, followed by the sound of leather reins slapping the horses' backs. She looked over at her father, who had turned an eerie grey colour.

'Will he be all right?' Oliver asked.

She could only imagine how much more stressful this would be without visuals to gauge the danger. 'Of course he will. It will take more than an arrow to be rid of him.' The humour fell flat, the situation too dire. She thought back to the last words she spoke to him.

Ita squeezed her hand this time. 'He'll be all right.' She

was in no condition to provide comfort to anyone, and yet she did.

Charlotte pressed her free hand to Ita's wound, causing the bodyguard to wince. 'Hold on.'

She looked back at her father.

Hold on.

CHAPTER 10

*T*atum stopped outside Charlotte's bedchamber door to gather his thoughts. It was late in the afternoon, and they had just finished questioning the shooter—another former rebel with a chip on his shoulder.

Exhaling, he dismissed the guard on duty, then knocked on the door.

'Go away' came Charlotte's reply.

Ignoring her response, he went inside to check on her.

She was seated by the window, barefoot and wearing only a chemise. The dress she had worn that day sat in a bloodied, crumpled pile on the floor. His gaze flicked to the basin of red water on the table. The metallic scent of blood hung in the air.

Despite the resilience she displayed earlier that day, she had likely never been exposed to violence up close before. She would naturally be shaken.

'Ita is all patched up and on her way to Maddock House,' he said.

She stared at him from across the bed. 'And my father?'

'Sleeping. The physician seemed optimistic.'

Charlotte rubbed at her head. 'I should go see him.'

Tatum walked over to the dresses hanging in the wardrobe, flicking through them briefly before tugging one down and throwing it onto the bed. 'You'll need to dress.'

She rose slowly to her feet, then covered herself with her hands. 'Turn around, please.'

He faced the door. 'Have you eaten?'

'This morning.'

'What about *after* this morning?'

Her silence gave him his answer.

'I'm afraid you're stuck with me as your personal guard now,' he said. 'Ita will be out of action for a while, and frankly, I don't trust the castle guards to replace her.' He glanced over his shoulder and, seeing she was dressed, turned back to her.

A curious look settled on Charlotte's face. 'What happens to you if my father dies? Will you get into trouble?'

'I'd rather not find out. No one is praying for his recovery more than I am right now.'

'Do you pray to Belenus? Your pagan sun god?'

He shrugged. 'The famine ended when the sun returned, did it not?'

She gave him a doubtful look, but then her face turned serious once more. 'Thank you for getting us out of there today. I see what all the fuss is about now. The defenders' ability to stay calm, protect, *and* catch the criminal was impressive.'

'I don't know about that. Your father *is* currently fighting for his life.'

She thought for a moment. 'Did you question the shooter?'

'We did.'

'And?'

Tatum rested his hands on his hips. 'We didn't get a lot out of him. He'll be executed tomorrow.'

'Hanged?'

He nodded, hesitating before adding, 'We believe the arrow was meant for Oliver and your father got in the way.'

'I see.' She pressed her eyes closed. 'I guess he was right.'

'Who?'

She opened her eyes. 'I overheard Lord Wybert speaking with my father this morning. He is of the belief that people think Oliver is cursed.'

'A handful of arseheads, maybe.' He exhaled. 'We all knew we had our work cut out for us coming into this. It's going to take time.'

'This is our third day here, and my father was shot.' She shook her head. 'It is the oddest thing in the world to have half the kingdom calling you "princess" and the other half wishing you dead.'

As a defender, he understood. 'Remember, you're here to change their minds. If you manage to win over your haters, you'll be the safest person in this kingdom. Every man, woman, and child will have your back.'

She threw her hands up. 'You keep saying that but with no advice as to how I do it. What is the actual process to get to this magical place and time? Do I invite the butcher and his hateful friends to dine with us?'

'Please don't. He's the one person in that village who has a better knife collection than me.'

A faint smile appeared on her face, quickly extinguished.

'There will be a way,' he assured her. 'An opportunity will present itself, and you'll be ready. There's a way to change the mind of every sceptic out there. Your situation is serious, sure, but not entirely helpless.'

'I will be sure to tell my father that. I am certain he will appreciate the sentiment in his current state.'

She had the kind of sense of humour that one could miss if they were not paying attention.

'Ready to see your father?'

She smoothed down her dress. 'Yes.'

He looked down at the bare feet poking out from beneath her dress. 'You don't want some shoes?'

Her gaze fell to her feet. 'Oh.'

He waited while she put on some boots, and then they went to see her father.

Charlotte passed Oliver in the doorway of their father's bedchamber. 'How is he?' she whispered.

'Awake.' Oliver leaned closer. 'This whole experience has done nothing to improve his mood.'

'I can hear you' came their father's voice.

Oliver winced. 'I shall be drinking in my quarters if you need me.'

Charlotte gave Sir Miles a quick pet, then watched Oliver make his way over to Hadewaye.

'I'll wait here,' Tatum told her when she went to step inside.

She nodded, then made her way to her father's bedside.

'Do not look so disappointed to see me alive,' Elis said when she reached him.

He looked so small in that huge bed. Perhaps it was the nightshirt. She could not recall the last time she had seen him in one.

'I knew you would be fine. Your pride would never allow one small arrow to be your end.' She noted the sickly grey tone of his skin. 'How is the pain?'

He blinked as though it were an effort. 'The physician has given me some rather strong herbs. I can barely feel a thing.'

She went to adjust the bedsheet.

'Do not fuss,' he snapped without looking at her.

Her hand fell away. 'Did Alveye tell you that they caught the man?'

'Yes.' He cleared his throat. 'Lord Wybert suggested a discreet, private execution. The last thing we want to do is rile up the locals.'

'That makes sense.'

A long silence stretched out between them.

'There is really no need for you to sit around,' Elis said.

She was being dismissed already. Her time was up.

A familiar feeling punched in the base of her stomach,

'He was clearly guilty, and we felt the need to be discreet. I personally oversaw the whole thing.' He returned his attention to Charlotte. 'I heard you were well received by many during your visit to Llanddeilo yesterday. People even addressed you with a royal title?'

He seemed genuinely impressed by this fact. It made life a little safer for him, she guessed.

'Yes, while the rest of the village fired arrows at my family,' she replied.

Wybert gave her a sympathetic look. 'Well, do not let a few unruly men get you down.'

She felt her blood heat at his response. 'That was just the trumpet call I needed, thank you.'

Tatum looked down at his feet to hide his smirk.

'I was about to check in on your father, if you would like to join me?' Wybert offered.

Charlotte stared hard at him. 'I think I will go later —alone.'

'Very well.' The duke bowed his head. 'I shall leave you to your day.' With that, he walked quietly away.

When he had rounded the corner, Charlotte saw that Tatum was trying not to smile. 'What is so funny?'

He looked off down the corridor. 'He's trying so hard. Was the fallout between the two of you really that bad?'

She headed off down the corridor towards Oliver's bedchamber. 'His efforts are too late. He is only *trying* because he needs something from me. The moment that changes, he will turn his back so fast I will be left spinning.'

Tatum jogged a few paces to catch up with her. 'I'm

not suggesting you trust him, only that you attempt to be civil for the sake of your own peace and sanity.'

'I am civil with those deserving of my civility.' She picked up her pace. 'Is my brother in his bedchamber?'

'Actually, he's training with Hadewaye.'

She pulled up and turned to look at him. 'What do you mean *training*? Training for what?'

'Just some basic weapons training.' He said it as though it were the most natural thing in the world for a *blind man* to be using weapons.

She stared at him, waiting for some sort of sign that he was joking, but he looked back with a straight face. 'Has Hadewaye lost his mind?'

Tatum shifted his weight. 'He has two arms, two legs, a functioning brain, and superb hearing. Yet no one has bothered to teach the man how to defend himself or take care of his sister if the need arises.' He paused. 'I'm afraid your father has failed him there.'

Her hands curled into fists. 'How dare you? My father has failed him in every way *except* that one.'

'He wanted to learn.'

'Did he?' Her voice was slightly raised. 'Well, I want him in one piece.'

Tatum gave her a tired look. 'He's your brother, not your child.'

'Your entire job is to keep him safe!'

'He's perfectly safe with Hadewaye.' Tatum sighed. 'You think we just handed him a sword and shield and started throwing knives in his direction?'

'Probably. Or perhaps you threw him over the edge of

a cliff to see if he could survive. That is what your kind do, is it not?'

He gave her a lopsided grin. 'That's not quite how that works—'

'Where is he?' She marched for the exit. 'I need to put an end to this madness before he gets hurt.'

He followed her once again. 'Does he not get a say?' When she did not reply, he said, 'They're in the outer-ward.'

Charlotte was shaking from anger by the time she made it outside. She charged ahead through the misty rain. When she finally reached them, she stopped to take in the scene before her. Her soaked-to-the-bone brother was holding a wooden sword, sparring an equally soggy Hadewaye. Somehow, he was *not* covered in blood.

Her gaze went to Sir Miles, who was lying calmly on the grass nearby, watching them. The dog was not tethered.

'Don't swing like that,' Hadewaye was saying. 'You'll use up twice the energy of your opponent. We want precise, calculated movements.' He moved behind Oliver. 'Now, listen for me.'

As if the scene was not confusing enough, standing under cover was Blackmane and a heavily pregnant woman with a giant bird perched on her shoulder.

Charlotte blinked. 'Is that an eagle?'

Tatum followed her gaze. 'Yes. That's Margery.'

'And is that Blackmane's wife?'

'It is. The lovely Isabel. She came to provide an update on Ita. Apparently she's doing well.' He looked over at them. 'And to see her husband, whom she's clearly missing.'

Charlotte scrunched her nose. 'Really? *Blackmane?*'

A chuckle escaped Tatum. 'The heart wants what the heart wants.'

Charlotte watched as Isabel pet Margery while chatting away to her husband. 'So that is the infamous Lady Isabel who leapt from the walls of Hampstead Keep into a moat to escape marrying Lord Hodge?'

'That's the one.'

Her attention was drawn back to the training field as Oliver spun around, jabbing the wooden sword straight at Hadewaye. The defender knocked it out of his hand before running his sword along the back of Oliver's knee.

'Better,' Hadewaye said, 'but if this were a real sword, you would be bleeding out right now.'

Charlotte's eyebrows pinched together. 'Wooden swords can still leave bruises.'

Oliver stilled at the sound of her voice and raised a hand in greeting. 'I did not realise I had an audience. Good morning!'

'Is it?'

Sir Miles got to his feet and sauntered over to her. She rubbed his head around the straps of the muzzle, wishing she could take it off.

It was at that moment that Isabel noticed her, and a smile spread across her pretty face as she made her way over. Blackmane remained where he was, but his eyes followed his wife.

'There she is,' Isabel sang. 'Her Royal Highness

Princess Charlotte.' She stopped three feet away and lowered into a curtsy. 'Welcome *home*.'

Charlotte looked the impossibly sweet woman over. 'There is no need to curtsy.'

'Of course there is. We only have one princess.' Her gaze fell to Sir Miles. 'Oh you poor thing. That thing cannot be very comfortable.'

She showed no fear of the dog, who was fixated on the eagle.

'Ita tells me we have a lot in common,' Isabel announced.

That seemed unlikely. 'Because we have both spent time in England?'

'There's that—and we both have guard pets.' Her smile widened.

Charlotte looked at the eagle, who was keeping a close eye on the dog. 'I see.'

'I was so sorry to hear about your rather rough start. People around these parts can take a little time to warm up to strangers.'

'I have definitely picked up on that,' Charlotte replied in a flat tone.

'But I assure you that you are in good hands. Commander Tatum is very good at what he does. Plus, he can be a lot of fun.'

Nothing changed on Charlotte's face. 'I shall take your word for it.'

Isabel looked over at Oliver. 'He is doing very well for his first time.'

'First time being repeatedly hit with a wooden stick?'

Isabel laughed a very pretty laugh. 'He is definitely

getting hit less now than before you arrived.' She faced Charlotte again. 'You will have to come visit us at Maddock House once you are settled. Ryder is not keen on me coming here, as you can imagine.'

Charlotte looked down at her bump. 'Congratulations, by the way.'

'Thank you.' She stilled suddenly. 'Oh.' Isabel reached for Charlotte's hand, and before she knew what was happening, it was pressed to her stomach. 'Our little fighter in the making. Can you feel it?'

Charlotte's first instinct was to pull away. It all seemed too intimate for two strangers. But then she felt the pulse of a foot, or head, or limb pressing against her hand. Her fingers relaxed against the fabric of the dress. 'Does it hurt?'

'Not usually.' Isabel's hand remained over Charlotte's. 'I actually find it comforting. If baby is moving, then baby is well.'

A loud 'Oof' from the lawn had Charlotte withdrawing her hand and looking to her brother. He was on his back, gasping for breath.

'That is quite enough,' she said, patience gone. 'I cannot stand by while you assault a blind man.'

Tatum spoke up at that. 'He is winded, not injured.'

Charlotte ignored him. 'This would never happen back home. In England, no one would expect a blind man to fight.'

A warm hand landed on Charlotte's arm. It was Isabel —always with the touching.

'You are not in England anymore. You are home in Carmarthenshire now. And here, if you can hold a sword,

96

then you can fight.' She smiled softly. 'Even if some of us are not very good at the fighting part.'

'What the lady lacks in skill, she makes up for in spirit,' Tatum said.

Isabel laughed. 'I try.' She kissed the eagle's beak before resuming the conversation. 'Tatum was telling me earlier that you are a very talented artist. I would love to see some of your work sometime.'

Charlotte looked up at Tatum. 'You told Lady Isabel that I am *talented*?'

'I don't think I used the word *talented*—'

'You definitely said talented,' Isabel said, cutting him off.

A gentle flush of colour appeared on his face.

Charlotte spared him further embarrassment and moved the conversation along. 'I shall paint you something and bring it to Llanelieu when I visit.'

Isabel reached out and squeezed her hand. 'Do not leave it too long. We love visitors. My mother will be especially thrilled, as most of our guests are usually soldiers.'

'Belle,' Blackmane called.

She looked over her shoulder.

'The carriage is waiting.'

Isabel nodded before returning her attention to Charlotte. 'It is time for me to return to Maddock House.' She looked down at Sir Miles. 'You take care of your people, dear sir. Hopefully next time we meet you are free of that torturous device.' She curtsied again and flashed a warm smile at Charlotte before leaving.

Charlotte watched her waddle away. 'How on earth did Blackmane secure such a woman?'

Tatum laughed. 'He's a big softie under all that armour.'

'I assumed under all that armour was another layer of armour.'

Oliver whistled for Sir Miles, and the dog ran to him. Soon, her brother was standing before her, face flushed with more life than she had seen in him in some time.

'What do you think?' he asked her. 'I got a few in.'

'I definitely saw Hadewaye get a few in.' She frowned at the defender, who had followed Oliver over to them.

'This afternoon it's laps in the outer-ward,' Hadewaye announced.

Charlotte's brow creased. 'You're going to make him *run laps*?'

'Sir Miles can run with me,' Oliver said. 'We will be absolutely fine.'

She bit her tongue because he seemed happy.

'The dog could certainly do with the exercise,' Tatum said.

Charlotte looked down. 'Ignore him. You are perfect just as you are.'

The rain began to fall harder. It had barely stopped since their arrival.

'What are your plans for the afternoon?' Oliver asked her.

She had not been prepared for the possibility of her brother being busy. 'I... had planned to visit Father.'

'That is three minutes of your day accounted for.'

'Then paint.'

Oliver took hold of the dog's collar. 'Well, I cannot wait to see the finished piece.' He winked, then stepped past her. 'See you at dinner.'

She watched him walk away, feeling oddly lost. She could feel the weight of Tatum's eyes on her and looked at him questioningly. 'What?'

'This is a good thing.'

She was going to ask what he was talking about but then realised she knew.

'Even Sir Miles knows it,' he added.

'Now you are a dog expert too?'

He looked after them. 'Sir Miles knows what Oliver can handle, even if you don't.'

He was right. The dog would have lost his mind if he thought her brother was in real danger.

Her gaze fell to the water pooling around them. 'Do you think Oliver knows what people are saying about him?'

Tatum was silent a long moment. 'I think he knows that arrow was meant for him, if that's what you're asking.'

She hugged herself against the rain. 'I pray they give him a chance, because he is so deserving. He is gracious, smart, patient, empathetic. He is everything one could want in a prince... but missing sight.'

Tatum studied her closely. 'You could choose to be all those things *with* the sight.'

She laughed in a humourless sort of way. 'No one has ever described me using those words, I assure you.'

'I described you as smart only a few days ago.' He sniffed. 'We can work on the rest.'

She bit her top lip to stop from smiling. 'Well, I am going to be *gracious* and go check on my father.'

'Great. You can practice *patience* while you're there.'

'And empathy.'

'And forgiveness.'

Her eyes narrowed. 'Are you adding to my list?'

'I could have sworn you mentioned forgiveness.' His eyes shone with mischief.

As much as she did not want to admit it, there were worse men she could have protecting her. Tatum was, if nothing else, amusing. 'Since we are on the subject of self-improvement, perhaps *you* could practice respect.'

He bowed his head. 'Touché, Your Highness.'

Charlotte gathered up her wet skirts and headed for the chambers.

CHAPTER 12

*T*atum was leaning against the inside wall of the turret, looking out the small window. The sky was a thunderous grey, contrasting the lush green landscape below. A flock of sheep was grazing in the distance. The sun had not been seen in days. He glanced over at Charlotte, who was painting. She held a wooden palette in one hand while she marked out River Tywi with the other.

'If you are trying to make me nervous by staring, it will not work. I simply paint over any mistakes later.'

He turned and rested his elbows on the window ledge. 'I watch only out of interest... mixed with boredom. Paintings take a long time, I'm realising.'

She ignored him.

'Are there any *short* recreational activities you enjoy?' When she did not reply, he said, 'I have some trousers you could mend.'

Her nostrils flared with silent laughter. 'One of my governesses used to make me do her mending under the pretence of preparing me for marriage. Horrid woman. I have not picked up a needle since she left.'

Tatum laughed through his nose. 'Glad I was not the only one with a less than desirable governess.'

'My father knew how to pick them. I swear they got progressively more horrid over the years.'

He looked up at the sky. 'My father just let the bailiff select ours. He had no idea what he was doing.'

She glanced sideways at him. 'Was your mother not around?'

'She was at her family home in Talybont.' His throat thickened. 'She has since passed.'

Her hand froze midstroke. 'How did she die?'

He cleared his throat. 'Pneumonia is what we were told. It was a long time ago.'

Charlotte turned to face him. 'You were *told*?'

He always felt claustrophobic when he spoke about her. 'She got out with my sister before the walls went up. They didn't return.'

She nodded slowly. 'I see.'

And now he felt the need to defend her decision. 'She saw the direction in which the kingdom was heading. It was a smart move.'

Charlotte was silent a moment. 'Why did she not take you also?'

He shifted his weight. 'Claudia was young and needed her mother.' When he noticed sympathy creeping into Charlotte's expression, he added, 'I don't blame her for leaving. Chadora was a difficult place to live for many years, and my father didn't make it any easier.'

Charlotte searched his face. 'Why did the whole family not leave?'

Normally, he would not bother trying to explain his father's actions or decisions to anyone, but he knew she would understand because her father was cut from the same cloth. 'Father's family all come from Chadora'—he made a face—'formerly Pembroke. He was too proud to leave. Everyone he deems important would have viewed him as a coward.' He paused. 'My brother stayed because he's to inherit the estate—'

'And you stayed because that is what men in your family do.'

He nodded.

'So your brother is to inherit, and you are to serve your kingdom?'

'Yes.'

She glanced in the direction of the castle. 'Ah, fathers, with their ridiculous pride and impossibly high expectations. Mine has never gotten over the disappointment of a blind son followed by a daughter.' She paused, wetting her lips. 'I remember overhearing a conversation between my father and my last governess. She was telling him that my beauty and fortune would appeal to any man—so long as I did not open my mouth before the wedding day.'

He winced. 'Ouch.'

She waved his sympathy away. 'She was right, though. One dinner with Lord Wybert's parents and the next day the wedding was off.'

'After one meal? What on earth did you say to them?'

'Too much. They made some comments about my

brother and mother.' She pressed her lips together. 'So I made some comments back.'

'Of course you did.' He had a very clear image of her completely losing her cool. 'That doesn't really explain the hate you hold for him. Is it because he didn't stand up for you?'

All the light left her face, and she turned back to the canvas. 'Among other reasons.'

The change in her demeanour had him dropping the subject.

Charlotte resumed painting. 'Tell me about your mother.'

He straightened. 'Why?'

'Because I am trying to gauge the impact her leaving had on you.'

At least she was honest.

'How much longer is this painting going to take?'

'It must have hurt when she left.'

It still hurt. 'It would be more of a concern if it didn't, don't you think?'

She glanced at him. 'Was she a warm person?'

His mind reached for memories of her without his permission. 'Yes, she was warm with everyone.'

Charlotte fell silent for a while. 'I cannot help but wonder if her departure and absence is the reason why you have relationships with unavailable women.'

'And who told you that?' He asked the question knowing full well it was Ita.

Charlotte dipped her brush in place of an answer. 'It makes sense. Married women cannot abandon you because they were never yours to begin with.'

He bristled. 'Are you done pretending you know what you're talking about?'

'Nearly.' She turned to him. 'You also hide behind humour. My brother does the same thing.'

He was done with the conversation now. 'It feels a lot like you're projecting and drawing convenient conclusions so you don't feel alone in your own grief. Yes, I make jokes.' He should have stopped there. 'Some of us prefer not to package our misery and carry it with us through life. Some of us are capable of happiness.'

Nothing changed on her face. 'You seem agitated. Now might be a good time for one of your little jokes.'

She was a real piece of work.

'Upon reflection, I see that you're right. Perhaps I'll try living *your* way. Copious amounts of wine, unbridled rage aimed at anyone who dares to cross my path, and a vicious pet to repel people.'

'You have several of those already. They are called *defenders*.'

They both fell silent, their stares heated. He was first to look away, bringing his hands to rest on his hips as he attempted to rein in his temper.

'Listen,' he said. 'We're stuck with each other, so as much as I would love to leave you here and watch you from afar as you struggle to carry all these supplies solo down that stairwell, I can't. And if you decide to storm off, I'll be forced to follow you.'

'You are right,' she said calmly. 'So let us simply agree to not speak for the rest of the afternoon unless absolutely necessary.'

'Agreed.'

'Good.' She waved a hand at him. 'Eyes away from me and on the job, please.'

He angled his head. 'You *are* the job.'

Colour rose in her cheeks as she crouched and began gracefully gathering up the pots and brushes around her. 'I think I have spent enough time painting today.'

He rubbed the back of his neck before stepping forwards to help her.

She thrust a hand towards him. 'I do not require your assistance.'

He pulled up and moved back from her, then stood awkwardly for a number of painful minutes while she loaded herself up like a pack horse. Once everything was balanced precariously in her arms, she made her way over to the stairwell.

'Careful,' he called to her.

Her gaze snapped to his, landing like a knife. She descended without saying a word.

CHAPTER 13

a knock at Charlotte's bedchamber door had her rising from the luxurious chair in front of the fire with a sigh and trudging over to open it. She found Tatum standing with an expression that was part concern and part curiosity.

His eyes moved over her. 'Are you unwell?'

She scowled. 'No. Why?'

'Because it's nearly noon, and you haven't left your bedchamber.'

She crossed her arms. 'To go where? To do what? With *whom*?'

He leaned his shoulder against the doorframe. 'Are you in a mood because your brother is busy doing things without you?'

'No.' The answer came out much too fast.

'The training is good for him. Mentally and physically—'

'I know.' And she did. He had been practically

bouncing off the walls at breakfast, desperate to get to the training yard with Hadewaye.

'Do you want to paint?' Tatum asked.

'At this rate, I am going to end up with twelve identical paintings.'

Tatum watched her for a moment. 'Get your supplies. I'm taking you out.'

'Out where?'

He pushed off the doorframe. 'Outside the walls. I know a spot that you're going to love.'

She felt an unfamiliar flutter of excitement in her belly. 'Outside the walls? Am I allowed?'

'You are if I say you are.' He stepped back from the door. 'Grab your riding boots, and let's go.'

Charlotte ran about grabbing parchment, charcoal, paints, and brushes, stuffing everything into a canvas bag. Tatum took it from her as she stepped past him out into the corridor.

'Ready?'

She nodded. 'Ready.'

Tatum sent word to Blackmane of their plans, and then they made their way to the stables.

It was drizzling rain by the time they were on their horses and heading for the gate, but there was no sugges-tion of going back—much to Charlotte's relief.

They walked their horses along the main road until it met with the winding path that ran adjacent to the river. Tatum pushed his mare into a canter, leaving Charlotte no choice but to do the same. Hers fell into a comfortable rhythm with his, and she found herself relaxing into the ride as the water flashed in and out of view.

Tatum slowed to a walk when they reached a wide part of the river, and Charlotte did the same. They rode in silence for a few minutes before the commander veered off the path entirely and pulled his horse up. Charlotte stopped beside him, looking out at the slow-flowing water and lush green surroundings. A chorus of frogs competed with the branches blowing in the breeze overhead. So much beauty in one glance.

'What do you think?' Tatum asked. 'Worthy of painting?'

The corners of her mouth lifted. 'Yes, most definitely.'

Tatum tended to the horses while Charlotte set up her paints beneath the cover of a giant elm tree, sitting on the thick blanket he had brought. The pair then sat in companionable silence, Charlotte sketching out the scene before them while Tatum trimmed a branch with his dagger.

Glancing sideways at him, Charlotte asked, 'Are you making a weapon or something?'

'A fishing spear.'

She paused to watch as he pulled some string from his pocket and attached his dagger to the stick. 'Have you ever caught a fish like that?'

He met her gaze. 'Are you seriously asking a Chadorian defender if he has the skills to catch a fish?'

It was a rhetorical question, so she returned to her painting without answering.

Tatum rose and walked to the edge of the river, watching the water for a few minutes. And sure enough, his patience paid off. He speared the water, then triumphantly held up a large trout.

'Well done,' she said.

He held the fish in place with his boot and yanked the spear free. 'You want a turn?'

She had never caught a fish in her life. 'I think I shall leave it to the experts.'

'Suit yourself.' He returned his attention to the water.

As Charlotte painted, she found her gaze drifting in his direction, moving over his broad shoulders and strong arms. She noticed the small details too: the creases between his eyebrows that appeared during moments of concentration, the darker shade of his hair due to the rain, the way he moved with effortless grace.

Giving up on painting, Charlotte leaned her back against the trunk of the tree, watching him.

When Tatum glanced in her direction, he straightened and lowered his spear. 'You all right?'

Realising how ridiculous she must have looked openly gaping at him, she sat up, bringing a hand to her brow as though she were shielding her eyes from the sun. 'Simply taking in the landscape. The light behind you is... mesmerising.' She winced at that particular choice of word.

'Is it?' He studied her for a moment. 'You sure you don't want a turn?'

Charlotte should have said no and picked up her brush, refocused her mind. Instead, she got to her feet. 'All right.' She walked over to him, stopping a polite distance away.

Tatum had other ideas, closing the distance between them. He was so close, in fact, that she felt the heat coming from his body. He showed her how to hold the spear, his hands covering hers in the process. Then he adjusted her grip and moved her arms so she could feel the weight of the weapon. His hands were still on her as he described how to look for fish darting beneath the surface, tracking them with small movements of the spearhead. Charlotte reminded herself to breathe, but not so deeply as to inhale his woody scent. He really was very close. This was confirmed when she looked up and realised his face was mere inches from hers.

Tatum's gaze fell to her lips, and then he stepped back. 'I think you're ready to give it a try.'

Charlotte tried very hard to focus on the water, painfully aware of the heat gathered in her cheeks.

'You need to quiet your mind,' Tatum whispered.

She laughed at that. 'There is no quiet in my mind, no peace, only a thousand thoughts shouting over the top of one another.'

He crossed his arms and angled his head. 'Except when you paint?'

'Sometimes they reduce to a murmur.' She straightened. 'I do not believe a person's mind can ever truly be quiet, can it?'

'Of course it can.'

She gave him a doubtful look.

Tatum took the spear from her hands and threw it aside. 'Come with me.'

Her brow creased in surprise. 'Where?'

He took her by the hand and led her towards his horse. 'A place where you can't hear your thoughts.'

'There is no such place.'

He mounted, then pulled her onto the mare behind him. 'There is such a place—trust me.'

She glanced in the direction of the other horse. 'Are we going far?'

'No, not far. Hold on.'

He kicked his horse into a canter, leaving her no choice but to grab hold of his uniform.

They rode upstream for about half a mile, the wind whipping Charlotte's hood off her head. She had no idea where they were going, but she knew she was safe.

When the river narrowed, Tatum slowed his horse. They stopped in front of some rocks with water surging over them in a majestic roar. The noise was deafening.

'Do you trust me?' he asked over his shoulder.

She winced at the noise. 'I am still deciding.'

He laughed. 'Climb down.' He held her arm as she slid from the mare's rump and landed lightly on the ground, then dismounted and gestured for her to follow him.

'It is so loud!' she shouted as they got closer to the water.

'That's the point!'

Charlotte turned her face away from the spray coming off the water.

'Nearly there,' Tatum said. They were practically balanced on the river's edge. Water gushed past their toes. He took her hand again. 'Now close your eyes.'

She shook her head and took a step back.

He brought her in line with him again. 'I've got you. You're safe.'

Charlotte looked at him and felt the tension she was holding start to melt. One thing she had come to realise about Tatum was that if he said she was safe, then she was safe.

She closed her eyes and felt his fingers tighten around hers. With the visual gone, there was just the noise of the river and the prickle of icy water hitting her face and neck.

'My mind is far from quiet right now. How long do I have to keep my eyes closed for?'

Tatum moved closer and said into her ear, 'Until the thoughts stop. Until the water is nothing but a gentle vibration in your mind and you barely notice the cold.'

With an impatient sigh, she resigned herself to freezing to death while she waited for a miracle.

Minutes slipped by, and her thoughts continued to race in all directions. But after a while, they began to blend with the noise of the water instead of competing with it, then reduced to something she could ignore. As more time passed, her arms began to relax and the tension left her jaw. At some point, the noise of the water softened, and she became aware of other noises, like birds and insects, and even Tatum's soft exhales beside her.

These sounds came and went.

'Charlotte.'

Her eyes opened, and she looked straight into Tatum's honey eyes.

'Quiet?' he asked.

She licked water from her lips. Much to her surprise, it had worked. She felt the calmest she had in a long time. And also the most vulnerable. That part was not as scary as she had imagined it would be—at least not with him.

They stepped back from the water, and Tatum released her hand. Only then did she notice the cold.

'Now are you ready to catch some fish?' he asked.

She nodded, eyes moving between his. 'Ready.'

They arrived back at Dinefwr Castle as the sun was setting—with half a painting and four fish. The outing had been just what Charlotte needed, and Tatum had clearly known that.

'Thank you for today,' she said to him as they made their way to the kitchen with their fish proudly in hand.

His gaze slid to hers. 'You don't have to thank me. I just wanted an excuse to fish.'

Charlotte smiled to herself.

They took the fish to the kitchen, handing them to the confused cook. Charlotte instructed him to deliver her meal to Oliver's room, where she would be dining. Tatum then escorted her back to her quarters, where her night guard was already waiting. She felt a pang of disappointment upon seeing him standing there.

'The princess will be dining with the prince this evening,' Tatum told the guard. He looked at Charlotte, eyes searching hers for a moment. 'I'll see you tomorrow.'

His departure each evening was becoming her least favourite time of day. It was logical to put it down to the level of safety she felt with him compared to the English guards, but it was more likely because she preferred his company. 'Goodnight, Commander.'

Charlotte watched him walk away until she realised

the night guard was staring at her. She quickly retreated to her bedchamber to get herself cleaned up for dinner.

When she arrived at Oliver's bedchamber half an hour later, she was greeted by an excited and concerned Sir Miles, who spent a few minutes thoroughly investigating the new scents she had brought with her.

'Why do you smell like fish guts?' Oliver asked, screwing his face up as she took a seat opposite him.

She laid her napkin across her lap, then sniffed her sleeve, smelling only the soap she had scrubbed herself with. 'Your nose never ceases to amaze me. I have washed thoroughly and changed, yet you can still pick it up.' She shifted in her chair and cleared her throat. 'I went fishing today. Rather successfully, I might add.'

'You did not.'

'I did.' She tapped the tray in front of him. 'The trout before you was caught by these two hands. The commander even taught me how to clean them.'

Oliver angled his head. '*Why?*'

It was a logical question. 'I had planned to paint, but then he offered to teach me... and we soon discovered that I am quite good.'

He looked suitably impressed. 'I had no idea you had such murderous gifts.'

'Nor did I.'

Oliver felt around for his fork. 'Come on, then. Let us sample the fruits of your labour.'

Charlotte served him up some trout, then put some on her own plate. They tasted it in unison.

He nodded his approval as he chewed. 'That is some

good fish, sister. You have done the family proud with your peasantry ways.'

She leaned back in her chair, looking him over. She noticed a bruise along his jawline. 'Is that another training injury I see there on your face?'

'No.' He touched the napkin to his mouth. 'Hadewaye sucker-punched me when I misspoke earlier.'

She pressed her lips together. 'That sounds exactly like something he would do.'

They resumed eating.

When Oliver's plate was clean, he said, 'I really enjoy the training, you know. I wish Father had thought to teach me instead of treating me like an invalid my whole life.'

Charlotte laid her napkin neatly beside her plate, waiting for him to continue.

'Today felt like a day *lived*.' He drew a slow breath. 'It is rather refreshing to feel like you are working towards something instead of simply existing the time away.'

His words made Charlotte's heart squeeze, partly due to the revelation that he was more unhappy than she had realised, and partly due to the revelation that she was too. They had been 'existing' together their entire lives.

'I wish I had known what you needed,' she said. 'Never in a million years would I have thought that putting a weapon in your hand would be good for anyone.'

He smirked at that. 'And never in a million years would I have thought that putting a fishing pole in yours would have the same effect.'

'It was a spear, actually. Tatum made it, right there in front of me.'

Oliver whistled. 'That man *really* knows how to be a man.'

'He does.'

Oliver pushed his cup forwards, and she refilled it.

'When I picture your ideal husband,' Oliver said, 'I always imagine someone submissive, some incompetent man prepared to hand you the reins and let you run his house the way it needs to be run. But here you are fishing with a soldier, blushing over his ability to attach a knife to a stick.'

Charlotte took a long drink before responding. 'First, I am not blushing in the slightest. Second, it was *one* soldier, *one* time. And third, it is a lot more involved than simply attaching a knife.'

'So defensive on his behalf.' He tapped a finger on the stem of his cup. 'I think you need a man like him. Someone to challenge you, someone who is not afraid to hurt your feelings.'

'I have you for that.'

'Someone *besides* me.'

Charlotte took another drink. 'You know very well that I have no intention of marrying.'

Oliver chuckled. 'Father might have other ideas now that you are the Princess of Carmarthenshire.' He paused. 'Though I do not think a soldier will be on his list of suitors.'

It was a joke, but she did not laugh.

The absence of laughter made Oliver sit up. 'That is some very distinct silence. Did I hit a nerve?'

He knew her far too well.

'No, I was having a drink.'

Oliver tutted. 'Liar.'

She cradled her cup in both hands. 'Shall we pretend this is our last drink, then request another jar of wine?'

'Absolutely. I better pop the muzzle back on Sir Miles. The chambermaid reports all bites to Father.' Oliver raised his cup in a toast. 'What shall we drink to?'

Charlotte thought for a moment, then lifted her drink. 'To a day lived?'

A smirk spread across Oliver's face. 'To a day lived.'

CHAPTER 14

Sir Miles's guttural barks pulled Charlotte from the depths of sleep. She looked to the window to gauge the time. It was still black outside. She inhaled sharply as she sat up, throwing the covers back and climbing out of bed. Even from that distance, she could hear the fear and urgency in the dog's bark.

Something was wrong.

Charlotte did not bother to dress, just grabbed her robe on the way to the door and threw it around her while fumbling with the lock. When she finally got it open, she found the night guard standing in the middle of the corridor, looking off in the direction of the noise.

'What is going on?' she asked him.

He looked at her. 'I don't know.'

She took off at a run towards her brother's quarters, the icy stone floor making her feet throb.

'My lady!' the guard called.

She did not slow until she rounded the corner and saw

the group of men gathered outside Oliver's room. Wybert was pounding on the door with his fist. 'Open up!'

Her brother's night guard was standing back, looking helpless. The defenders were there, too, their expressions pensive and bodies tense.

Charlotte continued forwards but at a walk this time, her legs not cooperating suddenly. Tatum looked in her direction, and the concern in his eyes almost propelled her backwards.

'We need to get in there,' Tatum said, gesturing for Wybert to move.

The duke stepped aside.

Tatum took off his belt and crouched, removing the two prongs from the buckle. He got to work picking the lock. Sir Miles lunged at the door, his body slamming against it.

Charlotte came up next to Tatum. 'Down,' she commanded through the door. 'It is me.'

But the dog did not stop. Sir Miles had lost the ability to follow commands.

'How much did your brother drink at dinner?' Hadewaye asked her.

They had gone through numerous jars of wine, but that was not unusual for them. 'Not that much.'

'He would have to be thoroughly intoxicated to sleep through this level of noise,' Wybert commented.

Everyone fell silent when the lock clicked open. Tatum glanced at Blackmane as he pushed the door open. Sir Miles burst through it, his muzzle thankfully still on. Charlotte grabbed him by the collar, but he pulled free with a yelp as though she had struck him. He was panting and drooling uncontrollably while turning in frantic circles.

'Easy, boy,' she said, her voice breaking.

The defenders rushed into the room, and she stared after them, her feet frozen to the floor. Then she smelt it, the pungent scent of blood. Her hand flew up to her mouth when the nausea hit. She watched Tatum approach the bed and caught the fall of his shoulders. Sir Miles jumped onto it, barking, warning everyone to get back. Hadewaye managed to secure him but had no luck calming him. The dog was choking himself in his efforts to get free.

Someone was shouting.

Someone was calling her name.

Someone was dead on the bed.

'Charlotte.'

She jumped at the sound of her name. Tatum was in front of her now, saying things she could not hear. His expression was painfully bleak, a reflection of everything she was feeling inside. She looked past him to the bed illuminated by candlelight, finding the courage to focus on the figure lying upon it. The sight stole all breath from her lungs.

Charlotte had no memory of her mother's death. She had heard the story second-hand from Oliver, whose adolescent mind had plucked out certain details and suppressed others. This time, this death, she would have a first-hand account.

Come on, feet.

They obeyed, carrying her into the room so she could experience the nightmare up close. She stopped next to the bed, knowing she would spend the rest of her life trying to understand the scene before her. Both of Oliver's wrists were cut, the linen beneath his hands soaked in blood. There was so much of it. His eyes were closed, his mouth open. His skin was a sickly shade of a colour she struggled to define.

'What do you see?' she imagined him asking.

She saw a man who had ended his own life, yet that seemed impossible. He had laughed through most of dinner. He had sparred in the morning and run laps in the afternoon. He had told her at dinner that it felt like a day *lived*. He had seemed more alive than ever before.

Charlotte climbed onto the bed and crawled over to him, searching for traces of life, but there were none. Nothing about him seemed familiar. He was too still, too quiet.

Sitting back on her heels, Charlotte pressed her palms to her eyes. 'Leave me.' When she did not hear the immediate retreat of feet, she said, 'Go!' Her hands remained over her eyes.

'Leave the dog,' Tatum said quietly to Hadewaye on their way out.

A moment later, Sir Miles leapt onto the bed, sniffing, yawning, and whining. Grieving.

Charlotte lay down on the bed next to her brother, waiting for the sob that was stuck in the centre of her chest to burst free. Instead, it suffocated her, making breathing so difficult that she was forced to roll onto her back to relieve the pressure.

'We were supposed to do life together.' She moved her

hand, her pinkie brushing his. For some reason, she expected him to be cold, but he was still warm.

Sir Miles came to lay between them, resting his head on Oliver but looking at her, listening for her words.

'We were going to grow old together. It was both funny and tragic, and we were fine with that.' She swallowed, then lifted a hand to pet Sir Miles, a tear sliding into her hair as she did so. The trapped grief finally worked its way free of her, climbing sharp and fast along her throat and exiting like a demon at an exorcism. The sound she made was so primal that it had Sir Miles climbing over her in an attempt to make it stop. She buried her face in his fur, holding him tightly with both hands. She held him until all of her strength was gone, until she was simply dead weight on the bed—like her brother.

The door creaked open, and footsteps approached. She rolled her head to look, the effort enormous. It was Tatum, looking as though he were carrying the weight of her grief on those strong shoulders of his.

'Tell me what you need,' he said.

How was she to know when her thoughts bounced and her stomach churned? 'Does my father know?'

He nodded. 'Yes. I can take you to him, if you like?'

That was the logical thing to do in such a situation, but she dreaded the things her father might say, or worse, the things he would *not* say.

She pushed Sir Miles off her and slowly sat up, closing her eyes and holding her pounding head for a few moments before looking back at Tatum. 'I need a horse.'

He frowned. 'A horse?'

'I need to go to Llanddeilo.'

'Now?'

A nod. 'Will you take me?'

He searched her eyes for a long moment. 'You're going to need some shoes.'

Tatum had Hadewaye escort Charlotte back to her bedchamber while he made arrangements. She put on the first dress she reached, her warmest cloak, and a pair of boots. When she exited the room, she found Tatum waiting for her. She was expecting five thousand questions, but he asked only one.

'Ready?'

They made their way to the stables, where Blackmane and Hadewaye were waiting. Alveye remained behind to watch over her father. Tatum helped Charlotte onto her horse, and the group headed for the gate.

As they made their way to Llanddeilo, the three men formed a protective triangle around her while allowing her to set the pace. Thankfully, they knew where they were going. She had only a vague sense of direction, which she did not trust in her current state.

She knew they were close to the village when she smelled the smoke from the hearths. Charlotte felt heavy and numb. It was likely the shock setting in.

'So, where are we going?' Blackmane asked, his tone gentler than usual.

She blinked. 'The church.'

'You could have used the church outside the castle walls if you wished to pray,' he replied.

She kept her eyes fixed on the steeple above the rooftops. 'I am in no mood for prayer tonight.'

Tatum and Hadewaye exchanged a look but did not comment.

When they reached the church, Charlotte dismounted and entered the building, grateful that the door was open so she did not have to break it down. She headed for the stairs that led to the small bell tower, climbing them two at a time in the dark.

'Slow down,' Tatum said behind her.

She ignored him.

When she reached the top, she marched out onto the platform and took hold of the rope, using her full weight to get the bell moving. Tatum stood to the side, watching with a concerned expression as she rang the bell over and over again, using all of her strength, so that it echoed throughout the entire village like a call to arms.

Only when she heard people coming out of their houses and gathering in the street below did she let go of the rope. Stepping back, she wiped sweat from her forehead with the back of her hand before turning and heading back down the stairs.

The crowd in the street was quite large by the time she exited the church. She marched fearlessly into the middle of the mass. What did she possibly have to fear at that point? She had already faced the thing she was most afraid of.

'People of Llanddeilo!' Her voice carried in the dead of night, echoing off nearby walls and drifting to those who were further away. 'Some of you believe that I do not belong here! You told me I knew nothing of your pain, that until I had suffered as you suffered, then I would never belong!'

People looked between themselves, confused.

Charlotte turned in a circle. She noticed Tatum and his men remained close while giving her some space.

'Well, here I am, joining you in this hell!' she shouted. 'My brother, *your* prince, is dead. His body grows cold as we speak, his blood seeping into every crevice of his bed.' She punched her chest with a closed fist. 'My heart is broken, my happiness crushed. His death feels like my own.'

It felt like a fire had been lit within her. She did not try to contain it, instead allowing it to consume every part of her.

'This is what you wanted for me, is it not? My father is confined to bed—after being shot in the *back*—and my brother is dead. So, come bask in my grief.' She threw her hands up. 'Are you happy now? I really hope so, because if that is not enough death and misery for you, then now is your chance to take me down too!'

All three defenders moved towards her, but she stopped them with a raised hand.

'Do not come any closer.' She pinned Tatum with a look so fierce that she saw his throat bob. 'This is their one and only chance to be rid of me.' Her gaze returned to the crowd, darting between faces. 'Where is the butcher? Where is he?'

People looked around, their expressions changing from wary to fearful.

When he did not come forwards, she said, 'Come on. Where is the man who had so much to say to me the other day?'

Some people in the crowd shrank back, revealing the stern-faced butcher standing there in his nightshirt.

She marched right up to him, not stopping until her face was mere inches from his. 'This is it. This is *me*—a broken mess before you. If I am still an outsider in your eyes, then I am all out of tricks. You can sleep easy now knowing that I have no more to offer this kingdom.'

The grief was swallowing Charlotte whole now.

'I have nothing left!'

She could not tell if she was going to claw his face or vomit all over herself. She was half crying and half fainting and—

Tatum caught her around the waist as her knees gave out. 'Get the horses,' he instructed Hadewaye.

'Back up!' Blackmane said, coming forwards to create some space around them. 'Show's over. Return to your homes—now!'

Charlotte held tightly to Tatum's cloak as the sounds around her became too loud.

'Hang on,' he whispered in her ear. 'I'm taking you home.'

*I*t rained relentlessly the day of the funeral, and Charlotte wondered if the heavens were grieving too.

They buried Oliver in the graveyard beside the church outside the castle. Everyone agreed to keep his cause of death private. A murder earned sympathy, whereas a suicide earned only disapproval. Elis did not want people thinking his son was weak. Wybert did not want people thinking their prince was burning in hell. And Charlotte... Charlotte could not even come to terms with the idea that her brother chose to end his life.

At the end of the day, he was gone. Nothing they said or did not say was going to bring him back.

Ita and Isabel attended the funeral, standing next to Charlotte. Her father was on the opposite side of the coffin with Wybert. He never even lifted his eyes to her.

It was a small gathering because they did not have many acquaintances in Carmarthenshire, and the kingdom was too dangerous for Englishmen to travel through for a reason as unimportant as a funeral.

The priest finished his sermon by asking for Oliver's soul to be given peace and rest. Then the coffin was lowered into the ground, landing in a pool of water at the bottom. Charlotte flinched at the splashing sound it made. She had been all right up until that point, but as soon as she lost sight of the coffin, she began to tremble. Ita must have noticed, because she slipped her arm through Charlotte's as the dirt was shovelled into the hole.

Charlotte stole another glance at her father, who was leaning heavily on his walking aid. She had never seen him cry and wondered if he would shed a tear in private for his son.

Wybert looked in her direction. His sympathetic expression only made her uncomfortable, and the fact that he stood there like the son her father always wanted made her angry. She looked away.

Tatum's steady presence behind her was another form of comfort. He had not left her side since it happened, even coming to check on her during the night. He simply made up reasons. She was aware that his job was to protect her, not hold all of the breaking pieces together.

'Are you all right?' Isabel whispered, pulling her from her thoughts.

Charlotte looked around. It was over. People were leaving. Her father was shuffling away, looking ten years older than when he had arrived at Dinefwr. Wybert followed at his heel, like a loyal dog. 'I am fine,' she assured Isabel.

They returned to Dinefwr on foot, where food and

drinks were served. The hall smelled of poached fruits and spices.

'I think I should stay a few days,' Ita said.

Charlotte immediately shook her head. 'That is entirely unnecessary.'

Concern was all over Ita's face. 'Some company might help.'

Nothing would help. That was why she was planning to hide in her room and sleep away the time. 'Thank you both for coming.'

The women exchanged a look.

'As soon as I'm fully healed, I plan to return as your guard,' Ita said, then lowered her voice. 'Give you some reprieve from Tatum.'

Isabel glanced in the commander's direction. 'I would not worry too much about that. The princess appears rather comfortable with the current arrangement.'

So others had picked up on the fact.

Charlotte looked over to where Tatum stood watching the room. He had more important things to do than stand outside her door. She knew that. Yet the prospect of him not being there when she opened it each morning made the empty space inside her feel even bigger.

As though feeling her eyes upon him, he looked straight at her, eyebrows tugging together in a question. She responded with a strained smile, communicating that all was well.

Soon, the hall was empty, and her father retreated to his private quarters without saying one word to her. He had barely uttered more than a few words to her since that night. Maybe it was because he was grieving. Or maybe he was afraid that if he asked how she was doing, she would reply with the truth. And what would he do with that?

Tatum escorted Charlotte to her bedchamber. When she went to close the door behind her, he blocked it with his foot. She gave him a questioning look.

'I'll be right here,' he said.

The impact of those four words was enormous. Her throat and chest began to ache. 'Can you have Sir Miles brought to me, please?'

He nodded.

'Then I wish to be left alone for the remainder of the day. I do not require any food to be brought to me. I only need sleep.' Her voice cracked a little when she said that last part.

He stared into her eyes for a long moment, then nodded. 'I'll make sure you're not disturbed.'

Charlotte did not know how long she slept for, but when she did finally open her eyes, it was light outside and still raining. That was all the information she needed. Her eyes sank shut again.

'Charlotte.'

She peeled her eyelids open and turned towards Tatum's voice. He was crouched beside the bed. Behind him was a rather worried-looking maid whom Charlotte did not recognise.

'I need you to sit up and drink something,' he said.

Her gaze went to the tray next to the bed. She was

about to say that she was not thirsty, but when she went to speak, her mouth felt as though it were full of cotton.

'You had us worried, my lady,' the woman said with a Welsh accent. 'It's too long to go without a thing to eat or a drop to drink.'

Charlotte slowly pushed herself up into a seated position, then took the cup of water from Tatum. She sipped at it as she eyed the maid. The woman had a round face with soft features. Her fair hair was pinned back in a neat bun.

'My name's Mevanou, my lady,' the young woman said, as though sensing Charlotte's questions. 'I'm your new lady's maid.'

Charlotte looked accusingly at Tatum.

'It was Ita's idea,' he said. 'She thought you might need some support in the coming weeks.'

'What I need is *sleep*.'

He added in a lowered voice, 'She's a family friend.'

'Perfect,' Charlotte muttered.

Mevanou stepped forwards. 'You can't be having soldiers coming in and out of your room and no lady present. People will talk.'

'Let them talk.' She did not care what other people said about her. Her gaze went to the window. 'How long was I asleep?'

'Two days,' Tatum said.

Two days? She was so groggy that she was sure it had only been a few hours.

Mevanou was fiddling with the food on the tray. 'We tried getting you up yesterday, but you refused to wake up. So we decided to let you sleep through the night, figuring we would have better success in the morning.'

'Well, you were right.'

She held out some bread with butter lathered on it. 'It's midafternoon, in case you're wondering.'

Charlotte absently took the bread, knowing she needed to eat despite the absence of appetite. Oliver would be horrified to see her moping about refusing food. She ate slowly, washing each mouthful down with water. Her stomach rolled.

'The soup is cold, but I can have it heated up for you,' Mevanou offered.

Charlotte shook her head. 'No, thank you.'

Tatum rose. 'I need you to dress and come with me.'

That sounded like far too much effort. 'I am so tired—'

'I know, but I need you to come with me anyway.'

His tone was firm but kind. It looked like she was getting out of bed whether she liked it or not.

'Out you go,' Mevanou said, ushering him from the bedchamber. 'I'll deliver her to you in a moment.' Closing the door, she returned to Charlotte.

'Where is Sir Miles?' Charlotte asked, looking around the room.

'Sir who?'

She was going to say 'Oliver's dog' but instead said, 'The dog.' The fresh stab of pain in her chest made her want to lie down again.

'Ah, yes. One of the defenders came and collected him this morning. He was going to take him for a run around the castle.' She laughed. 'I've not seen a dog that big before. I thought you had a calf lying across you.'

Charlotte could not take the talking, so she stopped listening.

A few minutes later, she was dressed, wrapped in a cloak, and delivered to Tatum.

'What is so important that it could not wait a few more days for me to finish my nap?' she asked.

He rewarded her feeble effort at humour with a half smirk. 'You up for a walk outside the walls? I want to show you something.'

She was only up for returning to bed but nodded.

They headed for the keep, their feet in sync. Tatum did her the favour of skipping small talk and meaningless questions like 'How are you feeling?'

One only had to look at her to know she felt like death.

When they approached the gate, Tatum signalled to the guard, and a moment later, the portcullis began to open. Charlotte looked up, spotting Blackmane atop the wall, bow in hand. He moved to the other side of the wall when they passed through it.

Charlotte's feet slowed when she saw an explosion of colour before her. So much colour. Bundles of flowers and foliage lining the roads, the edge of the moat, and filling the empty space in between. 'What is all this?'

Tatum looked around at the display. 'Bouquets laid in honour of your brother. People have come from villages all over Carmarthenshire to pay their respects.'

She blinked. 'They have?'

Tatum paused and plucked a bouquet off the ground, handing it to her. Charlotte took it from him, then, spotting the note tucked inside, fetched it out.

. . .

We are deeply sorry for your loss. May the prince rest in peace.

Charlotte pressed her eyes closed.

Prince.

Oh, how he would have loved the fuss.

She strolled on, retrieving any notes she came across and reading them aloud to Tatum. She felt like she gained energy from the outpouring of sympathy. There was more warmth in the words sitting in the palm of her hand than she had experienced in her entire lifetime.

Further down the road, she spotted a young couple and their son laying a bunch of wildflowers at the end of the display. The boy raised his hand in a wave, and she waved back. A moment later, they were headed towards her. Charlotte expected Tatum to warn them back, but he did not say a word.

'Your Highness,' the woman said when they reached her. 'We're awfully sorry for your loss.'

The man gave a small bow. 'I raised a cup in his honour yesterday.'

Warmth filled her. 'My brother would have truly appreciated the gesture, thank you.'

The boy had picked his bouquet back up to hand to her in person. 'They're a bit soggy from the rain.'

She was grateful that Tatum did not snatch them from her and start pulling them apart and sniffing them, declaring them a risk. 'These are lovely.'

'More foliage than flowers, I'm afraid.' The woman looked to the sky. 'This weather.'

Charlotte looked the bouquet over. 'I think I shall put these in my bedchamber. It could do with some colour.'

The woman gave her a sad smile. 'The grief feels like it will never loosen its grip on you at first, but it will.'

Charlotte's eyes began to prickle. 'Thank you for travelling all this way. It was very kind of you.'

The family left, but Charlotte noticed more people arriving on horseback.

'United by grief,' Tatum said quietly beside her. 'There's no doubt you're one of them now.'

Her hand instinctively reached for him, fingers grazing his. Then she realised what she was doing and withdrew it. It was gratitude she was feeling and nothing more. The last thing she wanted was to embarrass herself by doing something she would have to explain away later.

People continued to arrive, undeterred by the rain. People of all backgrounds and ages.

Charlotte remained outside for a long time accepting waterlogged offerings and wishing madly that her brother were alive to witness the outpouring of love. She was in no rush to return inside, choosing instead long conversations with people, asking questions about their lives, meeting their children, and even holding infants as she listened to them describe the people they had lost over the years. It seemed everyone had lost someone: parents, siblings, children, cousins, neighbours.

The one thing they had not lost was *hope*.

Eventually, the light began to disappear, and so did the people. Fatigue hit Charlotte once more.

'I am going to return tomorrow and paint this scene,' she told Tatum, stifling a yawn. 'I am afraid I will forget it otherwise.'

He looked around. 'I can't think of a better scene to hang on your bedchamber wall.'

They began walking slowly back towards the castle gate. When Charlotte looked up, she saw that Blackmane was still atop the wall, keeping watch over them. Another figure caught her eye at the far end. It was Wybert. He was leaning on the embrasure, taking in the sight below.

Tatum must have spotted him, too, because he said, 'I suspect His Lordship is wishing he had not listened to his mother all those years ago. A Welsh princess would bring endless benefits for a man in his current position.'

She looked at the ground before her. 'My title does not change the fact that women in my family carry children with defects and die birthing them.'

Tatum slowed midstep. 'What? Tell me that's not the reason the marriage did not go ahead.'

'It was certainly the excuse given to my father.' She looked up in time to see Wybert disappear.

'What a clod,' Tatum said. 'Women die in childbirth all the time, and there are far worse things than being born without sight. Your brother lived a good life from what I saw.'

She swallowed. 'It was a good life, mostly. Of course, after seeing how happy he was training with Hadewaye the other day, I now wonder whether I unknowingly prohibited him from living a *full* one.'

He waved a finger. 'No, no, no. We're not doing that.'

'Doing what?'

'The guilt. Imagining ways you've fallen short instead of celebrating the ways in which you stepped up and cared for him.'

Her hand reached for his again, seeking the warmth of his fingers. And this time she did not pull away when they touched. She left the hand right there in case they accidentally wanted to touch again.

The portcullis rose in front of them.

'Thank you for this,' she said without looking at him.

'All I did was not scare the mourners away.'

A smile started on her face, quickly extinguished by guilt. It was too soon. Though it helped to know that there were moments of reprieve. 'You did more than you realise.'

The backs of his fingers pressed the backs of hers. 'Happy to be of service, Your Highness.'

CHAPTER 16

The defenders stood in a circle in the courtyard, arms crossed, passing the letter from the warden between them.

'You definitely told the warden it was suicide?' Alveye asked. 'You were clear on the details?'

Tatum emitted a laugh. 'I was *very* clear on that part—because I value my life.'

Blackmane shifted his weight. 'I can go to Chadora—'

'No,' Hadewaye interrupted. 'I'll go. Isabel's due to give birth soon, and Oliver was under my protection. I should be the one to face the warden.'

The group fell silent.

Alveye rocked on his feet. 'It *was* suicide, right?'

The death had taken all four of them by surprise. None of them had picked up on any signs that something was wrong that day, and Hadewaye could normally sniff out a troubled man a mile away.

'The door was locked from the inside,' Tatum said.

'There was no one else inside that room and no sign of a struggle.'

'He's hardly going to struggle if he's asleep,' Blackmane pointed out.

Tatum inhaled, then looked to Alveye. 'I'm a little surprised that Lord Elis hasn't raised the subject.'

'He's barely spoken a word since it happened,' the defender replied.

Blackmane spoke up at that. 'What about the princess? What does she say on the matter?'

'You have to be awake to speak.'

'She still sleeping a lot?' Hadewaye asked.

The commander nodded. 'She wakes, paints, then returns to bed.' He shook his head. 'Right. It's settled, then. Hadewaye will go to Chadora and report to the warden.' He looked around the group. 'In case he doesn't make it back, should we go around the circle and share something we'll miss about him? Like his swoony ability to make any female fall instantly into friendship with him.'

Alveye smirked. Blackmane pinched the bridge of his nose. Hadewaye tilted his head and gave him a tired look.

Tatum clapped the youngest defender on the arm. 'Give my love to the warden. Be safe, and update me as soon as you can.'

'Assuming I live to tell the tale.' Hadewaye saluted the men before striding away.

Alveye exhaled heavily. 'I should go relieve the night guard. I'll see you both later.'

Tatum watched the men walking away for a few moments, then turned his attention back to Blackmane. 'When *is* this baby of yours coming? It's been months.'

Blackmane frowned. 'Yes, it has been months. Seven, to be exact. Babies take nine to grow.'

'Not elephants. Did you know they're pregnant for eighteen-plus months?'

Blackmane blinked. 'I did not know that entirely useless piece of information, no.' He looked Tatum over. 'Are you all right?'

'Fine. Why do you ask?'

'Because I heard you leave the room last night.' Blackmane rested his hands on his hips. 'Were you checking on the princess?'

Tatum scratched at his jaw. 'I'm just making sure no one else dies on my watch.'

Blackmane continued to stare at him. 'Right.' He looked up at the wall. 'Well, you know where to find me.'

Tatum did his best impersonation of someone who was in control of himself and the situation. 'I certainly do.'

Blackmane hesitated. 'Unless you want me to guard Charlotte today.'

'So I can catch up on my beauty sleep? Get out of here.'

Blackmane left without another word.

Tatum watched the defender until he disappeared around the corner. Only then did he allow himself a small smile. Drawing a deep breath, he went to take over from the night guard.

When he arrived at Charlotte's quarters, he found both the guard and Charlotte missing. The maid tending the fire directed him to Oliver's old bedchamber. He went in search of her.

He found the night guard standing outside the door.

The men exchanged a nod as he stepped inside, unsure what to expect.

Charlotte was on the other side of the bed, looking at the floor. She was dressed, which was a good sign. Her hair was braided loosely to one side.

'Morning,' he said, letting her know he was there.

She looked up. 'Good morning, Commander.'

The room had been thoroughly cleaned and aired. All of Oliver's belongings had been put into trunks and the bed stripped bare. All that remained was an ancient sword hanging on one wall and a large map of the kingdom on the other.

'What are you doing?' he asked, stepping past Sir Miles, who would not go any further than the doorway.

She pointed to the floor. 'Looking at the scratches.'

Tatum followed her gaze to the deep scratches in the wood she was referring to. 'Sir Miles's nails?'

She nodded. 'He must have been beside himself that night.'

Tatum crouched down and ran his fingers along the deep grooves left by the dog. Sir Miles watched him, panting heavily as though it were a hundred degrees where he stood.

'What's going on in that head of yours?' he asked Charlotte as he rose.

'Nothing.' Then her brow creased. 'I suppose I still cannot believe he took his own life, knowing Sir Miles would be forced to watch that life drain from him.' Her voice was quiet, her eyes red. Her heavy gaze went to the dog.

Tatum looked away. 'Have you eaten?'

'Yes.'

'This morning?'

Silence.

He hated feeling helpless when it came to her grief. 'Would you like to paint?'

Another shake of the head. 'I am quite tired. I think I shall return to bed for a while.'

She went to step past him, but he put a hand out to stop her.

'How can I help?' His tone was almost pleading.

Charlotte finally met his gaze. She looked like she had not slept in weeks despite doing little else.

'I do not need help. I need time.' She forced a smile. 'I am still here, still me. Tomorrow I will get up and try again. Today is not the day.'

Tatum reached a hand up and brushed the backs of his fingers along her jaw, immediately withdrawing it when her breath lifted in response.

'Tell you what.' He took a small step back. 'If you eat something, I'll let you go back to bed.'

She nodded slowly. 'Deal.' Then she stepped past him and exited the bedchamber, Sir Miles rejoining her at the door.

Tatum's gaze returned to the scratches on the floor. He ran the toe of his boot over them, then exited the room.

CHAPTER 17

*C*harlotte woke before sunrise the next morning. She lay with a heavy feeling in her chest, mind racing with thoughts of her brother, her future, her own death. It was when those dark thoughts entered her mind that she knew she had to get up.

She reached for Sir Miles, who was curled in a giant ball at the end of her bed, rubbing his head. He did not wear the muzzle when they were in her bedchamber, so he enjoyed it all the more. His eyes followed her as she sat up to light the candle.

Once he realised they were starting their day, he climbed on top of her, shoving his face in hers. She tried to push him off, but it was no good. He was too strong, and she was forced to accept her fate: death via big dog kisses.

When she was finally able to crawl out from beneath him, she headed over to the basin and filled it with cold water. She had a thorough wash, cleaned her teeth, then got herself dressed. It was a relief to step out from beneath the cloud of fatigue that had followed her for days. She could go for a walk, maybe even a long one. Walking and painting. Mind and body covered. She could alternate between the two and reward herself with sleep.

The night guard must have been dozing, because he startled upright when her door opened.

'My lady,' he said, blinking rapidly. 'Everything all right?'

'I wish to go for a walk.'

He glanced down the dark corridor. 'Now? The sun's not yet up.'

'Do not be afraid. I will scare the monsters away.'

He looked conflicted. 'Perhaps you should wait for Commander Tatum. He's still training.'

She bent to adjust Sir Miles's muzzle. 'I am going for a walk. Now, you are welcome to follow me or remain here. But I must warn you that if you do decide to come, I require space. If I can hear your boots, then you are *too close*.' With that, she strode off down the corridor before he had a chance to respond, Sir Miles trotting alongside her.

Charlotte headed for the wall in hope of catching the sunrise that was on its way. She climbed the steps and tugged up her hood when she emerged into the rain. She looked out over the valley where the hills were beginning to glow. But the sound of weapons clashing had her feet moving once more.

She continued walking until she came upon the defenders training in the outer-ward. Blackmane and Tatum were sparring while Alveye ran laps of the perimeter. Her palms flattened on the embrasure as she watched.

She could recognise Tatum by his size, frame, and the way he moved. He was familiar now.

His laughter drifted up to her. She had come to recognise that too.

She was aware of the change in her breathing as her eyes followed his every move. He had stripped down to trousers and a cream shirt that clung to his skin, displaying every curve of muscle. She forgot about the cold—and the sunrise too. In fact, the longer she looked, the warmer she felt. She did not even care that her night guard stood ten feet away, looking thoroughly uncomfortable.

Commander Brock Tatum had her *full* attention.

But then Tatum looked up suddenly, eyes locking on hers. She took a fast step back from the edge, hands still extended in front of her, heart pounding against her ribcage.

'Are you all right?' her guard asked.

She pressed her eyes closed and took a moment to collect herself before turning to him. 'You know, I think that is enough walking for today.' She kept her gaze on Sir Miles as she passed the guard and headed back to the turret at the other end.

The rain fell heavier, but instead of hiding from it, she turned her face up and let it wash away the heat in her cheeks. It felt so cleansing that she slowed down to enjoy the sensation. If only it could wash away the grief.

Charlotte ran a hand down her face as she entered the turret. Droplets of icy water trailed down her neck, soaking the collar of her dress beneath her cloak. She descended the steps at lightning speed but was forced to pull up quickly when she almost clashed with someone coming from the opposite direction. She sucked in a breath when she came face to face with an equally soaked Tatum. His hair was darkened by water and sweat, and something in his expression undid all of the rain's work. Heat rushed back into her cheeks. She waited for him to say something, but he only licked water from his lips.

'You are dismissed,' she said to the night guard standing awkwardly behind her.

He cleared his throat and slipped past them, forced to turn sideways due to the lack of space. Charlotte barely noticed because her eyes were back on Tatum.

'What were you doing up on the wall?' the commander asked when they were alone.

She swallowed. 'Walking. Clearing my head.'

'Walking?'

She nodded.

Neither of them moved or spoke.

Sir Miles's ears pricked forwards, and then he wandered off down the stairwell, probably to sniff around for rats. He seemed comfortable leaving her side when Tatum was around, giving himself permission to be a dog.

'You're shivering,' Tatum said after a long silence.

She had not even realised.

He was standing on the step below her, which brought them to equal height. He was so close she could see every detail of his face, every bead of sweat on his forehead. She did not know if his skin would feel hot or cold, so she reached up to touch it, her thumb tracing the curve of his cheek. It was a delicious blend of both.

He was still watching her lips as though he were

waiting for words she was yet to speak. 'What are we doing?' He angled his head slightly when he asked the question.

'I suppose we are deciding whether to make this mistake.'

He ran his finger down her wet neck.

'No good will come of this,' she added.

He leaned closer so his lips were mere inches from hers. 'Tell me to walk away and I will.'

She brought her lips to his, kissing him firmly. Her heart pounded away at twice the speed it had been beating earlier. He returned the kiss with equal ferocity, his hands roaming, overly familiar. The cold, bleak setting seemed to fuel her desire. She sucked in a breath as he pushed her against the stone wall, chest pressed to hers. His lips moved down her neck, collecting the rain from her skin. She moaned when his hand found its way beneath her chemise.

'Want me to stop?' he whispered against her skin.

She shook her head. If he stopped, she might come to her senses, and then all that heat would remain trapped inside her for eternity. What she wanted was some *relief*— from everything.

He broke the kiss and looked into her eyes. 'Either way, you're safe with me.'

She guided his mouth back to hers, probably too forcefully. Now was not the time for safe. She wanted the opposite of safe.

Why does the rain taste so good from his lips?

He pulled back again. 'I think we can do better than a stairwell—'

'Stop talking.' She was forced to take charge since he seemed more focused on making it magical than getting the job done.

He pulled back a third time, and she almost cried in frustration.

'What now?' she asked.

His hand stilled beneath her dress. 'I don't think—'

'Stop thinking. I beg of you. If you want me, then the moment is now.'

He searched her eyes, then descended on her once more. There was no holding back from that point. The defender had an assignment, and there was no stopping him.

He lifted her off the ground, the heat between them building. The icy buckle of his belt slid along her inner thigh as he found his way to her. Then it was pleasure reaching every part of her.

For a few moments, she felt elated. She felt her soul leave her body.

For a few short moments, she was out of the dark and *free*.

But they were only moments. And then they were gone.

As Charlotte sat there with her back pressed against the frozen wall, limp and trembling, she felt her soul crash back down to earth.

Tatum's arms were still around her, his breaths coming fast against her neck. He was as drunk on the moment as she was. That was all well and good, but she knew the next part was the difficult bit. Cue the shame, the embarrassment. It was a dance she had danced before with Wybert. He had made it seem like no big deal because they were to be married, then dismissed her quicker than her father at a family reunion afterwards. She had felt as cheap as wood leaving that room.

'Put me down,' she instructed Tatum.

He drew back to look at her. Upon seeing her expression, he lowered her onto the step. One of his hands was still cupping her face. When he did not remove it, she gently pushed it away, then proceeded to fix her dress.

'Charlotte—'

'I would like to return to my bedchamber,' she said over her shoulder as she walked away.

When she reached the bottom of the steps, she clicked her fingers in Sir Miles's direction, and the dog trotted over to her. Charlotte marched on and did not look back, slow, or stop.

When she reached her bedchamber, she quickly closed the door behind her and leaned her back against it. She covered her face with her hands and released a long, shaky breath.

CHAPTER 18

*T*atum stood before a glaring Blackmane outside the keep, squinting against the rain. He braced for the sermon.

'You fucking idiot,' the defender said, getting straight to the point. 'I knew this would happen. I knew the day she arrived here.'

Tatum went to speak but was cut off before he got a word out.

'What in Belenus's name were you thinking? How did it even—' He held up a hand, objecting to his own question. 'You know what? I don't want to know.'

'She started it.'

Blackmane's expression darkened, a warning. 'You're going to get us all booted from the army. Hadewaye hasn't even returned from dealing with the dead brother and you're already creating more issues.' He crossed his arms. 'The warden will be shouting across the border, demanding our uniforms the moment he learns of this.'

Tatum's eyebrows lifted. 'To be clear, I wasn't planning on *telling* him.'

'You won't need to. He'll find out, because he's the warden. The most likely outcome is that Lady Charlotte will tell her father that you took advantage of her grieving state—'

'That's not what happened—'

'It doesn't matter. The reasons don't matter. Your excuses *don't matter*. You crossed a line.'

Tatum shifted his weight. 'Well, I recall you crossing a line or two in the past.'

'That was very different.'

'Oh really? How so?'

Blackmane looked around the inner-ward. 'I wasn't scratching some itch.'

Tatum was not expecting those words to hit so hard. He stepped towards him. 'Watch yourself, defender. I'm still your commander.'

Blackmane stared at him for a long moment, his expression thoughtful. 'Oh shit.'

Tatum's forehead wrinkled. 'What?'

'It's not an itch. You're falling in love with her.'

He laughed. 'Love? No, no, no. Love is for needy freaks —like you. I'll admit to feelings.' He waved a hand. 'Lust, fascination, curiosity, maybe, but not love.'

Blackmane linked his hands atop his head and turned in a slow circle, stopping with an exhale. 'Right. Well, do you think you can keep your *curiosity* bridled and your trousers belted for the next few weeks until Ita returns?'

'Given that she hasn't spoken one word to me since it happened, I don't think that will be a problem.' He hesitated before adding, 'I've never had a woman use me like that before. She took what she wanted, then left without so much as a word.'

Blackmane sucked his teeth. 'I'm not sure I can muster the sympathy you're after.'

'Fair enough. We'll move on.' Tatum crossed his arms in front of him. 'What is it you wanted to see me about?'

'I came to tell you that the town square in Llanddeilo is now underwater.'

'Underwater?'

Blackmane nodded. 'The river's so high it's washed away entire crops. We should prepare for food shortages.'

Tatum pressed his eyes shut. This was too familiar for his liking. It was how the famine started. A few 'shortages' had turned into dead livestock followed by decade-long starvation. 'What about the rest of the village?'

'If this rain doesn't ease soon, the whole kingdom is going to be underwater. Word from the border is that it's missing most of Chadora.'

'And England?'

Blackmane cast a dark look at the castle. 'I'm sure the lords of Dinefwr will have more information about that part of the world. I've no doubt they'll be putting their hand out for more grain at some point.'

Of course they will. 'Are Tolly's men keeping an eye on things?'

He nodded.

'Good.' He pinched the bridge of his nose. 'Time for me to take over from the night guard. Wish me luck.'

'She was likely acting out of grief and is trying to erase the whole thing from her mind.'

Tatum blinked. 'And you have a nice day too.'

The defender gave him a casual salute. 'You need to do the same.'

With that, he strode away.

Charlotte never usually had a problem staring a man straight in the eye, but she was barely able to lift her gaze to Tatum after their entanglement in the stairwell. Everything about their encounter had her thrown—walking away *satisfied* being one of them. She had spent the better part of that night imagining what they could have achieved with those wet clothes removed in an *actual bed*.

Because of these thoughts, Charlotte knew the man protecting her was now her biggest threat. She had clearly caught feelings, which meant she was vulnerable to having them crushed. She had been hurt enough. There was no space in her for more, no whole pieces left for him to break. What was she supposed to do? Offer up the jagged leftovers of herself for him to pulverise?

'Are we going to talk about what happened the other day?'

She was setting up her painting equipment in the North Tower when he threw this question at her. 'There is really nothing to discuss. We made a bad decision, and then we moved on.'

He angled his head, visibly annoyed. 'Oh, we have, have we? Glad we have that sorted.'

She gave him a tired look. 'What do you want me to

say? What is it you need to hear? An apology? A compliment?'

He leaned his shoulder on the wall. 'Out of curiosity, what would the compliment be?'

'A compliment?' She threw her hands up. 'All right. You have great balance.'

'Balance?' There was disappointment in his voice.

'It could not have been easy to hold me up like that while perched on those uneven steps.'

'I've carried sacks heavier than you across a one-foot-wide bridge while suspended in the air.'

She rolled her eyes. 'All that training came in handy after all. Well done, Commander.'

He watched her closely as she began to mix paint. 'Why did you mention an apology? What could you possibly have to apologise for?'

'I am sure you will think of a reason. There is always something for women to apologise for—like existing.' She tried not to let the bitterness creep into her voice.

He fell silent after that. But after a few minutes of staring mindlessly out at the wall walk, he looked at her and asked, 'Can I have a board and brush?'

The question completely caught her off-guard. She turned to him, meeting his gaze properly for the first time since the stairwell incident. To her horror, her cheeks began to burn. Apparently she was incapable of looking at him without replaying said incident in her mind. 'Why?'

'I'd like to paint too.' He said it all casual, like it was the most normal thing in the world for him to join in.

'You do not even paint.'

'That's true.' His gaze fell to the supplies on the ground. 'Today will be my first time.'

She laughed once, waking Sir Miles, who had been sound asleep against the wall. 'And what did you have in mind?'

'I thought we could paint each other.'

'If you say naked—'

'If we were to do this naked, you would need a much bigger board.'

Her nostrils flared with the threat of laughter. 'You flatter yourself, Commander.'

'I'll accept that feedback, but only because of our shared history.' He winked.

The man was crude and obnoxious, but admittedly, his antics helped reduce the awkwardness between them. 'I think a portrait might be ambitious.'

'I'm a defender—ambitious by nature.'

'Do they not teach humility at that little training camp of yours?'

'Humility can't be weaponised, so no.'

With a shake of her head, she bent to pick up a board and brush and handed them to him. 'You will have to share my palette.'

'What's a palette?'

She was about to chastise him for not knowing but then noticed his smirk. 'Please do not make a mess. You only need a small amount of paint. Add a few drops of water for larger areas.'

He set himself up two embrasures down, positioning his board so he could see her while he worked. She did the same, resting the paint palette on the embrasure between them.

'We work until the sun reaches the horizon,' he said. 'Then we turn our boards—ready or not.'

She was going to suggest that it was not enough time, then realised it did not matter. 'Fine.'

Tatum put too much paint onto his brush, most likely to annoy her, then made some bold strokes on his board. As tempting as it was to correct his technique, she decided to let him be.

The time passed quickly and quietly, each of them focused on their own work. Charlotte wanted to capture everything from the freckles that dotted Tatum's cheeks to the shadows cast by his eyelashes. Every time she glanced at him, she noticed his mouth was turned up. It was possible he was enjoying himself.

After a few hours, Tatum slowed down, taking great care with the final details. Charlotte began to wonder if perhaps he *had* painted before.

She would soon find out.

When the sun reached the horizon, Tatum dropped his brush onto the palette. 'Time's up.'

'I need to—'

'Brushes *down*, Princess.'

She exhaled, eyes meeting his as she laid her brush next to his. 'All right. Since you are so clearly ready, you should go first.'

There was no objection. He flipped his board around and held it up so she could see every absurd detail. Her mouth fell open. It was a lot to take in at once. She stood in stunned silence, unsure which part to focus on.

He had painted her with comically large fists, which

were perched on her hips, and thick downturned eyebrows that made her look like an angry man. Then there were the green lips and the hair poking up in all directions. Or perhaps not hair.

Charlotte narrowed her eyes. 'Are they… horns on my head?'

He turned the board slightly so he could see. 'Well spotted. I went with a devil theme.'

'I see that.' She dropped her gaze a few inches. 'The black teeth are a nice touch.'

He gave her a hurt expression that she did not buy for one moment. 'You hate it.'

'No. I think it is rather good for someone who has been hit in the head as many times as you.' She forced a smile. 'Would you like to see mine now?'

He grinned. 'Very much.'

She watched him closely as she turned her board, waiting for his smug expression to collapse. She did not have to wait long.

'What in the book of mythical creatures is that?'

She held it a little higher so they could both see it. 'That is an artist's impression of you.'

'You mean *your* impression?'

She crinkled her nose. 'I am the artist in this instance, so yes.'

His confusion intensified. 'Are you… really bad at painting people?'

'No, not at all. In fact, I am quite gifted when it comes to the human form. Oliver used to say my impressions were *uncanny*.'

'Your *blind* brother said that?'

She pressed her lips together, surprised by how thoroughly she was enjoying the moment.

He placed his own painting down so he could really focus on hers. 'You don't think the chin is a little small?'

'Do you mean weak?'

His jaw ticked. 'And my ears aren't that big.'

She pursed her lips. 'Oh dear. I hope this very *accurate* depiction of you is not hurting your feelings.'

He gestured to the ropelike arms. 'Are these famine-inspired limbs?'

'I really wanted to capture you without all the bulk of armour.' She gestured to his shoulders when she said that.

He nodded slowly. 'And the stomach hanging over the belt?'

'Much less noticeable when your armour is on.'

'Is that right?'

She was enjoying herself far too much now. 'This is yours, by the way. You can hang it in the guards' quarters.' She held it out for him to take.

He tugged it from her hands with a facetious smile, then replaced it with his. 'And this is for you, to hang above your bed. If you hang it upside down, it will look like a mirror image.'

Involuntary laughter tore from her throat when he said that. Her first instinct was to clap a hand over her mouth in an attempt to contain it, but then Tatum cracked up, and that only made her laugh harder. She gave up trying to hold it in. Her hand fell away, and it poured from her.

'This is the biggest commitment to insulting someone I've ever witnessed,' Tatum said, pointing at her painting.

'The effort and care you put into making me look like one of the Panotti—'

'You gave me devil horns!'

'And a tail.'

She looked back at the painting and saw what did appear to be a tail. Her head tipped back, more laughter erupting from her. 'You have the artistic abilities of a small child, and for some reason, that makes it funnier.'

His deep laugh mixed with hers, and neither of them seemed able to stop. Tears ran down Charlotte's cheeks, and her ribs ached. Her entire body was laughing, and she felt the grief shift inside her, settling into place instead of taking up every inch of space.

After a few minutes of trying to catch her breath, the laughter finally eased. When she looked back at Tatum, she found him watching her. He was no longer smiling.

'Not to ruin the moment,' he said, 'but you are truly beautiful when you laugh.'

Guilt hit her. Guilt from laughing so hard and so soon after her brother's death. 'I suppose that is what happens when you refuse to cry. Grief finds a way to exit your body somehow.'

He nodded and looked down at the ground.

A different sort of guilt hit her. 'I am sorry about the other day.'

He looked up again. 'Which part?'

'All of it.'

Disappointment flashed on his face. 'It's me who should be apologising. You just lost your brother. I took advantage—'

'No you did not—'

'I shouldn't have let it happen.'

She drew a breath. 'And I should not have fled when it did.'

He studied her in the fading light. 'Why did you?'

'I suppose…' She swallowed, wondering if she had that level of honesty in her. 'I suppose I was getting in first. Better to hurt you before you have the chance.'

'I would never hurt you.'

He said it so fast and firm that she almost believed him. 'I have heard that before.'

His throat bobbed. 'From Lord Wybert?'

She looked away. 'This might be hard for you to believe, but once upon a time, I trusted him.' She adjusted the fold of her cloak. 'He promised me the world, invited me to his bed, then exited my life in a way that had everyone wondering what I did to mess things up.'

Tatum shifted his weight. 'I'm sorry.'

She dismissed his words with a shake of her head. 'I was really more embarrassed than hurt. He was my father's choice, not mine.'

'Who was your choice?'

One corner of her mouth lifted. 'Rumours spread—via the servants, no doubt. I was labelled a harlot. There were no men to choose from after that.' She looked at him. 'I bet you wish you had stayed in that training yard after hearing that.'

Tatum appeared genuinely taken aback by that suggestion. 'Why? Because some fool took advantage of you when you were young? That's not your shame to carry. It can be divided between Wybert and your father, who should have protected you from men like him.'

His words made her throat burn, even though she had heard the same ones from Oliver many times before. 'Thank you.' She blinked hard and cleared her throat. 'For the painting, I mean. I am looking forward to seeing it every morning when I wake.'

His eyes creased at the corners. 'As am I. The absolute confusion of my men when they realise it isn't me in the flesh but, in fact, a painting will be priceless.'

They watched each other for a few moments.

'I'll help you pack up,' Tatum said.

She began cleaning up, reminding herself that the lightness in her chest was a symptom of her laughter—nothing more.

CHAPTER 19

Charlotte could not sleep through the weather. Violent sheets of rain came in sideways, rattling the shutters and seeping through the gaps. She rose to deal with the water pooling beneath the window, then dressed. She wanted to see how high the river had risen after watching it swallow entire houses earlier that day. There were only so many high places for people to escape to.

After layering up, she stepped out into the corridor, locking Sir Miles in the bedchamber behind her. He whined as the door clicked closed.

The night guard straightened when he saw her.

'I would like to go to the wall,' she said as she stepped past him.

'It's raining, my lady.'

'Yes, I am quite aware of that.' She tugged the hood of her cloak up and continued down the corridor.

The rain was falling so heavily outside that Charlotte

could barely see the path in front of her. Her feet splashed in puddles with each step, the rain falling faster than it could drain away. The air felt thick and difficult to breathe. Undeterred, she trudged on, guided by the light that was coming from the North Tower.

When she made it to the top of the stairwell, she was surprised to find others already gathered there. Her father and Wybert were looking out the window into the darkness, and the three defenders were liaising with a handful of castle guards a few feet away.

'What is going on?' she asked.

No one had heard her approach due to the noise. They all looked in her direction.

Her father's glower was instant. 'What are you doing up here? You should not be wandering about in the middle of the night.'

'I second that,' Tatum said, glaring at the night guard behind her.

Charlotte crossed the wet stones to the window and looked out, but she could not see a thing. Though she thought she could hear people below. And animals.

'Is someone down there?' she asked, looking to her father for an answer.

Wybert spoke on his behalf. 'Some people have been forced to flee their homes. Dinefwr is a safe place to gather due to it being elevated.'

Her breathing slowed as that information sank in.

'Llanddeilo is completely underwater,' Tatum said. 'As are many other villages.'

Charlotte looked back at the window. 'These people are out there in the rain? Families? *Children?*'

Elis blinked slowly, already losing patience with her. 'What would you have us do? Erect shelters in the dark while being pummelled by rain?'

'Why has no one let them inside?' She could barely believe she had to ask the question.

Her father scoffed. 'I am still recovering from my last encounter with these people.'

She glanced at Tatum, who gave her a small nod of encouragement.

'So you are going to leave them to suffer in the rain?' she asked Wybert. 'Then expect to be welcomed back into Llanddeilo when the water goes down?'

He inhaled slowly in place of a verbal reply.

Charlotte addressed her father then. 'We need to open the gate.'

'And put them where?' he asked.

'We will figure it out.' She tried to sound as confident as possible despite having no plan beyond inviting them in.

Elis looked past her to Tatum. 'Are you not going to say something? It is your job to keep her safe.'

'To keep her safe while she performs her role,' Tatum replied. 'This is her role, isn't it? You brought her here to advocate for these people.'

Wybert spoke up at that. 'Remember that these walls are the only thing keeping us safe right now.'

'Keeping us safe or keeping us separate?' Charlotte asked.

'Both,' Elis snapped.

'If you are so concerned for your safety, then I suggest you remain in your quarters.' She turned to leave.

'Wait,' her father called. 'Where are you going?'

She kept walking. 'To let those poor people in.'

'And if they turn against you?' Wybert asked.

She rolled her eyes. 'Then you can feel superior about being right.'

Tatum and Blackmane followed her down the stairwell while Alveye remained with her father.

When they reached the bottom, Charlotte glanced sideways at Tatum. 'Am I gambling with our lives?'

Tatum and Blackmane exchanged a look she could not translate.

'You're trusting your gut,' the commander said. 'When you get to the gate, check in with yourself again. If something feels off, we'll find another way to help them.'

She had never had someone back her the way he did. It warmed her insides. If Blackmane had not been with them, she might have been tempted to hug him.

The three of them stopped in front of the portcullis. The guard on duty cast a wary look in their direction.

'We doing this?' Blackmane asked.

Charlotte could see nothing beyond the latticed grille. 'Yes. Open the gate.'

Tatum nodded at Blackmane, who went to inform the guard.

Another, rather concerned, guard exited the keep when the portcullis began to rise.

'Have someone wake the servants,' Charlotte instructed the man. 'We shall need help settling our guests.'

The guard glanced at Tatum before jogging off. Within a few minutes, the castle came to life.

A bleary-eyed Mevanou found Charlotte amid the growing chaos. 'What can I do to help, my lady?'

Charlotte narrowed her gaze at the people wrapped in soggy blankets on the other side of the moat. 'I need the hall cleared so we can fit as many people in there as possible. Prioritise women, children, and the elderly.'

Mevanou nodded. 'Yes, my lady.' She hurried away.

Then something unexpected happened. The villagers began moving back from the gate instead of towards it.

'Why are they not coming in?' Charlotte asked Tatum.

He looked over his shoulder to where a line of castle guards now stood. 'They're afraid.' He turned and shouted, 'Back up!'

Charlotte waved her arms at them like she was scaring off crows. 'Make some room, please!'

The guards exchanged confused looks but then backed up to the wall.

Charlotte decided to go out and encourage them inside. The villagers tensed up when they spotted Tatum coming towards them.

'Perhaps you should wait at the gate,' she told him.

He shook his head. 'Not a chance.'

Charlotte glanced sideways at him. It was clear from his expression that he was not leaving her side any time soon. She stopped just outside the wall, brushing rain off her face.

'It is all right!' she called to them, trying to project her voice as far as possible. 'Come inside! I assure you that you will be quite safe!'

Two men at the front of the crowd exchanged a

cautious look. 'What about our livestock?' asked one. He had a half-drowned chicken tucked under one arm.

Charlotte looked to Tatum for an answer. 'What do we do about the stock?'

He looked around at the menagerie of animals and birds. 'We could put them in the outer-ward.' He lowered his voice. 'They need a way to feed themselves when this is over. There won't be enough food.'

She acknowledged the comment with a nod, then addressed the crowd again. 'Bring them with you! We shall find room!' She waved them through. 'Just ignore the men with the swords!'

Once the people at the front made the decision to go, the rest followed. They filed slowly into the castle grounds, holding tightly to whatever possessions they had managed to bring with them, various animals trailing behind them. Blackmane waited inside the gate, one hand on the hilt of his sword.

'God bless you, Your Highness,' one woman said as she passed by, her voice heavy with exhaustion.

They were watching from the edge of the road when Tatum suddenly lurched forwards, catching someone by the arm. The man turned with a fearful look, and that was when Charlotte recognised him. It was the butcher from the village, the one who had very clearly, and publicly, articulated his thoughts on her coming to Carmarthen-shire. The same man she had attacked the day her brother died.

Tatum looked back at Charlotte. 'You don't have to let him in.'

The people around him stopped, watching to see what she would do.

She moved closer to avoid shouting. 'What is your name?'

'Iwan, my lady.'

She glanced at the young woman holding her breath next to him, likely his daughter. 'You will behave in my home, Iwan. If you show me or anyone else inside those walls the slightest bit of disrespect, I will have you thrown out—no matter the water level. Do you understand me?'

He nodded. 'Yes, my lady.'

The woman beside him resumed breathing.

'Good.' Charlotte waved him through. 'In you go.'

Tatum released him, and Iwan trudged off with his back hunched against the rain.

'I am going to look like a fool if he kills me in my home,' Charlotte said once Iwan was too far away to hear.

Tatum stared after him. 'Honestly, I think he's more scared of you after your last encounter.'

'Fair, given my behaviour.'

She spotted Wybert weaving through the crowd towards them. He stopped next to her, watching the people for a moment. 'Your father is safely in his quarters.'

She merely nodded.

'I hope you know what you are doing,' he said after a short silence. 'We are about to be severely outnumbered.' He paused. 'The only reason I am going along with this plan—'

'Is because you are a guest here, Lord Wybert,' she said, unable to hide her irritation. 'This is my family's home now. You have no authority when it comes to this matter.'

Tatum coughed into his hand, then looked away.

Wybert was focused solely on Charlotte. 'The only reason you are here is in support of English trade. You are here at *my* request. The castle might be in your father's name, but Dinefwr belongs to England. You would do well to remember that.'

Charlotte turned to face him properly. 'You know, if my blood was as English as yours, I would not feel comfortable with my back to all this Welsh rage. Do take care, my lord.' She stepped past him and headed for the gate.

Tatum followed, saying nothing.

Once everyone was safely inside the castle walls, they began the tedious task of figuring out where to put people. The men tended the animals while the rest of the families settled into the hall. When the space filled up, they directed everyone else to the keep and tower. Charlotte organised dry clothes and blankets for those who arrived empty-handed. Then they lit a fire outside, out of the weather, and got some food cooking. They needed to be able to feed people when the sun rose.

They all worked alongside the servants, ensuring people were warm and able to sleep.

'We'll not forget your kindness,' a young mother told Charlotte when she was handed a small portion of cheese. 'We have long memories.'

Charlotte gave her a tired smile. 'Get some rest. Who knows how long this rain will last?' She straightened, stifling a yawn as she looked around at the families huddled beneath blankets.

'You're done for the night,' Mevanou said, appearing

seemingly out of nowhere. 'Go lie down before you fall down.'

'She's right,' Tatum agreed. 'Time to go.' He gestured to the door.

Charlotte was far too exhausted to argue. She exited the hall amid murmurs of gratitude, focused only on changing out of her wet clothes and falling into bed.

Outside, Wybert was leaning against the wall in the dark, out of reach of the rain. He looked in her direction when she appeared.

'Done?' he asked.

She nodded with great effort.

'You were right,' he admitted.

Her eyebrows pinched together. 'You will need to be more specific.'

He pushed off the wall and ventured closer. 'You made the right decision.' He gestured to the hall. 'It was a smart move.'

She had not done it to be strategic, but she was far too tired to explain that to him.

'The Last Princess of Carmarthenshire,' he said, testing out the title.

Tatum looked around. 'Where's your guard? You shouldn't be out here unprotected.'

Wybert's gaze went to him. 'Do not worry about me, Commander. I can take care of myself.'

Before Tatum could reply, Blackmane appeared on the path in front of them. 'A word, Commander.'

Tatum turned to Charlotte. 'Don't move from this spot.'

She watched him walk over to Blackmane. They were

only twenty feet away, but Tatum kept looking back to check on her as they spoke.

Wybert followed her gaze and exhaled. 'Please do not waste your title on a soldier.'

She looked at him. 'What are you talking about?'

'Commander Tatum. He is a good man, a great defender. I would never take that away from him.'

'You cannot take that from him.'

He met her with a neutral expression. 'You need to let go of the malice, Charlotte. It no longer serves you.'

'I disagree.'

He blinked. 'I am the only son. I am to inherit everything. My family wanted to ensure their bloodline continued.' He held a hand up. 'I am not suggesting that it would have ended with us.'

'That was exactly what *they* were suggesting.' She waved a hand. 'It does not matter now. I am eternally grateful for their high standards. Can you imagine us married?'

'I can, actually. We are different people now. Older and wiser.'

'I will grant you the older part.'

He emitted a tired chuckle. 'Well, this old man needs some sleep.' He looked in the direction of the chambers. 'Goodnight, Charlotte.'

'Lady Charlotte,' she corrected.

He lifted a hand in recognition.

She watched him walk into the darkness. He was right about one thing: they had both grown up. The insults she threw his way were more habit than anything else.

Tatum and Blackmane finished speaking, and Tatum returned to her with a quizzical look. 'Everything all right?'

'Yes.' She looked away from Wybert. 'Yes, everything is fine.'

CHAPTER 20

One look at Lord Elis's face told Tatum he was not happy about Dinefwr's guests. He approached Charlotte like a storm cloud, prompting the commander to step in front of him.

'I need a word with my daughter,' Elis said.

Tatum looked past him to Alveye for some sort of clue as to what was going on, but the defender shrugged, suggesting he was none the wiser.

'It is all right, Commander,' Charlotte said from her chair. They were out in the courtyard, where everyone was enjoying the absence of rain. 'How can I help you, Father?'

Tatum reluctantly stepped aside. Elis went to move past him but froze when he saw his daughter. There was a young boy on her lap petting Sir Miles's big head, which was resting on the arm of her chair.

'That animal should not be around children,' Elis said once he had recovered from the shock.

'Why not?' Charlotte asked, looking up at him. 'He likes children.'

'Since when?'

'Since he was permitted to be around them.'

Elis scowled. 'Well, be sure to keep that muzzle on to be safe.'

Charlotte whispered something to the boy, and he climbed down and returned to his mother. 'Please,' she said, gesturing to the empty stool beside her.

Elis sat. 'One can barely move sideways in this place right now.'

Charlotte waved a hand at Mevanou, who was sewing nearby. 'I am going to need some wine.'

The maid shook her head, then disappeared inside.

'Wine before noon?' Elis asked, disapproval etched on his face.

She picked invisible lint off her cloak. 'If you would prefer I not drink in the morning, then perhaps you should visit in the afternoon.'

He ignored the comment. 'I still cannot believe you let all these people in. A handful of families would have been a good deed, but no, you had to let every man and his goat into our home.'

'What did the poor goats ever do to you?'

Elis eyed the children playing with sticks nearby. 'It has been two days. How long will they be here?'

'Until their homes are above water.' She looked up at the sky. 'At least the rain has finally stopped.'

'I think you forget that half of these people wish us dead.'

She rolled her eyes tiredly in his direction. 'I think *you* forget that I am here to change that. I would argue there are very few people who wish me dead right now, if any at all.'

He leaned forwards, resting his elbows on his knees. 'If I offered you a bowl of berries and told you two of them were poisoned but the rest were perfectly fine to eat, would you eat from that bowl?'

'That would depend on what type of berries they are. And am I sober in this scenario?'

He brought a hand to his forehead, clearly losing patience with her.

'What is it you wanted to speak to me about?' she asked.

He glanced at Tatum. 'It is regarding Oliver's estate.'

Tatum gestured to Alveye, and the pair wandered further away to give them some privacy.

'At least no one has died yet,' Alveye said quietly.

'Dreams really can come true.' Tatum watched someone throw wood on a nearby fire. 'Blackmane get away all right this morning?'

'Well, he hasn't returned, so that's a good sign.'

The defender had set off through flood waters, determined to check on his wife and the rest of the family. Maddock House was built on high ground, but Blackmane was not taking any chances.

Tatum snuck a glance at Charlotte, who was listening carefully to her father, then turned his attention back to the guests. The mood of the castle was relaxed. It was just family caring for family. The only violent thing that had occurred since their arrival was the slaughtering of a goat for soup.

'Looks like they're done,' Alveye said, nodding towards Elis, who was now on his feet. 'I'll see you later.'

Tatum watched them leave, then strolled back to Charlotte, who was staring into the cup of wine Mevanou had brought her.

'Everything all right?' he asked.

She placed the cup down on the tray and rose, folding her arms against the cold air. 'Yes.'

He was not convinced by her answer but decided not to push her.

Charlotte was silent for a few minutes. 'I did not even know Oliver was any good at business,' she said suddenly. 'We never really spoke about money because we had more than enough. I never questioned where it came from.' She looked at Tatum. 'Turns out he was quite the businessman.'

Oliver had clearly been smart and played to his strengths. 'Good for him.'

She exhaled. 'He wanted everything to go to me should anything happen to him. It is all in writing.'

'Are you surprised? You were his only family, in a sense, and his closest friend for the entirety of his short life.'

She closed her eyes. 'I am an unmarried woman. Therefore, everything goes to my father until I marry, and then it goes to my husband.'

'Ah.' Tatum looked down. 'I imagine you'll receive a very healthy allowance in the meantime.'

She opened her eyes and looked at him. 'Dinefwr Castle was supposed to go to my brother.'

He realised what the matter was then.

'When my father dies, the castle will be in English hands once more, and I will have no say over what happens here.' She bit the inside of her cheek. 'I will no longer have a home. Neither here nor back in England. I will be forced to rely on the generosity of a distant cousin or uncle who may decide not to carry out my father's wishes.'

He hated the thought of her wasting away in some English manor. Charlotte was royalty. She deserved a castle.

'Then you need to marry.' The words stuck a little as he spoke them.

Her bright eyes bored into his. 'My father is constructing a list of eligible English lords as we speak.'

His hand twitched. 'I would accuse him of bias, but Carmarthenshire is running a little low on noble suitors right now.' He looked back at the fire. 'I hope you at least get pick of that list.'

'It will be more a case of who is willing to marry me given my family history.' She hesitated before adding quietly, 'And romantic history.'

'They would be a lucky man' was his reply. 'I mean, look at this place. Who wouldn't want to live here?'

Her lips curled up. 'You joke, but I have never felt more at home.'

A realisation hit Tatum in the chest, winding him. *He* wanted to be on that list. He knew with absolute certainty that she would soften with the right man and become a walking nightmare with the wrong one. He wanted to be that man.

A throat clearing made them both turn. And there was Wybert, watching them.

Charlotte sighed. 'Good morning, my lord.'

Wybert was staring hard at Tatum, and something in his expression made the commander wonder if he could read minds.

'The river has dropped,' Wybert announced. 'The main road is now clear. I thought I might send some men into Llanddeilo to gauge the state of things.'

'There's no need,' Tatum said. 'Tolly dispatched men all over Carmarthenshire, and they'll send word when the area is safe for travel.'

Wybert gave a small nod. 'Very good.'

A woman approached with something in her hands, and Tatum instinctively reached for his sword. He relaxed when he realised it was fabric. It was the young woman who had arrived with the butcher that night. Tatum looked over at the fire and found Iwan watching.

'A little something for you, Your Highness. We noticed you didn't have one.'

Charlotte held it up and let it fall open. It was a flag.

'It's your family's emblem,' the young woman said. 'It should be flying proudly.'

A genuine smile spread across Charlotte's face. 'I agree.' She walked to the nearest flagpole.

Tatum followed. 'Here,' he said, taking it from her. He proceeded to lower the English flag, replacing it with the new one. The breeze picked it up as it neared the top. Everyone in the courtyard stilled to watch it, pride on their faces. It was a declaration of sorts.

The villagers looked back at Charlotte. Then, one by

one, they bowed and curtsied before her in a display of gratitude and respect.

Tatum felt a swell of emotion in his chest as he watched Charlotte. Her eyes were shining as she looked around, taking it all in.

The butcher shuffled forwards, prompting Tatum to reach for his sword again. Iwan raised his hands to show he meant no harm.

'Welcome home, Your Highness,' he said, bowing. 'We're happy you're here.'

Tatum knew this marked a shift in public opinion that would spread across the kingdom soon enough. And Wybert's face suggested he knew it too. She had won them over without the need for rehearsed public displays. She had done it with her grit and rough edges, edges that mirrored those of the people before her.

'What do you think, Lord Wybert?' Charlotte asked the duke.

He looked up at the flag, then to the English one flying on the far wall. 'I think they complement each other.' He paused and glanced around before adding, 'Your Highness.'

Pride radiated off Charlotte as she looked up with newfound confidence—confidence that had been missing until that point.

One by one, people returned to their pastimes and chores. Iwan gave Charlotte a crooked smile before going to tend the fire. Wybert glanced at the flag a final time before retreating indoors.

'Thank you,' Charlotte said quietly.

Tatum turned to her. 'For what?'

'For pushing me to do better than a smile and a wave.'

He swallowed. 'I knew you could. I saw your strength.'

'When everyone else was blinded by my bitterness.'

'I was blinded by it initially but eventually saw past it.'

She bit back a smile. 'Well, then thank you for your persistence.'

His fingers itched to hold her hand, to touch her in some way, but he kept them firmly by his sides. 'Anytime, Princess.'

CHAPTER 21

*I*t took four days for the water levels to fall. When all the roads were open, the villagers packed up their belongings, harnessed their animals, and returned to their homes to begin the clean-up. Tatum accompanied Charlotte to Llanddeilo to inspect the damage. Many homes had disappeared altogether, swept away by the flow of the water, a layer of sludge left in their place. Tolly volunteered men to help with the rebuilding, but he pointed out that they would have to rely on donations and items they could scavenge. The army did not have spare money for materials.

When Tatum and Charlotte returned to Dinefwr, Charlotte went to speak with her father. She exited his quarters an hour later.

'You can inform Tolly that we will be contributing funds to help with the rebuild,' she told Tatum.

So that was what she had been up to.

'You didn't have to do that.'

'No need for a fuss.' She smiled weakly. 'I would rather

it go to people who need it than a rich English lord who has plenty already.'

His chest tightened at the mention of her future husband. 'I'll let Tolly know.'

The following day, Blackmane returned to Dinefwr, bringing Ita with him. She had recovered from her injury and wanted to be of use.

'What about Lady Isabel?' Charlotte asked. 'The baby is due any day.'

'Babies are rarely on time. Isabel has her mother and brother with her. They'll send word when it's time.'

Tatum's eyes met Charlotte's during this conversation, and he wondered if she was thinking the same thing he was. He was not ready to be separated from her yet. They had reached a point of familiarity where they were entirely relaxed in each other's company. The conversations were easy. The silences were comfortable. They had inside jokes that other people did not understand.

'It is settled, then,' Charlotte eventually said. 'At least it is a much safer working environment for you now.'

'So I have heard, *Your Highness*.' Ita threaded her arm through Charlotte's and walked her away from the defenders. 'Everywhere I go, people are talking about you. All good things, I promise.'

Charlotte glanced over her shoulder at Tatum.

He did not follow because he was no longer needed. Instead, he went with Blackmane to see to castle security —though the processes they had put into place were so seamless now that there was very little for him to do there either. With the afternoon still in front of them, the defenders wandered the grounds.

'Ita's with her,' Blackmane said when he noticed Tatum looking for Charlotte. 'You don't have to watch her so *intensely* now.'

Tatum kept his eyes forwards. 'Habit.'

Blackmane smirked at the ground. 'Habit bordering on obsession.'

Tatum ignored the comment. 'Do you know who's really been getting on my nerves of late?'

'Besides the night guards?'

'Lord Wybert. He's been hanging about like a bad smell these past few days.'

Blackmane looked at him. 'You think he's had a change of heart since the villagers claimed Charlotte as one of their own?'

'It's not a change of heart. The man's an opportunist. It's a change of business direction.'

Blackmane watched him for a few paces. 'I can't imagine you're jealous of that man.'

'I'm protective.'

Blackmane stopped, waiting for Tatum to turn before speaking. 'That's it? Or is there something else going on?' He paused. 'You sleep with her again?'

'No.'

'Then what?'

Tatum struggled to find words.

'Ah. You fell for her,' Blackmane said, finally looking away.

He opened his mouth to disagree but said instead, 'It doesn't matter. I'm a defender. Her father's got this big plan—'

'I don't doubt it.' His gaze returned to Tatum. 'What's *your* plan?'

Tatum did not respond straight away. '*My* plan? My plan is to stay out of the way and not get into any more trouble.'

Blackmane nodded. 'I said the same thing once.' He looked around before adding, 'As inconvenient as it is, we don't get to choose who we fall in love with.'

Tatum could barely believe those words had come from Blackmane's mouth. 'That's something Hadewaye would say.'

Blackmane stepped back. 'Aaaand we're done.'

A messenger jogged up to Tatum, catching his breath as he handed him a letter. 'From Chadora, Commander.'

Tatum took it from him. 'Thank you.' He waited for the man to leave, then examined the seal. 'Shit.'

'From the warden?'

Tatum nodded. He opened it and read it all the way through. Then he read it again to ensure he understood.

'Speak,' Blackmane said, losing patience.

'We're to leave Dinefwr Castle. You're to return to the camp, and Alveye and I are to return to Chadora.'

Blackmane snatched the letter from him. 'What?'

'Immediately.' Tatum's mind raced. 'At least he let you remain here for the birth of your child.'

'Because he knows I would hand my uniform over the same day if he tried to make me leave.' Blackmane pointed to a part of the letter and read it aloud. 'Dinefwr Castle has been deemed safe and will be under English protection moving forwards.' He shook his head as he handed the letter back to Tatum.

There was no point standing around disputing the warden's decision. If he was ordered back to Chadora, then he had to go. 'I need to go speak to Lord Elis, let him know I'll be gone a few days.'

Blackmane quirked a brow. 'A few days is optimistic, especially since the warden has announced that Dinefwr will be under English protection now.'

He needed to be optimistic or he would struggle to leave. 'Shapur needs all the facts before making that decision.'

Blackmane looked doubtful. 'I'll go fill Alveye in, then head to the stables.'

Tatum felt ill suddenly.

Blackmane went to leave, then turned back to him. 'Ita can stay with Princess Charlotte for a few days.'

While that helped Tatum breathe a little easier, he was dreading telling her the news.

He visited Lord Elis in his quarters to explain his departure. The lord did not seem at all surprised, like he was expecting the announcement. When Tatum finished speaking with him, he found Charlotte waiting outside in the corridor, a hand pressed to her stomach and her cheeks drained of colour.

She already knows.

'We ran into Blackmane and Alveye outside the stables.' She struggled to look at him. 'Ita is helping them pack.'

His mouth was dry suddenly. 'She'll remain here with you for the next few days.'

Charlotte nodded—barely.

He struggled with what to say next. 'Listen, Blackmane will be in Llanelieu. If you need anything—'

'I am going to need you to stay.' She grew a little taller, her expression going from shaken to determined.

His eyebrows lifted in surprise. 'I can't—'

'You can if I order it.'

'My orders come from Chadora, as you know.'

She punched a finger at her chest. 'I am Princess Charlotte of Carmarthenshire, and I order you to remain at my side.' Her voice was raised now, her breaths coming fast.

His shoulders dropped an inch. 'I have to go. I'm sorry.'

Her eyes filled with tears, which she blinked back. 'I forbid it.'

Tatum took hold of her face and dropped his forehead to hers. 'Charlotte,' he whispered.

She pulled away from him. 'Fine. *Go*. Back to your walls.'

'Stop.'

She shoved him. 'Go!'

Tatum caught her by both wrists. She struggled to free herself, but he kept a firm hold of her until she gave up. Then, looking into her eyes, he said, 'Enough.'

'*Let go of me.*'

'Not until you stop behaving like my leaving is my choice. I am a defender. We don't get choices—we get orders. If I had the option, I would stay here with you.'

She went limp in his grip and swallowed.

He released his hold on her. 'I'll come back.'

'When?'

'I don't know.'

She searched his eyes, then closed the distance between them, pushing up onto her toes and kissing him. Her lips melted against his as his hands went into her hair, fingers curling around her impossibly soft locks. She pressed against him.

He had to break the kiss before things got out of hand. 'I can't kiss you like this, then leave,' he said, running his thumb over her lips.

'Good.'

He dropped his forehead to hers, eyes closing. 'I'm going to Chadora, as per my orders, and when I return, we're going to figure this out.'

'This?'

He gestured between them. '*This.*'

'How will we do that?'

'I don't know yet.'

That would have been a good time to disengage, but his lips found hers again, committing her taste to memory. The temptation to back her all the way up to her bedchamber was strong. But then Lord Wybert appeared around the corner, and Tatum's mood evaporated.

The duke stopped when he saw them, looking between them for a moment. He did not seem surprised nor embarrassed by what he saw. 'I hear you are leaving us.' There was no malice in his tone. He took a few lazy steps towards them.

Tatum would have told him to piss off if it were not for the uniform he wore and the oaths he had made upon receiving it. 'I have orders to return to Chadora as soon as possible.'

Wybert nodded. 'Yes. Alveye told me. He is waiting for you at the stables.'

It felt like a hurry-up. Wybert continued to stand there, staring at them, making it clear that whatever the commander had left to say would have to be said in front of him.

Tatum looked back at Charlotte, who was poised once more. He bowed. 'Stay safe, Your Highness.'

She swallowed audibly. 'And you, Commander.'

His gut twisted as he stepped away from her, pausing briefly in front of Wybert. The men stared hard at each other.

'My lord,' Tatum said, bowing his head.

Wybert returned the gesture. 'Thank you for everything you have done, Commander. Safe travels.'

Tatum left without looking back.

CHAPTER 22

Tatum and Alveye stood inside the warden's quarters, waiting for him to arrive.

'He does this to make you nervous,' Alveye whispered. 'You end up waiting until your anxiety renders you useless for the conversation ahead.'

Tatum glanced at the array of weapons hanging on the wall, knowing Shapur Wright had mastered every one. 'Maybe he's just busy.'

He had barely gotten the words out when the door flew open and the warden's large frame filled the door-way. Shapur looked between the two men, appearing to immediately disapprove of their presence despite giving specific instructions for them to wait for him there.

The defenders saluted.

'At ease,' Shapur grunted, closing the door and making his way over to the large wooden table that took up half the room. It was covered in neat stacks of parchment and carefully placed maps. He insisted on order in all areas of his life.

'You actually obeyed orders for once,' he remarked.

'Like loyal dogs, sir,' Tatum said before he could stop himself.

Shapur pinned him with a glare. 'I was very sorry to hear that Lord Oliver Livingston took his own life. He was a good man, by all accounts. For *once*, the blame does not land on your heads.'

The man loved to assign blame.

'It was very sad for the family,' Tatum said.

Shapur nodded. 'I can only imagine.'

'Might I enquire after Hadewaye?' Alveye asked. 'We've been waiting for him to return to Dinefwr.'

'And I have been waiting for you to catch the Earl of Cornwall's killer. Not so much as a lead, I hear.'

Tatum had been expecting him to bring that up. 'General Blackmane has been—'

'Yes, yes.' Shapur took a seat and began sifting through one of the piles of parchment. 'He was preparing to depart for Carmarthenshire when I received a letter from Lord Wybert.'

Tatum tensed at the mention of him. 'Really? And what did he have to say?'

'His letter stated that the Livingston family is now settled and safe in Carmarthenshire. Princess Charlotte has made strong progress. He seems to think your services are no longer required.'

Fucking Wybert.

'And he said some other things too,' Shapur said, staring pointedly at Tatum. He held up what appeared to be the letter and began to read from it. 'He goes on to describe, and I quote, "an inappropriate relationship with

Princess Charlotte while she was in a vulnerable state".'
He lowered the parchment and stared at Tatum, waiting
for him to explain himself.

Alveye looked down at the ground, which acted as
confirmation that Tatum was guilty.

'The duke doesn't know what he's talking about,'
Tatum said.

Shapur's face darkened. 'Did something happen
between the two of you or not?'

The commander reached up to loosen the collar of his
uniform. 'Not... in the way Lord Wybert is making it
sound.'

Shapur rose, chair scraping. 'You were there to protect
her.'

'I did protect her.'

'Before or after you seduced her?'

Tatum thought about all the things he could say in his
defence but realised none of them would be sufficient.
The warden had already made up his mind that Tatum
had behaved inappropriately, and that was that. 'I assure
you the lady was safe at all times, sir.'

Shapur looked far from impressed as he lowered
himself into his chair. 'I am not sure her father would
agree with you, Commander.'

Tatum dropped his gaze to the floor. The fatherly
disappointment was too much.

'You are hereby stripped of your rank,' Shapur said.
'You will both remain here in Chadora on a strict training
schedule until I can figure out what I am going to do with
you.'

A tense moment passed. It took Tatum another

moment to process everything that had been said. Once the words had settled, he reached up and removed his gold commander pin, then stepped forwards and placed it on the table.

Shapur looked down at it, then immediately busied himself with another task. 'You are both dismissed.'

The pair saluted, then left the room.

Outside, they found Hadewaye. A smile stretched across the defender's face when he saw them. 'I heard you were back.' The smile vanished when he saw Tatum's expression. 'What did I miss?'

They moved away from the door and kept walking so the warden could not hear them.

'Shapur stripped him of his rank,' Alveye said quietly.

Tatum blinked slowly. 'I don't care about that. It's being held here like a prisoner that's a problem.'

Hadewaye looked down at his cloak where the pin had been. 'Did he find out about you and Charlotte?'

Tatum looked between the men. 'Does everyone know my business, then?'

They nodded innocently.

'Lord Wybert *wrote* him about a certain princess,' Alveye explained.

Hadewaye tutted. 'What's it to him? He had his chance with her and blew it.'

'The absolute nerve of that ball sack to paint me as the morally grey character in this story,' Tatum said.

Hadewaye grinned at Alveye. 'His painting references are really quite sweet.'

'Do shut up,' Tatum replied.

Hadewaye walked backwards a few paces, studying

him closely. 'Is it serious between you two, then? Or is it the separation from Blackmane that has you all broody and wounded?'

'I'm not broody,' Tatum said in a distinctly broody tone.

A smirk settled on Alveye's face.

'I suppose I'll need to write Blackmane, tell him that we'll be here having our arses handed to us on the training field for a while,' Tatum said, splitting from the group. He would write to Charlotte, too, and let her know he had arrived safely. 'I'll see you later.'

Hadewaye stopped and looked after him. 'You're going to write to him *now*?'

He kept walking. Instead of heading to the barracks, he went straight to the port borough, to the beach, to the water's edge. He stood with the icy wind hitting his face and the roar of the ocean drowning out his thoughts.

Except the sound was not loud enough to drown out thoughts of her. Suddenly he was back at River Tywi, telling her to close her eyes and holding her hand. She had trusted him. She *still* trusted him.

The waves crashed down with rhythmic force, sending thick foam rushing up to meet the toes of his boots. He had promised her that he would return, so he would find a way to make that happen.

If he failed, she would never trust another man ever again.

CHAPTER 23

For the next two weeks, Charlotte spent most of her time atop the wall, painting and staring out at the western tree line. That was the direction he would come from. There was a heaviness in her chest that refused to let go and a lump in her throat that would not subside no matter how many times she tried to swallow it down.

This was grief of a different kind.

It did not help that she had written three letters to Tatum in the short time he had been gone and received no reply. It was Ita who had informed her that Tatum was safely back in Chadora under some intense training regimen. However, no one seemed to know how long for.

Mevanou appeared in her peripheral vision, casting a worried glance at Ita, who was standing on the other side of the wall carving a piece of wood into what appeared to be a spoon.

'Yes?' Charlotte said, looking tiredly in her direction.

Mevanou walked over to her. 'Your father wishes to see you, Your Highness.'

The maid had been using the formal address ever since the day the flag had gone up.

'He's waiting for you in his quarters,' she added.

Charlotte gave a resigned nod. 'Tell him I will be there in a moment.' She glanced a final time at the trees before leaving the wall walk, Ita in tow.

Technically, Charlotte was under English guard now. Ita was simply being kind by showing up each day to stand on a wall with her.

'You should be at Maddock House with Lady Isabel,' Charlotte said as they headed to her father's quarters.

Ita glanced sideways at her. 'Don't worry, I'll go when the baby arrives.' She walked a few more paces before adding, 'You should really think about getting some Welsh guards when I go. The castle guards here are mediocre at best.'

'I doubt General Blackmane will go for that idea.'

'You're Welsh royalty. I can't see why he wouldn't.'

Charlotte could see plenty of reasons but refrained from listing them.

'I'll wait out here for you,' Ita said when they arrived at her father's quarters.

The fact that Wybert's personal guard was also waiting outside had Charlotte on alert. 'That is not necessary.'

Ita looked Wybert's guard up and down. 'Let's decide that after the meeting.'

Charlotte had no idea what she had done to deserve such a friendship, but she was grateful for it. 'Thank you.'

She knocked and then entered the room, more nervous than she cared to admit.

Her father and Wybert were seated on either side of the table. Light filtered in through the large window, drawing her eye to the intricate carvings on the wooden beams. The furniture in the room was heavy and ornate, and relatively new since so much was destroyed by fire during the famine.

Her father gestured to the empty seat by the fire.

'I will stand, thank you.' She looked to Wybert. 'Is there a reason you are here?'

Her father cast a hard look in her direction. 'Do not start. And yes, there is a reason he is here.'

She was afraid of that.

'We need to talk to you about the plans we have made,' her father began.

'*We?*'

Wybert said nothing.

Elis leaned forwards, linking his hands atop the table. 'We are all here for the same reason.'

Charlotte looked at Wybert when she replied, 'I doubt that.'

Elis cleared his throat. 'We have spoken at length these past few days about what is best for everybody and made some decisions.'

The fire in the room suddenly felt stifling to Charlotte. 'What decisions?'

Wybert joined the conversation. 'Your brother is sadly no longer with us, which leaves the matter of who will inherit Dinefwr Castle in his absence.'

She blinked. 'I do hope you are not losing sleep over

business that does not concern *you*, my lord.'

'Except that it does. Dinefwr Castle is an integral part of the current trade agreement, as you know. Without it, both England *and* Carmarthenshire will suffer.'

She crossed her arms in front of her. 'I suspect England is quite nervous given the inevitable food shortages they are facing.'

'Trade is not the only concern here,' Elis interjected. 'I want to know that you are taken care of should anything happen to me.'

It was one of the most fatherly statements he had ever made, so Charlotte had no idea how to respond to it.

'We have put our heads together and come up with a solution that we believe benefits everyone,' Wybert said.

Charlotte's stomach dropped. 'What solution?'

Her father's drawn-out pause before answering made it drop further.

'You will marry Lord Wybert,' Elis said.

She had known it was coming, but it still landed like a slap. 'Absolutely not.'

Elis rose to his feet. 'Before you go off on a rant, I want you to listen.'

'My response at the end will be the same.'

Her father took a step towards her. 'I plan to leave Dinefwr Castle to Lord Wybert. As his wife, you will be free to live here for as long as you wish, even if he decides to return to England. This will remain your home.'

She barely heard a thing after the word *wife*.

'Before you say no,' Wybert began, 'I want you to consider the fact that I know you. My expectations going into this union are grounded in reality. You will not be required to play the doting wife, but you will be respectful and faithful.' He paused, letting those words settle. 'Your father told me of Oliver's wishes regarding his estate. I support that. When we marry, you will be free to use that wealth as you see fit.'

'You would give me access to my own money?' She pressed a hand to her heart. 'What a lucky princess I would be.'

Apparently he was not done.

'The castle will be passed down to our children—as will your royal blood, and I believe you care about that. The people of Carmarthenshire certainly do.'

She stiffened. 'You dare to speak to me about children and bloodlines after walking away for those very reasons. Where are your concerns about our children being born with impairments now?'

Wybert pinched the bridge of his nose. 'Charlotte—'

'Your Highness,' she corrected.

Wybert threw his hands up, giving up on the conversation.

Drawing a breath, Elis took over from him. 'Once you see past your pride, you will realise that this match benefits you more than any other I could bring to fruition.'

Tatum's face flashed in her mind, filled with disappointment upon hearing the news. 'I am afraid I must decline.'

Elis slammed his fist down on the table, making her jump.

'This is what I have decided,' he shouted. 'This is the plan I have made for you. It is not a negotiation.'

She fought back tears. 'You are sentencing me to a life

with a man I cannot stand.'

'You cannot stand most people, so what am I supposed to do?'

'That is not true,' she said, head shaking in defiance.

Wybert cleared his throat and looked straight at her. 'Addressing the elephant in the room, I think we are all aware that you developed feelings for a certain commander while he was in your service. However, I am sure we all agree on the impracticalities of those feelings. His departure was well timed.'

Elis rubbed his forehead. 'Foolish girl. He is a defender, for God's sake.'

To hear him reduced to that one word was unbearable. 'He is more than the uniform he wears. Just because he is a soldier—'

'It is more than that,' her father snapped. 'He is Chadorian. Meanwhile, England is holding their breath, unsure if they are going to have enough grain next month.'

'Do not put that on me,' she replied.

Her father took a fast step towards her. 'It is already on you. That is why we are here. Whether you like it or not, you are the link between England and Carmarthenshire.' His eyes were ablaze. 'You cannot put your personal feelings before the needs of your country.'

Silence fell over the room. She had no response because his point was valid.

'You are a smart woman,' Wybert said, rejoining the conversation. 'You would be a fool to risk everything you are building here for an unavailable man, and you know it.'

Charlotte wiped sweat from her brow and looked

accusingly at the fire, expecting to find it roaring. But it glowed gently.

'I need some air,' she said, turning and heading for the door.

'We are not done,' her father said.

Charlotte was. She was very much done. She pulled the door open and stepped out into the corridor, taking greedy breaths.

Ita turned with a concerned look on her face. 'Are you all right?'

Charlotte shook her head before walking off down the corridor towards the exit. Ita's footsteps sounded behind her. Outside, the cold air stabbed at her lungs in the most cleansing way.

Ita gave her a moment before asking, 'What on earth did your father say that has you in such a state?'

Charlotte held on to her hips and walked in a circle, breathing deeply. 'Tatum said he would come back. Was he telling the truth?'

It took Ita a moment to respond. 'If he's ordered to, then yes.'

Charlotte stilled and looked at her. 'Of course. Orders first.' She closed her eyes tightly. 'I am to marry Lord Wybert. That is what my father wanted to tell me.'

Ita exhaled slowly. 'Oh.'

'And the worst part is that all the reasons he gave make perfect sense.'

Ita's face filled with sympathy. 'What are you going to do?'

Charlotte pressed her palms to her eyes. 'I have no idea.'

'Where are you off to?' Wybert asked, stepping in front of Charlotte's horse and taking hold of the reins.

He had followed Charlotte to the stables to act like an overprotective father. He had been constantly popping up in her life ever since the conversation with her father two weeks earlier, despite the fact that she had yet to agree to this plan of theirs. Her stalling time was definitely running out.

'Llanddeilo,' she said, glaring at his hand on the reins. 'I have business there.'

He glanced suspiciously at Ita on the horse beside her. 'What business is that?'

Charlotte resisted the urge to ride over the top of him. 'That would be *my* business.'

Ita pressed her lips together and looked down at the pommel of her saddle.

Wybert let go of the reins but did not move out of her

way. 'Need I remind you that your business will soon be my business?'

'I do not recall agreeing to that.' Resentment laced her words.

The duke looked between the women, then took a slow step back from the horse. 'Have a safe journey, ladies.'

The pair pushed their horses into a trot and headed for the gate. They crossed the moat, which still contained water despite being designed as a dry channel, then headed for the village.

The sun was high in the sky by the time they reached Llanddeilo, though it was hidden by heavy clouds that threatened more rain. The black sludge swept from people's houses sat in heaped piles outside their homes. Decaying furniture lined the road. They made their way along the muddy streets, stopping briefly to speak to a few of the families.

'They say it's like this all over Carmarthenshire,' Ita said when they were back on their horses. 'And to think that England is still holding their hand out for grain.'

Charlotte had questioned Wybert about that. He had told her that they could not bring business to a halt every time it rains. She had wanted to send some of Dinefwr's supplies to struggling families, but the suggestion had been quickly shut down by their cook, who was keeping a close eye on their grain bags.

The women dismounted outside a tall stone house covered with dead ivy, and a moment later, the two Black-mane brothers stepped outside. It was Charlotte who had suggested the meeting with the general. She thought it best to do it as far away from Wybert as possible.

'Morning, Your Highness,' Blackmane said as he stepped up to take her horse.

Being with Tatum's friends was the closest she had felt to him since he had left. 'Good morning, defender.'

He led her horse away, leaving her with Tolly.

The general bowed his head. 'Your Highness.'

'Thank you for coming, General.'

When Blackmane and Ita returned, the four of them went inside. Charlotte was surprised to find a bare room with filthy floors.

'Who lives here?' she asked.

'No one,' Blackmane said. 'It was a church before the famine. Now it's mostly used as a fortress for children's games.'

Tolly looked around. 'We'd offer you a seat, but...'

Charlotte waved a hand dismissively. 'I prefer to stand.' She looked over at Blackmane. 'Have you heard from Commander Tatum?' She failed to keep the hope out of her voice.

Something flashed in the defender's eyes that she could not identify.

'He remains in Chadora,' Blackmane replied. Hesitating, he finally added, 'And it's just "defender" now. He was stripped of his rank.'

Her stomach fell when she heard that. 'Why?'

Blackmane's eyes moved between hers. 'Inappropriate conduct while abroad.'

Charlotte dropped her gaze to the ground. She had done that. She was the other half of that 'inappropriate conduct'. And now his life was crumbling. 'I gather he will not be returning to Carmarthenshire any time soon.'

'Not to my knowledge, no.'

Charlotte swallowed against the thickening in her throat. She had written to him two weeks earlier, after her father had revealed his plan for her. She had told him everything, including the fact that she did not want to marry Wybert. He had not replied. He had not replied to any of her letters. Now she was left wondering if *any* of it had been real on his part. The man had a reputation with the ladies, after all.

'You wanted to speak with me?' Tolly said, moving the conversation along.

Charlotte tried to focus. She might not have been able to help Tatum, or herself, but she did have a rare opportunity to help the rest of Carmarthenshire. 'Ita has been telling me about some of the current challenges the army is facing.'

Tolly glanced in Ita's direction. 'Has she now?'

'I may be able to help,' Charlotte added.

Tolly returned his attention to her. 'I'm listening.'

'Is it true that the Carmarthen Militia is dependent on charity?'

He nodded. 'Yes. That's the cost of remaining independent of the crown.'

Charlotte pulled a piece of parchment from the pocket of her cloak and unfolded it. 'I have been playing around with some figures.'

Tolly and Blackmane exchanged a surprised, and slightly sceptical, look.

'Each soldier receives around six pounds per year,'

Charlotte began. 'That money is donated by the church, which relies on donations from the people—who currently have nothing to give.' She looked up at Tolly. 'Who pays for your weapons?'

He shifted his weight. 'Most of our weapons are donated also—by English soldiers.'

She was about to ask him how that worked, then remembered what Oliver had told her during their carriage ride to Dinefwr. 'Oh.' She moved on, referring to her notes. 'At present, your barracks consist of canvas tents. You have no uniforms, physicians, cooks.'

'The cooking is a shared responsibility, and we rely on local healers.'

She looked up again. 'I am guessing all of the horses you have in your possession right now were also donated by English soldiers.'

His silence answered that question.

Charlotte looked to Blackmane, who was leaning against the wall with his arms crossed. 'Even the training provided is donated by another kingdom.'

'For the record,' Tolly said, 'the defenders are the highest paid soldiers in Carmarthenshire.'

Blackmane's lips twitched. 'Paid by King Becket.'

Charlotte checked her notes again. 'At present, you have eight hundred men, most of whom are distributed along the borders, correct?'

'Correct.'

She nodded. 'These past few days, I have been liaising with blacksmiths, attiliators, seamstresses, and cooks, trying to gauge what it would cost to get our army properly set up.'

'*Our* army?' Tolly asked.

'Yes. If I am to provide funds, then I expect the same protection as any other person in this kingdom.' She paused. 'Plus personal guards.'

Tolly stared at her for a beat. 'You have a castle full of guards.'

'English guards. Men loyal to Lord Wybert and my father. I want men loyal to *me*.'

He appeared amused by her answer. 'Basically, you want to *buy* an army.'

'It is not about ownership.'

Blackmane straightened. 'Control, then?'

'What I want is an effective army.'

Tolly exhaled slowly. 'I'll tell you right now that a soldier's loyalty can't be bought. They would sooner go without the money.'

Everyone waited for her response.

She looked between them. 'I am not naive enough to think I can tell you who to fight or what to fight for.' Her gaze settled on Tolly. 'I can fund everything mentioned, including five years of wages.'

The silence that followed was the loudest she had ever heard.

Tolly took a small step towards her. 'You're going to pay *twenty-four thousand* pounds in wages over the next five years?'

She shook her head. 'The current wage amount is barely enough to live on, and these people have families to support. So I am going to pay *thirty-six* thousand pounds.'

Blackmane pushed off the wall. 'Do you even have that amount of money?'

'Would I be here having this conversation if I did not?' She swallowed. 'My father has control over the funds at present.'

'And he'll agree to this?' Tolly asked, his tone wary.

'He will if incentivised.' She drew a shaky breath. 'He will if I agree to marry Lord Wybert.'

Blackmane uncrossed his arms. She kept her eyes on Tolly.

'I do not want my brother's wealth to fall into the duke's hands. Oliver would hate that.' A faint smile appeared. 'Do you know what he would have loved? Hearing me describe the soldiers walking about in vibrant uniforms with our family emblem sewn into them. And he would have loved knowing that every person in Carmarthenshire was better off because of him.'

'Including you,' Ita said with a smile. She turned to the men. 'For God's sake. The princess is offering to give you all of her wealth and wants a few guards and a bit of reassurance that you have her back in return.' She looked between the brothers. 'You know very well that she does not want to marry Wybert. She's trying to make wine from sour grapes, so hand the girl some sugar. Give Carmarthenshire the army they deserve and protect this woman at all costs.'

The brothers looked doubtfully at each other, and then Tolly asked, 'You spoke to seamstresses about uniforms?'

'Yes.'

He drew a breath. 'How fast can they sew?'

When Charlotte returned to Dinefwr Castle, she went straight to her father's quarters. She knew he would never agree to release all of Oliver's money to her unless there was something to gain from it. This was a business transaction, pure and simple.

'He will see you now,' the guard said when he emerged after announcing her arrival.

She strode into the room and stopped in front of his desk.

He looked her up and down. 'What is it?'

'I have a proposal, and I would like you to hold all questions until the end.'

He crossed his arms and leaned back in his chair. 'I see. Go on.'

She told him of her plans, and he listened without interrupting her once. After she had shared every detail, he sat in silence, mulling it over. When she could bear his silence no longer, she said, 'It is your turn to speak now.'

His eyes never left her. 'When you marry Lord Wybert, you will behave as a wife should. You will not muddy my family's name. Do you understand me?'

She clasped her hands in front of her. 'Yes.'

'I will give you half the amount now and the other half after you are wed.'

That was clever—and expected. 'Always the businessman.'

He cast her a tired glance before calling to his guard, who appeared a moment later. 'I will be travelling to England tomorrow. Make the appropriate arrangements.' He plucked his quill from the inkpot, then looked back at Charlotte. 'Is that all?'

The correct answer was 'Yes', then exiting as she always did, but she remained there with a question burning on the tip of her tongue.

Growing impatient, Elis said, 'Spit it out, girl. I have much to do.'

Her palms were heating up. 'Do you miss him?'

Elis did not ask who she was referring to. He dropped the quill back into the inkpot. 'Am I sad that my only son is dead? What a silly question.'

'Is it? You have not said a word about him since his death.'

He drew a breath. 'What would you have me say? He chose to leave this world, chose to leave us—despite the fact that he wanted for nothing.'

Charlotte could not tell which part of that statement she found more upsetting, the part about Oliver choosing to leave her or the suggestion that they wanted for nothing. She decided to focus on the last part because it was easier to direct her anger at her father. 'Are you serious? *Wanted for nothing?*'

Elis scowled. 'I have always provided for my children. He had everything he desired over the years.'

The sad part was that he actually believed the words coming from his mouth. 'If you are referring to food, shelter, education—'

'And every luxury item he could fathom.'

She swallowed, twice. 'We were both well provided for in that sense.'

'Why do I feel a "but" coming?'

Charlotte looked around the room, caught off-guard by

the burn at the back of her eyes. 'Those are all things that can be bought. There were other things he wanted and needed, like your time and approval.' She forced herself to look at him again. 'Oliver wanted to feel like a real son.'

Elis did not say anything, and Charlotte was encouraged by this. He was listening, and he never listened to her, so she went on.

'Me? I wanted recognition for always being there for Oliver when you were not. And when Wybert trampled over my life at such a young age, I wanted you to be angry on my behalf.' She paused. 'Then when he suggested we try again, I wanted you to tell him no, that I was too good for him, that I deserved better.' There was no stopping her now. 'Also—'

'There is more?'

'I wanted stories of my mother so I did not have to imagine them. And I wanted you to tell me that her death was not my fault.'

Elis brought a hand to his forehead, rubbing at the creases of skin. 'That goes without saying.'

'I was a child. You should have said it anyway.'

His hand fell away. His face held no anger, which surprised her.

'At age six you were already a better parent to Oliver than I ever was,' he said, looking at the door behind her. 'When I was home, I almost felt like I was intruding.'

'We still needed you.'

He gave a defeated nod. 'Your mother would have agreed with that assessment.'

It was such a revealing comment, and she had no idea

what to do with it. He never spoke of her, and they had learned at a young age never to ask about her.

'Am I like her?' Charlotte was desperate for any pinch of information he was prepared to share.

Elis shook his head. 'No. I am sorry to say that you are a lot like me.'

'Did you love her?'

The way his body involuntarily stiffened in response to that question gave Charlotte her answer.

'I married her.'

'And I am marrying Wybert, yet I can barely tolerate him.'

Elis's expression softened a fraction. 'Your mother and I were lucky that it was both a sound match and we cared for each other.'

It was the closest he would come to speaking of love, so she did not push him any further.

He picked up his quill again. 'Now, is that all?'

'Yes.' It was as though a knee had been lifted off her chest. 'Yes, that is all.'

With that, she went to take care of the thing she had been dreading most.

She went to write her final letter to Tatum.

CHAPTER 25

*I*t was week three of their new excruciating training regimen, designed to break mind and body. Tatum arrived at the training yard early after another sleepless night, greeted by the smell of sweat and mud. He had just gotten settled in when he looked up and spotted his father striding towards him.

'Shit,' he muttered.

Hadewaye, who had been dragged there early, too, followed his gaze. 'Lord Brinley! Good morning!'

Brinley nodded at him. 'Morning.' He stopped five feet from Tatum, looking him over. 'I heard you were back.'

Tatum had been meaning to go see his family but kept putting it off, knowing they would have plenty to say on the subject of his return. He did not have the energy for it. 'I had planned to come visit later in the week. The warden has me on a rather tight training schedule.'

Hadewaye looked awkwardly between father and son, then cleared his throat. 'I'm just going to duck off and grab us a couple of axes.'

He jogged off towards the armoury before Tatum could stop him. They both watched him for a moment before looking back at each other.

'His family has seen him at least a dozen times since his return,' Brinley pointed out.

Tatum had known it was coming. 'He returned a few weeks before I did.'

'Yes.' Brinley looked around at the sparring defenders. 'I had dinner with the warden last night. I wanted to get a better sense of where things are at before coming to see you.'

Tatum bent to pick up a shield and began fiddling with the back of it. 'And now you know.'

A nod. 'Nothing like physical exercise to clear one's mind.' There was an awkward silence before he added, 'I was concerned about some of the things he told me.'

Tatum dropped the shield back on the ground. 'It's just a title.'

'I am not worried about that—well, not only that.' He wandered closer. 'You allowed a woman to distract you from your duties.'

Tatum looked heavenward. 'The woman you speak of was the assignment. My focus was exactly where it was supposed to be.'

Brinley pinched the bridge of his nose. 'Do you think me a fool? Shapur did not share all the details, but I was able to put the pieces together.'

Tatum wet his lips, saying nothing.

'Your brother bears the responsibility of carrying on the family name so you do not have to. This life you live is a gift, and you came very close to throwing it away for a *woman*. A foreigner, no less.'

The foreigner part of that comment stemmed from his own wounds. Tatum's mother had been a 'foreigner', and she had returned home to her family with barely a backwards glance.

'Not every relationship ends like yours, you know. There are other outcomes—even happy ones.' Yet as he said that, he was reminded of the fact that Charlotte had not responded to a single one of his letters. It was possible she had come to her senses.

Brinley closed the distance between them and rested a hand on Tatum's shoulder. 'Are you prepared to risk your position—which you are holding on to by a thread, by the way—in order to find out if you are one of the lucky ones?'

Hadewaye returned before Tatum could reply, an axe in each hand. He realised fairly quickly that he had arrived at a bad time. Looking over his shoulder, he said, 'Actually, I should get us a couple of maces too.'

Tatum stepped out of his father's grip. 'We don't need any maces.' He snatched an axe from Hadewaye's hand. 'Let's begin.'

Brinley sighed. 'Will you at least come for dinner this evening? I know your brother wants to see you.'

Tatum glanced in his direction. 'I'll try my best.'

'Brock,' his father said, waiting for Tatum to look at him.

He reluctantly obliged.

'Come to dinner.'

Tatum leaned his weight on one leg, realising that he

could not avoid facing his judgemental family forever. 'All right. I'll come.'

'Good.' Brinley finally backed up. 'Then we shall see you this evening.' He nodded a farewell at Hadewaye before striding off across the muddy lawn.

When Tatum looked back at Hadewaye, he found the defender staring at him. 'What?'

Hadewaye released a heavy sigh. 'What's going on?'

'Nothing.' He spun his axe a few times in an attempt to loosen up his shoulder.

Hadewaye was not prepared to let the subject go. 'It's one thing to skip meals with us, but your *family*?'

'They only want to sit across the table and point out how ungrateful I am.'

Hadewaye frowned. 'Ungrateful?'

'For the freedom he supposedly handed me. My father has no expectations of me outside of serving my kingdom. He views it as some remarkable act of generosity on his part, a life without the burden of family. Imagine his disappointment in learning that I almost chose that for myself.'

Hadewaye went to speak, but Tatum cut him off.

'I don't need to hear from everyone, over and over again, that being with her was a mistake, that loving her is somehow a fault in me.' Heat climbed his neck. 'Do I know the relationship is impractical? Of course I do. I don't need every man and his horse pointing out how hopeless the situation is. I fucking *know*.' He was breathing hard by the time he got that out, as though he had run a lap before saying it.

When Hadewaye went to speak again, Tatum raised a

hand. 'Can we skip the awkward reply and go straight to the part where I get to swing this axe at you?' He looked at his friend. 'Please.'

Hadewaye swallowed and nodded. 'Now I'm going to feel bad if I knock you out.'

'Don't.' Tatum picked up his shield again. 'I could do with the sleep.'

Before they had a chance to get started, a young recruit ran up with a letter in his hand. 'From Maddock House, sir.'

Tatum let his weapons fall to the ground and took it.

'From Blackmane?' Hadewaye asked, tossing his axe up and catching it.

Tatum waited for the recruit to leave, then checked the seal as he opened it. 'Yes.' He read quickly, slowing when he reached the bottom.

Hadewaye glanced in his direction, straightening when he saw Tatum's expression. 'What does it say?'

Tatum read the last part again, then looked up. 'Charlotte has invested her fortune in the Carmarthen Militia.'

The defender relaxed a little. 'Wow.' He inspected the blade of his axe. 'She's really leaning into her new role.'

Tatum's hand fell to his side. 'She doesn't want her brother's money falling into her future husband's hands.'

'Future husband?' Hadewaye was visibly confused. 'What are you talking about?'

He blinked repeatedly. 'She's to marry Lord Wybert.'

CHAPTER 26

'Ican't believe no one ever taught you how to play chess,' Ita said as she moved her knight on the board.

They were seated at the table under the window in Charlotte's quarters, fire blazing and shutters open for fresh air.

'My only companion through childhood was blind, and all of my governesses believed anything fun landed a person in hell, so...'

Ita screwed up her face. 'I suppose chess without sight would come with its challenges.'

Charlotte's finger tapped the table as she considered her next move. When she went to reach for her pawn, a large bird appeared at the window, its giant wings beating against the bars. She almost tumbled off her chair as she reared back from it. Sir Miles leapt up from the rug, his bark deafening.

'Margery,' Ita said, shooting up out of her seat. 'Are

you trying to scare the princess to death?' She gave Charlotte an apologetic look. 'Sorry.'

Charlotte went to Sir Miles and tried to calm him down. 'That is quite enough.' He fell silent when she took hold of his collar.

Ita slipped her hand through the bars and stroked the eagle's chest. 'What are you doing here?' It was then that she spotted the note attached to Margery's leg. She untied it.

'What is that?' Charlotte asked, walking close enough to see but well out of reach of the eagle.

Ita unfolded it and read. 'It's from Blackmane.'

'What does it say?'

Ita turned to her with a bright smile. 'Isabel's in labour.'

'Well, you must go to her. I am certain she will want you by her side.'

'What about you?' Ita looked past her to the door. 'I hate the thought of leaving you here alone. Why don't you come to Maddock House with me?'

'I am not alone.' Charlotte gestured to Sir Miles.

'I suppose Mevanou is here to keep you company.'

'And talk my ear off,' Charlotte added quietly. 'Besides, my guards will be arriving in the next few days. They might be a little thrown if they get here and find me missing.' She glanced at the eagle, who was watching them through the window. 'That said, I will definitely come visit when Lady Isabel is up to visitors.'

There was a knock at the door, and before Charlotte could ask who was there, Mevanou barged in.

'Afternoon, Your Highness. Some painting supplies

arrived for you.' She walked over and placed them on the table, spotting the eagle in the process. 'And good afternoon to you, too, Margery. What are you doing this far from Maddock House?'

Ita held up the note. 'Isabel's in labour.' She grabbed her cloak from the back of the chair.

Mevanou clapped her hands together excitedly. 'Oooh. I pray she has an easy time of it.' She made the sign of the cross. 'Not like my poor mother with my youngest brother.'

'I should get going.' Ita looked to Margery. 'Wait right there. I'll come and get you.'

The eagle spread her wings and took flight instead.

'Brilliant,' Ita muttered. She flashed a smile at Charlotte and lowered into a curtsy. 'I'll keep you updated.' She was out the door before Charlotte could reply.

Mevanou walked over to the window. 'Not that you want a bird that size flying about your bedchamber with a dog that size in pursuit'—she looked pointedly at Sir Miles—'but you can remove these bars if you need to.'

Charlotte gave her a questioning look. 'What do you mean?'

Mevanou walked over to the window, running her fingers around its edges. 'There should be a hook...'

The maid came upon a latch at the bottom, then reached for the top. After fiddling for a few seconds, she gripped the iron grille with both hands and gave it a hard yank. The whole thing came away in one piece.

Frozen in place, Charlotte stared at the window.

'My grandfather helped rebuild the place after the fires, *before* King Edward moved in,' Mevanou said as she lifted the grille and wrestled it back into place. 'I remember him telling me that every window in every bedchamber can be removed from the inside—so no man, woman, or child might ever burn alive again.'

A cold sensation ran through Charlotte, starting at the top of her head and spreading all the way to her fingertips. Without saying a word, she fled the room, leaving Mevanou chatting away to herself.

Charlotte made her way down the corridor, her steps hurried, coming to a grounding halt outside Oliver's old bedchamber. She pushed the door open and stepped inside, heading straight for the window. Her heart was pounding hard and fast as she felt around the frame for anything resembling a hook. She froze when she came upon it, then took a breath and reached up to unhook the top. She tore the grille from the window and let it fall to the floor with a clang.

All of the air left her lungs. 'Oh, Oliver.'

Heat pumped through her. If Mevanou knew about the windows, then it was likely others did too. It was possible, was it not? That someone unlocked the window when he was out training that day, came through it that night, held him down, and...

Is Father in danger? Am I in danger?

No. If someone wanted them dead, they would be dead already.

She needed to get out of there. *Not* knowing was the best way to keep safe.

Carefully and quietly, she put the window back in place and exited the room, pulling the door closed behind her. A wet nose brushed her hand. She looked down at Sir

Miles. He had followed her but refused to enter the room. She crouched and wrapped her arms around him.

'I understand,' she whispered. 'I would not want to go in there either if I had seen the things you have seen.' She pressed her eyes closed. 'I promise that if someone else was in that room, I will find them.'

Rising once more, she clicked her fingers at Sir Miles, and they walked slowly back to her bedchamber.

CHAPTER 27

The warden requested an audience with Tatum, Hadewaye, and Alveye, summoning them to his quarters. The defenders arrived within minutes, slightly on edge as they stood shoulder to shoulder before Shapur. The silence stretched out as they waited for him to finish the letter he was writing. Finally, he laid down his quill and leaned back in his chair, looking between them.

'It has come to my attention that Princess Charlotte has invested a considerable amount of money into the Carmarthen Militia.'

Tatum had not been expecting to hear her name, and his mind buzzed in response to it. The warden sifted through some papers and plucked one out. Even from that distance, Tatum recognised Blackmane's handwriting.

Shapur began to read. 'Barracks, horses, uniforms, cooks, blacksmiths, physicians.' He dropped the letter on the table. 'Add to that a wage increase that will have farmers laying down their tools and running to sign up.'

Tatum stared at the warden as the words settled. It was a smart move on her behalf. A kingdom is only as strong as its army.

Shapur linked his hands together on the table. 'Now is not the time to be withdrawing men from Carmarthenshire. Now is the time to keep our allies close and remain watchful.' He sniffed and looked straight at Tatum. 'I was considering sending a new unit. However, your knowledge of the area and established relationship with General Blackmane work to our advantage.' He paused and spent a few long and painful moments shuffling papers. 'I am sending the three of you back to Carmarthenshire.'

Tatum's lungs resumed working.

'You will continue to assist with training and keep me updated with any changes,' Shapur continued. 'And I want weapon production tracked. If the relationship ever sours, we need to know what we are up against.' He paused. 'Perhaps you could find the earl's killer while you are at it—since you failed to do it last time.'

Tatum was about to point out that the English had also failed in that regard but knew better than to interrupt him. He waited for Shapur to continue.

'There are some strict conditions.' The warden looked between the three defenders. 'You are to stay away from Dinefwr Castle unless you are invited there by Lord Elis or Lord Wybert. I will not tolerate any disruptions to their business or personal lives. Is that clear?'

Hadewaye and Alveye nodded. 'Yes, sir.'

The warden glared at Tatum, and the defender realised he had not responded.

'Yes, sir,' Tatum said.

Shapur's scowl deepened before he shifted his gaze to Alveye. 'Since *someone* has to lead the unit, I am promoting you to commander for the duration of your deployment. Will that be an issue for any of you?' He looked specifically at Tatum when he asked that question.

'No, sir,' Tatum and Hadewaye replied in unison.

The warden nodded. 'Good. I have already written to Blackmane so that everyone is clear on expectations.' He opened a drawer, retrieved a gold pin, and placed it on the table before sliding it towards Alveye. 'You will depart for Carmarthenshire in the morning.'

Alveye stepped forwards to take the pin. 'Thank you, sir. I won't let you down.'

He nodded. 'Just make sure everyone returns here in one piece.'

'Yes, sir.'

He returned to his work and said, 'You are all dismissed.'

The three defenders filed out of the room.

Hadewaye pulled the door closed behind them, then reached for Alveye's shoulder. 'Congratulations, *Commander*.'

Alveye exhaled. 'Thank you, but it feels wrong accepting it, knowing it's rightfully Tatum's.'

Tatum clapped him on the back. 'What on earth are you banging on about? I can't think of anyone more deserving—except Hadewaye.'

Alveye smirked at the ground and began walking.

'Besides,' Tatum said, 'we all know I won't listen to you anyway.'

The new commander glanced sideways at him. 'Oh, I know.'

Hadewaye came up between them, one hand on each of their shoulders. 'It will be so good to see Blackmane. Bet he's missed us.'

Tatum snorted. 'I doubt that. He's likely enjoying the peace.'

Hadewaye ignored the comment. 'Every time I think our period of serving together has come to an end, fate says, "Not yet, my friend."'

'That definitely sounds like something old fate would say,' Tatum replied, making Alveye smirk again.

Hadewaye drew a long breath. 'Well, back to Carmarthenshire we go.'

And all Tatum had to do was stay away from Dinefwr Castle, away from the woman who had consumed his every thought since leaving that place.

'Yes, back we go.'

'They're here, Your Highness,' Mevanou announced as she flew through Charlotte's bedchamber door—without knocking. Thankfully, Sir Miles was used to sudden entrances now and did not lunge at the door.

'Who is here?' Charlotte asked, putting the letter from Ita aside and getting to her feet.

'Your new guards! In their uniforms, no less. Proper soldiers they are.'

Charlotte smiled to herself. 'Where are they?'

'With Lord Wybert in the courtyard.'

Charlotte clicked her fingers at Sir Miles, who immediately sprang to his feet. 'Let us go save the poor men from His Lordship, shall we?'

They made their way to the inner-ward, where the two men were speaking with Wybert. Her soon-to-be husband turned to her when she came into view. 'So, this is what you have to show for the thousands of pounds your father handed over to the Carmarthen Militia.'

He had naturally objected to her spending the majority of her fortune without any consultation with him. But to his credit, he had not interfered or tried to prevent her father from travelling to England to make the arrangements. Though that was most likely because her father was also changing his legal will so everything went to Wybert upon his death.

'Need I remind you that my men would have protected you for *free*,' Wybert added.

Charlotte met his gaze. 'As previously explained, a Welsh princess should have Welsh guards.' She stepped past him in order to address the waiting men. 'Welcome to Dinefwr Castle.' Her gaze fell to their bold green tunics with a red lion sewn onto the sleeve, and she felt a pinch of pride.

'Your Highness,' the men said in unison as they bowed.

She waited for them to straighten before continuing. 'I know I ask a great deal of you in coming here and working alongside English soldiers, so thank you both.' She was well aware that Wybert was listening a few feet away. 'However, that is how we ensure trade continues, benefiting the kingdom long-term.' She looked between the soldiers. 'What are your names?'

The taller soldier spoke up first. 'Dudley Stroude, at your service.' He gestured to his comrade. 'And this is Dafydd Bowen.'

'Stroude and Bowen. I will try to remember that. I gather General Blackmane has briefed you?'

'He has, yes,' Stroude replied.

She smiled. 'Good.'

Bowen cleared his throat. 'We understand the safety

risk is low at present, but that could change with the announcement of your impending nuptials.'

Charlotte glanced over her shoulder at Wybert. 'Something to look forward to.'

The duke did not respond.

'Now that I have adequate protection, I need to go to Maddock House in Llanelieu. Lady Isabel gave birth to a son recently. I would like to visit them.'

Wybert had something to say about that. 'Llanelieu? That is many hours away.'

'Well, I just so happen to have many hours to fill.'

He was visibly displeased. 'It seems like an unnecessary risk.'

'A risk my guards are more than capable of managing,' she replied, glancing at the men.

Wybert frowned. 'And will you be staying overnight?'

'It would be a rather ambitious journey to do in one day.' His discomfort was likely due to Isabel being the wife of a defender, and he clearly wanted her as far away from them as possible. 'You are welcome to join me if you fancy an afternoon of baby doting. However, I will be in the carriage, and you will be on horseback.'

His eyes searched hers. 'I have business to take care of here. You go ahead, enjoy the visit. I shall see you tomorrow when you return.'

She shook her head as she watched him stride away.

Back in her quarters, Mevanou helped her pack for the journey, even including a gift for the family.

'A mother can never have enough linen wraps and blankets,' the maid said as she let the lid of the trunk drop shut.

Charlotte gave her a small smile. 'Thank you.' She went to fetch one of her paintings to put with it.

'You sure you don't want me to come with you?'

As much as Charlotte liked the chatty maid, she could not think of anything worse than being trapped in a carriage with her for hours on end. 'Very kind of you to offer, but I am quite comfortable with my own company.'

An hour later, Charlotte was in her carriage on her way to Maddock House, watching the landscape slip by. She let her mind wander wherever it pleased—and of course, it went to Tatum. The hollowness in her chest grew. She had not heard one word from him since he had left Dinefwr. She rationalised that it was not too surprising post-news of her engagement, but what about the long weeks she had endured before that? She had delayed the betrothal for as long as possible, a childish part of her waiting for Tatum to show up and 'figure this out' like he said he would.

Like he had promised.

Charlotte leaned her head on the window, trying to envisage her life with Wybert. He would work. She would paint. There would be social commitments, and likely children. Weirdly, she could not think about that without feeling like she was betraying Tatum.

With her mind full and heart empty, Charlotte drifted off to sleep.

She woke when the carriage rolled to a stop and looked out the window at the modest-sized house surrounded by immaculate gardens. Livestock grazed in nearby paddocks, and various poultry foraged freely.

The carriage door swung open, and the driver

appeared, extending a hand to her. As she stepped down, she heard the front door of the house open, and Ita came out with a giant smile on her face.

'You came!'

She was followed by a middle-aged woman who Charlotte guessed to be Lady Isabel's mother.

Ita stopped in front of her with a small curtsy. 'Your Highness, this is Lady Gwenore, proud grandmother of the new arrival.'

'Congratulations.'

Gwenore smiled. 'It is so very kind of you to travel such a great distance to visit, Your Highness. Please, come inside.' She glanced at the guards, who were standing back from them, watchful. 'Your men are free to access the stables. We have a lot of soldiers coming in and out of here, so it is set up like a second house.'

'Thank you, Lady Gwenore,' Stroude replied, then looked at Charlotte. 'We'll be nearby if you need us, Your Highness.'

She nodded, then followed the women inside the house.

The main room was a cosy space with smooth timber floors and elegant silk tapestries hanging on the walls. Comfortable armchairs sat on either side of the fireplace.

'I was very sorry to hear about the passing of your brother,' Gwenore said, gesturing towards the lounge.

Charlotte breathed through the pinch in her chest. 'Thank you. He is sorely missed.'

Before she had a chance to sit, the stairs creaked, and Isabel appeared with a bundle of baby in her arms. A smile spread across her face when she laid eyes on Charlotte.

'Oh, what a wonderful surprise.' She handed the baby to her mother before walking over to Charlotte, where she curtsied.

Charlotte waved her hand. 'That is completely unnecessary. You just had a baby.'

'It is not every day we have *royalty* calling by the house. Most of our visitors are soldiers in need of a good bath.'

A smile came and went on Charlotte's face. 'Well, congratulations on the safe arrival of your son, Lady Isabel. I was pleased to hear everything went smoothly.'

'You can call me Belle. Everyone else does.' Isabel went to collect her son. 'Here he is. Do you want to hold him?'

Charlotte was about to politely decline, but when the tiny boy came into view, her entire body softened in response. He had the sweetest nose, and his whole head was covered in fluffy black hair.

'He is like a miniature Blackmane,' Charlotte said, taking the baby into her arms.

'I told Blackmane he looked just like Hadewaye,' Ita said. 'He didn't like that.'

Charlotte fought back a smile. 'What did you name him?'

'Domangard,' Isabel said. 'We call him Dom for short.'

'Is it Irish?'

Isabel nodded. 'It was Ryder's father's name.'

'Hello, Dom,' Charlotte whispered, brushing a finger down the baby's pink cheek.

The front door opened, and she looked to see who it was. Blackmane was halfway through the door when he spotted her and immediately froze. She thought she saw panic flash in his eyes. It was an out-of-character reaction for a man who was rarely fazed by anything.

'Are you waiting for a written invitation?' came a painfully familiar voice behind him. '*Move.*'

Charlotte's gaze snapped to the figure behind the defender, and there was Tatum, preparing to shove Blackmane out of his way. He glanced in her direction, gaze snagging on hers. His face fell.

'Charlotte.'

The way he spoke her name cracked something inside her.

Blackmane entered the house, but Tatum did not follow. He stared at Charlotte for a long moment, then disappeared entirely.

Charlotte looked accusingly at Ita.

'I wanted to tell you,' she said, face twisting with guilt.

Charlotte glanced down at the baby in her arms. He was awake and watching her, like everyone else in the room. She handed him back to Isabel, then smoothed down the front of her dress. 'Please excuse me for a moment.'

Her eyes met Blackmane's as she exited the house.

Outside, the carriage was gone, and her guards were at the stables tending their horses. She looked around and saw Tatum's retreating back heading for one of the paddocks. She followed him, legs moving fast to catch up.

'Tatum!'

He whipped his head in her direction, his stare cold as he waited for her to catch up. 'Your Highness.' His tone was equally as cold.

She stopped a few feet away, unsure what was going to come from her mouth.

An awkward beat of silence passed between them.

'You are back,' she said, stating the obvious.

He nodded. 'I am.'

'Were you planning on telling me you had returned to Carmarthenshire?'

He shrugged. 'I figured you'd find out eventually. No need to make a big announcement of it.' He crossed his arms. 'Your soon-to-be husband would likely be aware of the fact given he's in direct contact with the warden. Did he tell you that?'

She understood that he had reasons to be angry, but so did she.

'Wybert's the reason we were summoned back to Chadora,' he added when she did not respond. 'Interesting timing, don't you think?'

The level of hostility caught her off-guard. Charlotte was momentarily lost for words.

'I guess he needed me out of the way.'

This was not the conversation she had imagined having with him when they finally crossed paths. 'You know I do not want to marry him, so please choose your next words carefully. I will not stand here and beg for your forgiveness. Marrying Wybert *is* the punishment.'

He nodded slowly. 'And *you* know that I've been following orders and staying out of the way.'

'Orders before all else, am I right?'

His jaw ticked. 'You should go back inside.'

He turned to leave, but she caught his arm. 'You lied to me. You said you would come back.'

'I'm here, aren't I?' His eyes were bright with anger now. '*You* were supposed to wait for me, remember?'

'I did wait!'

He leaned closer. 'You were engaged to someone else six weeks after I left. *Six weeks.*'

Charlotte's guards came at a run, clearly having heard her yell. They stopped in their tracks when they saw Tatum with her.

'I am fine,' she assured them.

They retreated a few steps but remained watchful.

Charlotte faced Tatum again. 'I had no idea when or if you would return. You did not reply to any of my letters—'

'Because I didn't receive any letters.'

She searched his eyes, her words jamming her throat. 'I wrote to you half a dozen times.'

His chest was rising and falling fast. 'I received nothing, despite writing to you frequently. I ceased only upon hearing news of your engagement, out of respect.'

Her hands went over her mouth. 'Someone intercepted the letters. My father, Wybert. Perhaps the warden.'

Tatum looked around the garden, visibly agitated. 'Not entirely surprising.' He shook his head, eyes returning to her. 'If you had just waited.'

She dropped her hands to her sides. 'They were pushing and pushing—'

'Since when are you a pushover?'

'I saw an opportunity to help people!'

He gestured to her guards. 'I see that. Fancy uniforms, by the way. I hope they bring you a lifetime of happiness.'

She threw her hands up. 'You are exhausting. All of you. You are all the same.'

'Don't lump me in with *him*.'

'I am so tired.' She covered her face. 'It has been weeks of negotiating and guilt and questioning everything you said to me.' Her hands fell to her sides once more. 'I do not even know if any of it was real. Perhaps I was simply another woman you could not have, and I imagined the rest.'

The flames in his eyes extinguished, and his shoulders dropped a few inches.

'It doesn't matter now,' he said, looking defeated. 'Real, pretend—none of it matters. It's done. Now we both have to get on with the job we're here to do. The main thing is you're safe.' He nodded towards her guards. 'We trained those men.' His eyes returned to her. 'You're in good hands.'

He was right about it being too late. There was nothing left to do but get on with things—a fact she resented with her whole self. As for the safety part… she was tempted to tell him about the window situation at Dinefwr, about her suspicions, but that felt like a selfish thing to do. He had a new assignment that had nothing to do with her. It was not fair to drag him back into her mess.

'You're the last Princess of Carmarthenshire,' he said quietly. 'I'm a Chadorian defender. It was always going to be him or someone just like him.' He went to reach for her but stopped himself. 'Go back inside.'

She blinked back tears. 'I wanted it to be you. I really did.' Turning slowly away, she headed for the house.

'Your Highness,' he called.

She paused and looked back.

'The uniforms are great.' His hands went to his hips. 'The barracks being built, the cooks, physicians, the wages supporting families. It's all great.' He pressed his lips together. 'Oliver would be proud.'

Charlotte averted her gaze so he would not see the tears rising, then resumed walking.

CHAPTER 29

*T*atum should have returned to the camp, to the safety of a tent. Even the bed of a certain married silk-weaver would have been safer than remaining at Maddock House, but he had missed Charlotte. In all the ways one can miss a person, he had missed her. So he loitered around the house, but not inside it, because that was too close. He ate dinner in the stables with her guards despite visits from both Blackmane and Ita asking what he was doing.

'Enjoying the cool evening,' he told them, his numb hands tucked beneath his armpits.

They gave up and left, heads shaking.

He swore under his breath when he saw Isabel walking across the lawn towards him. They had sent their most effective weapon.

She took a seat beside him, hugging herself against the cold. Stroude and Bowen glanced between them, then announced they were going to check on their horses.

Isabel waited for them to leave before looking at him. 'What are you doing?'

'Working up the energy to return to camp.'

'You have your own room inside the house, but that is not what I was asking.' She placed a hand on his arm. *'What are you doing?'*

He did not reply because he did not have an answer. He had no idea what he was doing. What he did know was that it hurt to be away from her, and it hurt to be close to her, so he was figuring out where on that scale he needed to be in order to breathe properly.

'I have seen you with various women over the last year,' Isabel said, 'but never have you looked at one of them the way you looked at her today.'

His eyes sank shut. 'She's getting married.'

'I, too, was getting married once, remember?' She withdrew her hand and sat up a little.

'This is different.'

'Because of her title? Her father's preferences?' When he did not answer her, she said, 'I will let you in on a secret. Love does not care about any of those things. Nor should you.'

'You and Blackmane fought for this life of yours. Not all of us are up for it.'

She laughed lightly. 'You are one of the best fighters I know. Do not let fear make a loser out of you.' She leaned forwards to catch his gaze. 'And in case you need to hear this, she is not your mother, and you are not your father.'

He blinked, saying nothing.

She patted his arm. 'When you are ready, come inside.

Do not freeze out here all night unnecessarily.' Standing, she headed back to the house.

Tatum decided to go for a long run to burn off his pent-up energy, despite having trained hard that morning. When he finally returned to the house, he found it quiet. Only Gwenore and Ita sat yawning in front of the fire.

Ita looked him up and down. 'She's already retired for the evening.'

'I didn't ask.'

'You didn't have to.'

It was a good thing she was already in bed. Better not to lay eyes on her again if he stood any chance of sleeping under the same roof as her.

He bid Ita and Gwenore goodnight and made his way upstairs, eyes on the guest chamber door where Charlotte was sleeping. He paused briefly, listening for movement, but all was silent. He was about to walk on when the handle turned and the door creaked open. His eyes met Charlotte's through the crack. She opened it wider and rested her head on the doorframe.

'Why are you sweating?' she asked.

'I went for a run.'

'Do you normally run at night?'

'Sometimes.' She was wearing only a nightdress, and he fought hard to keep his eyes up. 'Can't sleep?'

She shook her head. 'I cannot believe you have your own room here.'

'It's not just for me. It actually has three beds in it.'

She laughed softly. 'Of course it does.'

Her laughter made his chest feel the lightest it had in months. 'For the record, it was all real.' He looked away before adding, 'At least for me, anyway.' He made himself walk away. 'Goodnight, Princess.'

Tatum was almost to his door when he heard, 'Goodnight, defender.'

He was grateful for the safety of his room. He closed the door and leaned against it before going to fill the basin with cold water. Stripping down, he had a wash. Then, with a towel wrapping his hips, he flopped down on the bed, a hand pressed to his forehead.

A knock at the door had him sitting up. He stared at the shadow at the bottom before rising to open it. It was Charlotte, now fully dressed. Her expression turned his legs to liquid.

'What's wrong?' he asked.

She looked off down the hallway. 'I do not feel safe alone in that room.'

He raised one arm, holding the edge of the door. 'Really?'

She nodded.

'Well, I'd invite you in, but then I wouldn't feel safe in *this* room.'

Her eyes returned to him, laughter in them.

'What exactly are you afraid of?' he asked.

The laughter in her eyes dissipated. 'Everything from tomorrow onwards.'

Without waiting for an invitation, Charlotte stepped inside the room, her floral scent taking over the air. The light from the lamp glinted off her neckline, drawing his eye as she passed him. He wondered if he had it in him to do the right thing and walk her back to her room. Yet at the same time he was having this thought, he also pushed the door closed and turned to her.

'If your plan is to have me against a wall, then leave without a word—'

'That is not my plan.' She stepped closer and rose onto her toes, laying a gentle kiss against his lips.

Sensation coursed through him, so strong that it took all his willpower to not press her up against said wall. 'Charlotte—'

'Do you want to waste time on questions, or do you want to take off my dress?'

He wanted to take off her dress. 'You're forgetting about a certain promise you made to a certain lord.'

'I forget nothing. I promised to be a faithful and respectful wife, and I meant it.' She swallowed. 'But we are not married—yet.'

The dismal amount of strength Tatum had dissolved, and his lips found hers. He kissed her thoroughly for a number of minutes before whispering, 'All right. Tonight you belong to me.'

Brock Tatum was the definition of comfort. As Charlotte lay in his bed, wrapped in his strong arms with her legs entwined with his, she knew she would never experience comfort like that again. There was no safer place in the world than with him.

'Should I leave?' she asked quietly in the dark, her heart beating gently against his ribs.

His arms tightened around her in response. 'We have at least two hours until sunrise.'

She looked up at him, studying the shadowed edges of his face. 'That was—'

'Better than a wall?'

She pressed her lips together. 'Yes. Better than a wall.' She reached up and traced a finger down his throat. 'Can I ask you something?'

'Anything.'

'In another life, in a world that made sense for us, could you have loved me the way Blackmane loves Isabel?'

He caught her hand and brought it to his lips, kissing the back of it. 'In this life, in this world that makes no sense, I love you.'

'You do?'

'Ask me again in the morning and I'll deny it, but under the cover of darkness, I'll admit it freely.'

She ran her thumb over his lips as all kinds of heat-fuelled emotions washed through her. 'How do we make it stop?'

'That's easy. You need to do or say something unforgivable. I'll replace the love with anger, which will eventually turn into indifference.'

'Like marry Lord Wybert?'

'Exactly.'

She suppressed a smile. 'And what will you do to rid me of *my* feelings, since I love you too?'

He drew her closer—if that were possible. 'You just sit tight. It's only a matter of time before I say or do something you deem unforgivable.'

She dropped her hand to his chest. 'Well, do not leave me hanging too long. I have a wedding coming up.'

His lips found hers in the dark, and he kissed her deeply for a long time. Then they lay in silence for the next hour.

The closer it got to sunrise, the more anxious Charlotte became about their time together coming to an end.

'What if we were to run away and marry?' she whispered. 'Oliver always used to say it is better to ask for forgiveness than permission.'

She was met with silence.

When she looked up, she saw he was sound asleep. On an exhale, she rested her cheek on his chest. Eventually, she fell into a dream-filled sleep charged by body heat and dread of morning.

When her eyes sprang open a few hours later, light was filtering in around the drapes, painting bright stripes on the floor. It took her a moment to realise that Tatum was no longer in the bed. She sat upright and looked around the empty room, eyes landing on the place where his boots and uniform had sat the night before.

They were gone.

He was gone.

The sound of a horse approaching had Charlotte climbing out of the bed and peering out the window. She froze when she spotted Wybert dismounting, then immediately stepped back from the curtain. With trembling hands, she went to the basin and got to work washing Tatum's intoxicating scent off her skin while the man she was due to marry made his way to the front door.

It took a few minutes to work the knots from her hair

before twisting it into a low bun. She could do nothing about the colour in her cheeks. Tatum had lit a fire inside her so large that no amount of powder seemed to be able to disguise it.

A knock at the door made her jump. She went to open it and found Isabel standing there with an apologetic expression.

'Oh good. You are here.' She cleared her throat. 'Lord Wybert has come to collect you.'

Charlotte felt her cheeks get hotter. 'Did he say why?'

Isabel shook her head. 'No.'

'Is Tatum here?'

'He and Ryder left an hour ago.'

Charlotte forced a smile. 'Thank you. I will be right down.'

After Isabel left, Charlotte brought a hand to her raw, sensitive lips. When she licked them, she could still taste him. Left with no choice, she put on her boots and made her way downstairs, where she found Wybert waiting in the main room. His gaze swept the length of her, as though assessing her for damage.

'Good morning, Your Highness.' He bowed his head.

'My lord.' Charlotte snuck a glance at Ita, who was openly glaring at the duke. 'What brings you to Maddock House?'

'I had business nearby and thought we could travel home together.'

'Did you now?' She waited for the guilt to hit her, but it did not come. The only guilt she felt was due to going home with the man in front of her when her heart so wholly belonged to Tatum.

She looked over at Isabel. 'Thank you for being such a wonderful host, Lady Isabel.'

She smiled. 'You are welcome at Maddock House anytime.'

'I'll come visit soon,' Ita said.

Charlotte exited the house, instructing Bowen to fetch her trunk.

'Shall I travel in the carriage with you?' Wybert asked.

She shook her head and picked up speed. 'You have your horse, and I would prefer to be alone.'

'Was that the case last night too?'

She stopped and turned, forcing him to pull up. 'You have a lot of audacity showing up here. I know you intercepted my letters to Tatum.'

'So you did see him.'

'Imagine my surprise. I did not even know he was here in Carmarthenshire—thanks to your interference.'

'That interference was for your own good *and* at your father's request.' He rubbed his forehead. 'Nonetheless, I am sure it was a heart-warming reunion.'

Charlotte angled her head. 'It was, actually. *Very* touching.'

Wybert's jaw ticked. He glanced at Stroude, who had one hand resting on the hilt of his sword. 'We have big plans, Charlotte. If we stay focused, we both get everything we want.'

She laughed through her nose. 'Not everything.'

Wybert stepped past her and headed for his horse.

CHAPTER 30

'Would you just come and have dinner at the house?' Blackmane said, losing patience.

Alveye and Hadewaye were standing on either side of him, waiting for Tatum's response.

He had not been back there since the morning he fled without so much as a goodbye. Charlotte *had* said she needed a reason to hate him. 'No, thank you.'

'Why?'

'Because they're going to peg me with questions and pity glances across the table.'

Alveye's eyebrows came together. 'Who?'

'Isabel and Ita.'

Blackmane looked thoroughly perplexed by this. 'You're scared of my *wife*, who does nothing but feed and dote on you?'

'That's not all she does, though, is it? She talks about feelings and—'

'Not *feelings*,' Hadewaye said with a gasp.

Alveye chuckled.

'And they judge me—harshly.'

'Because you sleep with married women' was Alveye's reply.

Blackmane gestured to the horses. 'Quit your whining and let's go.'

Tatum let out a noisy breath. 'Fine.' He headed for his horse. 'I'll go. But let me be very clear about something. There's to be no discussion about the princess.'

Blackmane did not reply.

An hour later, he was seated at the large table at Maddock House holding a sleeping baby who had been forced upon him as he walked in.

'Thank you,' Isabel said to Tatum as though he had offered.

He looked down at the boy who was too adorable for his own good.

'Suits you,' Ita said, getting in first.

Hadewaye leaned in and said, 'He's a little sensitive right now.'

Lady Gwenore gave him a sympathetic smile. 'Because you are in love with the princess?'

Tatum gave Blackmane a look that said 'I told you so'.

'It is a little early to be throwing your hands up in defeat,' Isabel said. 'She is not married yet.'

Ita nodded in agreement. 'But keep in mind that once our darling princess *is* wed, we will all be telling you to steer clear. You're not to muddy up her life.'

Tatum looked around the table. 'I knew this dinner was a trap.'

Alveye swallowed his mouthful of food. 'The problem is everyone knows you spent the night together.'

Gwenore coughed, then touched her napkin to her mouth. 'Excuse me. I think I shall go find Everard.'

Isabel tutted at Alveye. 'You know she is sensitive to scandal.' There was a ghost of a smile on her lips when she said that.

'You all know that a Welsh princess marrying a Chadorian defender is a wasted opportunity for this kingdom,' Tatum said. 'So can we all move on to another topic now?'

Isabel laid her cutlery down. 'Does that mean you have spoken of marriage?'

'No.' His mind returned to the last thing Charlotte had said to him.

'What if we were to run away and marry? Oliver always used to say it is better to ask for forgiveness than permission.'

He had pretended that he was asleep, then left shortly after.

Hadewaye waved his knife in the defender's direction. 'But you've clearly been thinking about it.'

Ita heaped some boiled carrots onto her plate. 'Such a wasted opportunity. She's perfect for you and you know it.'

'And a princess,' Tatum said tiredly.

Ita stabbed a carrot with her fork. 'People in Carmarthenshire don't care if you have a title or not, only that you treat her well and support her work here.'

'They would celebrate a love match,' Isabel said. 'Lord Wybert, on the other hand, will be tolerated at best.'

Tatum kicked Blackmane's leg under the table. 'Now's the time to back me up.'

Blackmane lifted his gaze from his plate. 'I can't.'

'Why not?'

'Because I happen to agree with them. You're both problematic yet somehow good for each other.'

Tatum's eyes narrowed. 'Did you say *problematic*?'

'Yes.'

'What my darling husband is trying to say,' Isabel interjected, 'is that you bring out the best in each other.'

Ita took a sip of her wine. 'That's true. Somehow, you level each other out.'

Tatum rose, handing the baby to Blackmane with an accompanying glare. 'This conversation is an enormous waste of all our time. If I'm able to move on, then all of you should be able to do the same.' He looked around the table. 'I need to get back to the camp.'

'No you don't,' Blackmane said.

If the man had not been holding his son, Tatum might have tackled him from his chair. 'I'm sorry, are you commander of this unit now? I thought that privilege went to Alveye.'

Alveye waved him off with a laugh. 'Go on, then. We'll see you back there.'

Tatum reached past Hadewaye and plucked a chicken leg off the tray, took a giant bite, and left.

CHAPTER 31

'No word from your father yet?' Mevanou asked as she set the tray of food down.

Charlotte was famished and reached for the chunk of bread. 'Not since he sent the funds.' Half of which had already been handed over to the Carmarthen Militia.

One positive thing about his absence was that the longer he was away, the bigger the delay until the wedding.

'What's the plan for this morning, then?' the maid asked. 'Another painting?'

There were only so many scenes a person could paint from Dinefwr's walls. 'Maybe I'll ask Stroude for some suggestions.'

Mevanou poured her a small amount of wine. 'They're not here, Your Highness. Their replacements arrived this morning.'

Charlotte covered her mouth while she swallowed her giant mouthful of bread. 'Replacements? What replacements? General Blackmane said nothing of this.' Rising, she walked over to the door and pulled it open. Outside was a man she had never seen before. Her eyes moved over his Carmarthen Militia uniform.

'Who are you?'

The man gave a small bow. 'Leuen Jenkins, Your Highness. My comrade Parry and I were sent to relieve Stroude and Bowen.'

Disappointment washed over her. She had liked her former guards. 'When will they be back?'

'I'm afraid I don't know.'

She nodded. 'I see.' Her bottom lip disappeared between her teeth. 'Well, I would like to go to the camp and speak with General Blackmane this morning.'

'I'm afraid that's not possible.'

Her brows lifted. 'Why not?'

He glanced off down the corridor. 'Because news of your engagement to Lord Wybert has spread through Carmarthenshire. Some are not happy. His lordship suggested you remain at Dinefwr until things settle down.'

'Hide away, you mean?' She marched off down the corridor. 'Where is he?'

'The stables, Your Highness.'

Charlotte called for Sir Miles, then went in search of Wybert. She found him inspecting a horse in the mounting yard. He turned when he noticed her and waited for her to reach him.

'You look upset,' he said when she stopped in front of him. 'What is wrong?'

She pointed at Jenkins, who had remained at the edge of the mounting yard. 'First, I liked my old guards, and the general sent me new ones. And second, everyone hates that I am marrying you, so now I am stuck here behind these walls again with only Mevanou for company'—she pinched the bridge of her nose—'and she is really lovely in very small doses.'

Wybert crossed his arms. 'Is that all?'

'For now.'

He sighed. 'First, we suspected news of our engagement might be met with some resistance because wastelanders hate the English.' He raised a hand when she went to interject. 'For reasons I understand. Second, you do not need to like your guards. Their job is to keep you safe.' He glanced over at her guard. 'He seems fit and strong. As for Mevanou, get rid of her. I can always invite my sister to Dinefwr to keep you company.'

Charlotte laughed. 'Your *sister*? Your sister who told people that you had dodged an arrow when we parted ways?'

'I forgot about that.'

'Well, lucky for you, I have a long memory and the ability to hold a grudge until death.'

'Which we are trying to avoid right now.' He gave her a patronising pat on the arm. 'Your father would never forgive me if anything happened to you in his absence, so do me a favour and listen to your guards.'

He turned back to the horse.

'Speaking of my father, have you heard from him?' she asked. 'I have written to him many times and have received no response.'

He picked up the horse's back hoof and inspected it. 'He is likely busy getting his affairs in order.' He glanced in her direction. 'Do not fret. We will not have the wedding without him.'

She rolled her eyes. 'If people continue to reject you as my future husband, there will not be a wedding.'

Wybert straightened and leaned on the horse's rump. 'It is your job to change their minds.'

'That is difficult to do while locked up here.'

Wybert said something to the groom, and the horse was led away. He then walked up to Charlotte, bringing his face close to hers. 'Please behave. People can hear you, and people talk. We need to present as a united front.'

She stared at him. 'I am not a child, so do not tell me to behave.'

'You are acting like one.' He stepped past her and called to Jenkins. 'Escort the princess back to her quarters, please.'

She marched after him. 'My guards do not take orders from you—' The words were snatched away by the breeze created from Jenkins's fast approach.

'Let's go, Your Highness.' He gestured for her to walk ahead.

Normally, that kind of behaviour would have had her seeing red, but she felt unease in place of anger. 'I will not be forced into my quarters by my own guard.'

He gestured again. 'Please, Your Highness. Do not make a scene. Let's go.'

Her gaze bored into Wybert's retreating back as she headed for the path.

CHAPTER 32

'Visitor,' Tatum said, pointing to the sky where a large eagle glided overhead.

Blackmane looked up as Margery came in to land, dropping gracefully down onto a post beside Ita at the edge of the new training yard. She retrieved something from the bird's talons and held it up to inspect it.

'What's that?' Blackmane asked.

Ita held up a piece of green fabric. 'I think Margery has been... let's say "playing" in the laundry area. I fear some poor soldier is going to find his uniform shredded when he goes to collect it.'

Tatum was about to pick up the weapons when Blackmane asked, 'Is that blood?'

Ita winced, then looked accusingly at the eagle. 'Please tell me you did not do this while the soldier was wearing it.'

Tatum inspected Margery's talons, which were blackened with a mixture of blood and mud. 'Is there any way we can find out where she got this?'

'She's not violent,' Ita said.

Blackmane coughed.

'Unless provoked,' Ita corrected. She sniffed the fabric. 'Though that is definitely blood.'

Blackmane and Tatum exchanged a look of concern.

'From a corpse?' Blackmane suggested.

'She does love a corpse,' Ita said. 'But there have been no deaths reported for months.'

Something did not feel right. 'Where's Alveye?'

'Mess kitchen,' Ita replied. 'Are we going hunting for corpses?'

Tatum was already walking away. 'Yes. Prep your bird.'

Blackmane jogged after him.

The defenders found their commander leaving the mess hall and spent a few minutes filling him in.

'Let me get this straight,' Alveye said. 'A pet bird brought its owner a piece of fabric, and now the three of you want to ride blindly around the kingdom trying to find the rest of the uniform?'

'There are only a few possible explanations,' Tatum said. 'Something feels off.'

Alveye looked at Blackmane. 'Do you second this bad feeling?'

The defender shrugged. 'I think it's worth a few hours of our time to ensure some poor soldier isn't lying injured somewhere waiting for help.'

'Unlikely,' Ita said, walking over to them with Margery perched on her shoulder. 'More likely dead.'

Alveye looked between them and sighed. 'Fine. Off you go. I'll update Tolly. Let me know if you find anything.'

The three of them made their way to their tethered horses, and then everyone looked expectantly at Margery.

Ita held up the fabric in front of the eagle. 'Show me.'

The bird spread her enormous wings and launched herself into the sky. The three of them mounted their horses and followed the eagle's large shadow away from the camp and over the Welsh terrain.

Around half an hour into her flight, Margery landed atop a tall pine tree.

Tatum cast a doubtful look at Blackmane.

'She's just resting,' Ita said. 'Give her a moment.'

Sure enough, a few minutes later, she took flight once more.

Two hours and three breaks later, they came upon a kestrel hovering above a stream. It flew off when it spotted Margery. They spotted twenty-plus crows gathered on the ground below.

'I think we've arrived,' Blackmane said. He looked at Ita. 'You can wait here if you want.'

She rolled her eyes in his direction. 'Because we wastelanders are so sensitive and have never seen death up close before?'

'She has a point,' Tatum said, nudging his horse forwards.

As they drew nearer, the crows took flight. Tatum's gaze narrowed on two muddy figures pressed up against the edge of the stream, collecting floating debris.

'Shit.'

Margery was now resting comfortably in a tree, watching them.

Everyone dismounted when they reached the water

and walked over to inspect the bodies.

'Maybe they drowned in the floodwaters,' Ita suggested.

Tatum and Blackmane dragged the men onto dry land and flipped them onto their backs. Their faces were crow-pecked and covered in mud.

'Their throats were cut,' Blackmane said, pointing. 'Likely dumped upstream.'

Tatum looked in that direction. 'This stream connects to River Tywi?'

Ita nodded. 'Sure does. With the speed of the water post-flood, they could have been thrown in miles away.'

Tatum went to his horse to fetch a bandage from his saddlebag.

'I think we might be a little beyond that,' Ita said as he passed by.

Tatum dunked the bandage into the stream and returned to the dead men, where he began washing their faces.

A few minutes later, Ita gasped.

'What?' Blackmane asked.

Ita stared at the corpses, a hand frozen over her mouth, unable to speak.

Tatum saw it then, the recognition arriving like a hot wave over him. He rose slowly, eyes never leaving their faces.

'Someone want to tell me who these two men are?' Blackmane said, losing patience.

Tatum met his questioning stare. 'It's Stroude and Bowen.' He leaned on his knees, feeling sick suddenly. 'Princess Charlotte's guards.'

CHAPTER 33

'Take a breath,' Blackmane told Tatum.

The defender was turning in circles, his hands linked atop his head. 'A breath? Charlotte could be *dead* for all we know.'

Ita still had not spoken a word. She was crouched on the ground with her hands covering her face, processing.

'I need to get to Dinefwr Castle,' Tatum said, striding off towards his horse.

'Wait,' Blackmane said, his tone firm. 'I'm with you. Whatever's next, I'm with you. But we need to keep a level head and be smart about how we handle this.'

Tatum shook his head. 'If anything's happened to her—'

'Take the blankets from the horses,' Ita said, standing up suddenly. 'We'll take the soldiers with us. They deserve better than to be left here to be picked apart by crows.'

She was right.

The three of them got to work wrapping the bodies, then loaded them onto the horses.

When they were ready to depart, Ita looked up at Margery. 'Time to go, pretty lady. Your work here is done.'

They rode at a steady pace back to the camp, shaving off time by taking a more direct route than the one Margery had led them on.

When they arrived at the camp, Alveye and Hadewaye appeared, looking between the corpses secured to the saddles.

'Stroude and Bowen,' Blackmane stated. That was all he had to say.

Hadewaye looked back at the corpses. 'Oh shit.'

'Go find Tolly,' Alveye said.

The defender nodded, then jogged off in search of the general.

Tolly marched into the mounting yard with a fierce expression. He looked down at the wrapped corpses now laid out on the ground, and his mouth flattened into a thin line. 'How did they die?'

'Their throats were cut,' Blackmane said.

The general's fists were clenched tightly at his sides, the veins in his neck bulging. 'I'm going to Dinefwr to find out what the hell is going on.'

'I'll come with you,' Tatum replied immediately.

Alveye looked at him. 'We've been ordered to stay away from the castle. If you go, there's every chance the warden will hear about it from Lord Wybert.'

'Assuming Wybert is alive long enough to write the letter.'

Hadewaye frowned. 'You think he had something to do with it?'

'Let's not jump to conclusions,' Blackmane said.

Tatum threw his hands up. 'Either way, I'm going.'

'Blackmane, go with him and make sure he behaves,' Alveye said with a resigned breath.

'Hadewaye and I will contact the soldiers' families,' Ita said. 'I would hate for them to find out some other way.'

Tolly nodded. 'Good.' Then he said to Tatum and Blackmane, 'Get some fresh horses, and let's go find out what the hell is going on at Dinefwr.'

They were forced to wait at the front gate of the castle while the guard on duty went to speak with Lord Wybert. Tatum spent that time pacing the length of his horse's reins until Blackmane grew tired of it and pinned him with a hard stare.

'We'll have a better chance of making it inside if you don't appear so unhinged.'

Tatum forced his feet to keep still as he looked up at the wall above. Charlotte loved to paint the scenery from that spot. But unsurprisingly, she was nowhere to be seen.

Approaching footsteps drew his attention back to the gate. A moment later, the portcullis began to rise. Two guards waited for them on the other side.

'His Lordship will see you in the outer-ward,' said one of the men.

Blackmane threw a 'Behave' glance at Tatum as they led their horses inside.

They found Wybert standing out in the open with his personal guard. Tatum looked around, feeling the eyes and arrows of archers upon him. It came as no surprise that the lord was taking precautions given the nature of his guests.

Wybert nodded a greeting. 'Afternoon, all.' His gaze narrowed on Blackmane and Tatum. 'I must say, I am a little surprised to see you two here given your orders to stay *away* from Dinefwr Castle.'

'Where's the princess?' Tatum asked, cutting straight to the point.

Wybert's eyebrows rose. 'I'll remind you of two things before we continue this conversation. First, you are in my home, so you will speak to me with respect or leave. Second, Princess Charlotte is no longer your concern. You are not her guard, or friend, or anything else you presume to be.'

'So she's safe? Alive?'

Wybert looked between them, confused. 'Of course she is.'

That was enough for Tatum in that moment.

'But currently unprotected?' Blackmane asked.

Wybert squinted. 'Quite protected, I assure you.' He looked between them. 'Why are you here?'

'Two of my men are dead,' Tolly said, anger gripping him once more.

Wybert pinched the bridge of his nose. 'While I sympathise—'

'They were the princess's guards,' Tatum added. 'Throats cut and thrown into the river, like dogs. Know anything about that?'

Wybert blinked. 'I have enough trouble keeping track

of my own men. Am I expected to keep track of yours also? Charlotte's guards were refreshed some days ago.'

Tatum looked past him. 'Where is she? I want to see her.'

'I bet you do,' Wybert replied tiredly.

'You said the guards had been refreshed,' Blackmane said. 'Who replaced the murdered soldiers?'

Wybert thought for a moment. 'Jenkins and another man whose name I cannot recall.'

Tatum did not recognise the name. He looked questioningly at Tolly.

'I'd have to see them to know,' the general said.

Tatum was done with the conversation. It was time to find Charlotte and figure out what in Belenus's name was going on. He marched off in the direction of the castle.

'Defender!' Wybert shouted after him. 'I warn you—'

'I'd be warning your own men first.' Tatum drew his sword, confident no archer would shoot a defender on Carmarthenshire soil unless they had a death wish.

'Wait,' Blackmane called to him. 'We're coming with you.'

Charlotte had been escorted from her bedchamber by her guards with no explanation, despite asking for one several times. They had insisted that Sir Miles remain in her quarters for 'ease', which translated to them being fearful of him.

Patience gone, she stopped in the middle of the wall

walk and turned to face them. 'I would like to know where you are taking me and why.'

The men exchanged a look, and then Parry said, 'His Lordship was concerned about some visitors at the castle and asked that we take you somewhere safe until they leave.'

She stared back at him. They had been painfully controlling her every move for the past three days—and she was done. 'You do understand that I requested Welsh guards for a reason? I wanted to feel safe in my home, in control. Lord Wybert's concerns are just that, *his* concerns. It is both your jobs to act on *my* concerns, and if you cannot do that, then I will have you both replaced—immediately.' She brought a hand to her forehead. 'This is ridiculous. I am going back to my bedchamber.' She stepped between them. 'And I am writing to General Blackmane—'

Jenkins caught her by the arm. 'Your Highness, it isn't safe at this time.'

Her gaze fell to his hand. 'Unhand me at once. If you do not, I will scream until the bricks we stand upon crumble beneath us. Do you understand?'

She was grateful that the slight tremble in her voice was not audible.

Jenkins let go. 'Apologies, Your Highness, but we're going to need to remain here for now. It's our job to keep you safe.'

There were really only two possible reasons Wybert would want her kept apart from these visitors: it was either a secret business deal or someone he did not want her near. Tatum immediately came to mind. Tatum her safe place. Tatum whose gaze could melt her very bones.

Charlotte marched towards the stairwell, afraid that if she slowed down or interacted with the guards, she would miss her chance to find out who Wybert was with and his motive for hiding her away. The guards followed, shouting things that she ignored.

She entered the turret and ran down the steps, taking them two at a time. Light blinded her as she headed for the exit at the bottom, but before she reached it, a hand clamped over her mouth and she was dragged into the shadows. She screamed into the hand as panic flooded her, but the sound was only loud inside her head. She kicked backward, connecting with a shin.

'Keep her quiet,' Jenkins hissed.

That was when she realised Parry had hold of her. The two men there solely for her *protection* were holding her captive.

'Calm down,' Parry said into her ear. 'I will let you go as soon as—'

His hands went limp on her, then fell away altogether. She could barely see through her panic but knew instinctively that she needed to run.

As she took off, she slammed into a body. At first, she feared it was Jenkins, but then familiar hands gripped her shoulders. She blinked rapidly in an attempt to clear her vision, afraid she was wrong.

'I've got you,' Tatum said, guiding her towards the exit as the putrid smell of blood filled the turret, making her stomach heave. Behind her, she could hear a commotion happening inside the turret, Jenkins protesting.

'Don't look,' Tatum said.

'What on earth is going on?' That was Wybert, marching towards them.

Charlotte headed straight for him, lashing out like a cat when he was within reach and scratching his cheeks.

'How could you?' she shouted.

Wybert pressed a hand to his bleeding face. 'For goodness' sake—'

'You turned my own guards against me!'

'Calm down. I did no such thing.'

She turned as Tolly and Blackmane emerged from the turret with Jenkins, who was bleeding from a cut above his eye.

'They're not your guards,' Tatum said. 'They're not part of the Carmarthen Militia.'

She blinked. 'Then who are they?'

'Clearly impostors,' Wybert replied. 'This is what happens when you entrust your safety to strangers.'

A realisation dawned on Charlotte. 'Stroude and Bowen—'

'Are dead,' Tatum said quietly.

Charlotte pressed her eyes shut. She had foolishly trusted the new arrivals, simply because they had shown up at her door in uniform. Her stomach swirled.

'Where's the other guard?' Wybert asked.

'Dead,' Tolly replied. 'We have a few questions for this one.'

Wybert gestured to the tower. 'We are more than capable of questioning him here. This is a Dinefwr matter, after all.'

'Actually, it's an army matter,' Tolly replied.

Tatum caught Charlotte's eye. 'You should come to the camp until we know what's going on.'

Wybert took a step towards them. 'Need I remind you, defender, that the princess's safety is *my* responsibility now, not yours.'

'Actually, it's the army's,' Tolly said. 'Let's go.'

Wybert took another step towards Charlotte, and Tatum had his sword drawn and the tip of it pointed at the duke's throat so fast that he froze with one foot still in the air.

'You're right,' Tatum said. 'You're also responsible for her safety—and you failed. Get this castle in order. Employ a better steward, better guards. If you don't know exactly who is coming in and out of that gate at all times, then ensure someone else does.'

Wybert's jaw ticked. 'The warden will hear about this.'

He sheathed his sword. 'I don't doubt it.'

CHAPTER 34

Tolly was still fuming when they arrived back at the camp. He did not take well to losing men, and the fact that no one knew a thing about it made matters worse.

'How do two guards die in that place and no one realise?' Tolly pointed at Jenkins. 'Put him in a tent. I want answers.'

Blackmane shoved the prisoner to get him walking. 'We'll have answers soon enough.'

It was late afternoon, and the soldiers at the camp were winding down for the day. The air smelled of the mutton cooking in the kitchen pots.

'What will they do to him?' Charlotte asked.

He looked at her. 'Whatever they have to in order to find out who killed your guards.'

She swallowed. 'I should have written to Tolly and questioned the changeover.'

'They were already dead by then. It wouldn't have changed that.'

That did not appear to ease her guilt.

Hadewaye and Alveye approached, eyes on the prisoner being led away.

'What happened?' Alveye asked.

Looking at Hadewaye, Tatum asked, 'Can you please take Charlotte to my tent? No one in, no one out.'

Hadewaye nodded. 'This way, Your Highness.'

Charlotte hesitated.

'Get some rest,' Tatum told her. 'I might be a while.'

She reluctantly left with Hadewaye.

Tatum spent the next few minutes updating Alveye. The commander stood with his hands on his hips, listening. When Tatum finished, he looked at the defender.

'The warden's not going to like this.'

Tatum nodded.

Alveye gestured towards the tent where Jenkins was being held. 'Go. We'll figure out the rest in the morning.'

All eyes were on Tatum as he made his way to the tent. He entered and found Jenkins tied to a chair, now bleeding from the eye *and* nose. Tolly was beside him, and Blackmane was standing off to the side, watching.

'What do we know so far?'

Tolly glanced in his direction. 'He claims he knew nothing of the deaths, never even saw the soldiers. The uniforms were given to them by the man who hired them.'

'Which man is that?'

Jenkins shook his head. 'I already told the general. We never dealt with him directly. It was always someone else.'

Blackmane drew his dagger and inspected the blade. 'A Welshman?'

Jenkins nodded as he eyed the dagger. 'Yes, Welsh.'

Now it was Tatum's turn. He approached the prisoner, leaning over him and holding on to the arms of his chair. Using a slow, steady voice, he began asking questions.

'Where are you from?'

'What were you sent to do?'

'Where did you meet the man who hired you?'

'Why were you selected for the job?'

'Tell me about Parry.'

Between stuttered denials and pleas for mercy, Tatum began to piece together how two misplaced wasteland rebels, struggling to adapt to the new way of things, had ended up posing as soldiers at Dinefwr Castle. It became clear an hour into their questioning that Jenkins did not care about the politics, or the monarchy, only the money he was supposed to receive at the end of the charade. He was not privy to any information outside the task he was sent there for. He was a pawn in a game he had little interest in understanding. The man had been told that no one would die, that he would be free to disappear when he was no longer needed.

That part caught Tatum's attention. 'And when was that supposed to be? When would you no longer be needed?'

Jenkins's eyes moved between Tatum's. He was trembling all over now. 'He would tell us when.'

Tatum straightened and looked at Tolly. 'Keep him alive.' He sheathed his bloodied dagger. 'He's the only one who can identify the man behind this.'

The three of them exited the tent.

'Wybert knows something. I can feel it,' Tatum said,

looking around. 'Wouldn't surprise me if he's behind the whole thing.'

Blackmane nodded slowly. 'It's possible he wanted some form of control over her given how little he has.'

Tatum rubbed his eyes. 'We'll regroup in the morning.' He clapped Tolly on the shoulder. 'Don't worry. We'll find the person responsible.'

Tolly nodded. 'I'll see you in the morning.'

Tatum headed straight to the wash area to clean himself up. He removed all the grime that had built up over the course of the day, scrubbing his skin until every bloodstain was gone. After cleaning his weapons, he put on a fresh uniform before heading to his tent.

He found Charlotte seated on his cot with a blanket wrapped around her. She looked in his direction when he stepped inside. There were tear streaks on her face. He crossed the floor and crouched in front of her. She sat up taller, putting on a brave face for his benefit.

'What did you learn?' she asked.

He reached up and tucked the loose hair behind her ear. 'You want to have this conversation now?'

She nodded.

He sat on the cot beside her and repeated everything from the interrogation, watching her expression change constantly as she took in all of the information. When he finished speaking, she sat with her shoulders rounded, blinking.

'I have no idea who to trust anymore,' she said, sounding defeated.

'You can trust me.'

'I know. But it would be nice if I could trust someone

inside the castle besides my chambermaid.' Her eyes sank shut. 'Everything is a mess, and my father is ignoring my letters. I do not even know if he is still in England.'

'We'll have the soldiers at the border advise us if he crosses.'

She studied his face in the fading light. 'You know I have to go back to Dinefwr, back to him. Sir Miles will be beside himself.'

'Shame. We could have run away together.'

One corner of her mouth lifted. 'The whole engagement thing is wildly inconvenient.'

The light in her eyes faded.

'I could help you get out of Carmarthenshire,' he whispered.

She laughed through her nose. 'And where would I go? Back to Livingston Manor? Alone? Until my father passes and I am cast from it anyway. No, my home is here now. At least I serve a purpose here.'

He nodded, knowing he was going to struggle to let her go again, especially with her safety at risk. 'I should go. The last thing you need right now is a scandal.'

'Agreed. The good people of Llanddeilo are still recovering from the church incident.'

A lazy smile came and went on his face. 'The tent will be guarded at all times, so you can sleep easy here.' He rose, standing awkwardly for a long moment. 'Goodnight, Princess.'

She stared up at him, her fingers twitching in her lap. 'Thank you for today.'

He nodded once, then left the tent.

CHAPTER 35

*C*harlotte was startled awake by men shouting outside. She was surprised to see that it was daylight already, and she had slept solidly through. Apparently all it took was the knowledge that Tatum was nearby to slip into a coma-like sleep.

'English horses approaching!'

That had her leaping from the cot and snatching up her boots. A childish part of her hoped it was her father, charging in at a gallop after hearing of what had happened.

That bubble quickly burst when she peered through the flaps of the tent and saw Wybert approaching at a trot, surrounded by his guards. The Carmarthen Militia were not taking any chances. They armed themselves and formed a circle around the visitors as they came to a stop.

Tolly arrived a minute later, striding straight up to Wybert. The defenders joined him in a pack soon after. When the English guards reached for their weapons, the duke held a hand up to stop them, then dug around in the pocket of his cloak. He produced a letter and held it out.

'For Commander Alveye.'

Charlotte emerged from the tent and made her way over to find out what was happening.

Alveye stepped forwards to take the letter. He read it, then handed it to Tatum.

'Who is the letter from?' Charlotte asked.

Tatum looked in her direction, and she could tell the letter meant she was leaving with Wybert.

'I have come to collect you and take you back to Dine-fwr,' the duke announced.

Her gaze remained on Tatum. 'Who is the letter from?'

'The Chadorian warden,' Wybert answered, even though she had been asking Tatum. 'It states that if there is any further interference from the defenders, they will be immediately recalled and disciplined.'

The bastard had gone straight to the warden, knowing it was the only means to get Tatum out of the way.

She looked to the spare horse intended for her. This was a simple business transaction, and she was the business.

'That was quick work,' she replied. 'What of my safety?'

'You will be protected by English guards. I have decided that there will be no one in and no one out until your father returns. All business will be conducted outside the walls. Your safety is my priority.'

Tatum laughed. 'So your idea of keeping her safe is to leave it to *them*?' He gestured to the English guards. 'I used to have to wake them when they fell asleep on duty.'

The insult had the guards' fingers brushing the hilts of their weapons.

'Perhaps you forget that the Chadorian warden has no jurisdiction over this army,' Tolly pointed out. 'Welsh guards are the obvious solution here.'

Wybert gave him a tired look. 'Like the ones who showed up in a stream recently?'

Tolly's face darkened. 'The men I assigned to the princess were exceptional soldiers.'

'Who unfortunately failed at their roles.'

Tatum took a step towards Wybert, prompting Blackmane to move in front of him, blocking his path. 'Easy.'

'*You* failed to keep Dinefwr secure,' Tatum said.

Charlotte realised they were going in circles. There were only two choices: she could stand there fighting the inevitable, which would land the defenders in more trouble, or leave peacefully with the duke.

'It is all right,' she said, adjusting the folds of her cloak. 'I am quite safe. If someone had wanted me dead, I would be dead already. Besides, I still have Sir Miles.' She looked at Wybert. 'I will come with you.'

It was the hardest thing in the world to walk past Tatum like he meant nothing, but that was what she did—until he caught her arm and led her a few paces away from the horses.

'This is your army,' he said, voice low. 'They *will* protect you if you ask them to.'

'To what end? No one is dying because of me.'

He held her in place for a moment, eyes searching hers. 'If you're in any sort of trouble, lower the flag on the east wall to half-mast.'

She swallowed, then nodded.

Finally, he let go of her.

Charlotte rushed forwards to the waiting horse, afraid she would change her mind if there were any more delays. She ignored the tightening in her stomach as she mounted the sturdy grey mare. 'Thank you for hosting me for the night, General.'

Tolly's dark gaze flicked to Wybert. 'Remember, Your Highness, that this army protects *all* its citizens.'

Charlotte had grown to both respect and like the general. She gathered up the reins. 'I look forward to seeing you all in proper housing when I next return.'

Her gaze went involuntarily to Tatum, whose shoulders were rigid, his eyebrows knitted together. She rode off before he was tempted to say or do anything else—or she was. Within moments, she was swallowed up by English guards.

Once they had exited the camp, Wybert rode up next to her. 'You did the right thing, the mature thing. I promise I will keep you safe.'

She did not even look at him.

Their journey through the countryside was done in complete silence. The only sounds were the heavy breathing of tired horses. The landscape seemed to mourn alongside her with its muted green tones and waterlogged trees. Civilisation felt sparse, strange, and deserted, likely because Wybert intentionally bypassed the villages to avoid unwanted attention. The handful of people they did pass looked upon them with suspicion. Charlotte felt displaced among the red tunics. The colour no longer fit her.

'Home at last,' Wybert said when Dinefwr finally came into view.

Its walls reflected the overcast sky, making for another sad scene.

Later, as she was leaving the mounting yard, she felt that the walls seemed higher from the inside. Her steps echoed off them as she was escorted to her quarters by both Wybert and his guards. He stopped outside the door to her bedchamber.

'Ensure Her Highness has everything she needs,' he said to one of his guards.

Charlotte looked at the man. 'Have Mevanou come to see me.'

Wybert dropped his gaze. 'Mevanou was dismissed.' He looked up. 'As I said, we need to lock the castle down. No one here knew her background or motives for being here—'

'*I* knew! How dare you dismiss one of my staff without consulting me.'

He rubbed his jaw. 'When your father returns, you can discuss it with him.'

Charlotte pushed the door open, preparing to be bowled over by an excited dog, but her room was empty. She looked back at Wybert. 'Where is Sir Miles?'

'Confined in the stables.'

Her teeth pressed together. 'I want him brought to me.'

'He was unmuzzled—'

'I do not care about your reasons! Bring him to me —now!'

The guard looked to Wybert for approval, and he

nodded his consent. 'That dog is going to tear someone's throat out one day.'

'I am counting on it.'

Wybert watched her for a few breaths, then sighed. 'We can make this work. You know we can or you would not have agreed to it.'

She stared at him for a long moment. 'I want to be very clear about something.'

'What is that?' he asked tiredly.

'I am not here for you. In fact, I am here for the benefit of everyone *but* you.'

Nothing changed on his face.

'I will never love you.'

He touched the scratches she had left. 'Oh, I know. Do not worry. I am not trying to recapture our youth.'

His words evoked sadness. Not because she wanted him to love her but because their transaction robbed her of experiencing love with someone else.

Brock Tatum.

Charlotte would never admit it aloud, but she wanted to love and be loved. She wanted everything she had experienced with Tatum. The impromptu smiles and free-fall feeling. The reprieve from life's difficult parts. It all seemed so manageable when he was around. Not to mention the mutual trust—her most precious commodity.

'Please remember why you are here,' Wybert said. '*I* secured this castle for your family. *I* made you a princess.'

She exhaled sharply through her nose. 'You get no credit for my blood, and it is the people on the other side of that wall who made me a princess, not you.' She looked at the second guard. 'Bring me some wine.' Her gaze landed briefly on Wybert. 'I will be drunk in my bedchamber if you need me.'

*F*our days. That was how long Charlotte gave herself to fall apart. Four days to sleep, and drink too much, and miss the people who had died or were miles away. Four days of skipping meals or liquid-only meals and cuddling with Sir Miles and wondering where the hell her father was while trying to solve the mystery of who killed her brother. It had to be the same person who killed the earl. And probably every other nobleman who had died within these walls.

Or maybe no one.

Maybe no one else knew about the window. Maybe she was hopeful they did because the alternative remained unbearable.

Maybe the fresh wave of grief and conspiracies was due to the wine.

After the four days, she emerged from her bedchamber, head pounding and arms loaded with painting supplies, and announced to the guard at the door that she was going up on the wall to paint. She was surprised to discover that not only was it not raining, but there were patches of blue sky peeking through the clouds. Too bad the glare was unbearable in her less-than-ideal state.

As she was setting up her supplies, her gaze went to the turret where she and Tatum had painted each other. The laughter had been so luxurious, so cleansing. So healing.

She turned away from it and focused on the hills in the distance. Sir Miles lay down at her feet, facing the guard. Even though he was familiar with most of them now, he still liked to stare them down until they took a step back —muzzle or no muzzle.

After a few hours of painting, Charlotte noticed that the pins in her hair were making her scalp ache. She pulled them out one by one, letting the stiff breeze passing over the wall walk take her hair in whatever direction it pleased.

She no longer cared.

'What do you think?' she asked the awkward guard, holding up her painting.

The man, whose name she had not even bothered to learn, ran his eyes over the splashings of green dotted with wildflowers. She had turned the whole sky to a bright blue, because she was officially sick of the grey, and added plenty of colourful birds.

'It's an interesting interpretation, Your Highness.'

She rolled her eyes and bent to pet Sir Miles. The sound of the portcullis opening brought the dog to his feet. He stood tall and still, listening. Charlotte laid her brush down and moved over to the embrasure, looking out. To her surprise, Sir Miles's giant paws landed beside her.

'What a nosy dog you are.' She tutted but made room for him. 'Just make sure those hind paws remain on the wall walk.'

They watched Wybert exit the castle—alone. Her gaze was drawn to a man waiting with his horse, likely a local businessman judging by his clothing.

Sir Miles emitted a low growl that seemed to rumble through his entire body.

Charlotte looked at him in surprise. 'That is a little dramatic, even for you.'

The dog's eyes were fixed on the man, or maybe the horse, and all the hairs along his back were standing up. Realising that he was about to lose his mind over the visitor, Charlotte took hold of his collar and attempted to pull him down.

'With me.'

Normally, that would be enough, but he attempted to jump up onto the embrasure instead. He would have succeeded had she not been holding him.

'I beg your pardon,' she said. 'Get down at once.'

The guard came forwards to assist, and Sir Miles whipped his head around and snapped at him. The muzzle might have prevented a bloodbath, but the force of the bite knocked the guard backwards.

'*Sir. Miles.*' Charlotte threw her body weight against him, terrified he was going to jump from the wall.

His front paws finally returned to the wall walk. That did not silence him, though. His barks grew more frantic, as if they were under attack. He was barking to intimidate. He was barking like... like...

He was barking like he had the night Oliver died.

The guard was back on his feet, saying something to her that she could neither hear nor comprehend. She let go of Sir Miles, and he immediately lunged for the embrasure again. Her guard was ready this time and somehow managed to wrestle him down and hold him in place. Not with ease, though. Sir Miles was twisting and snapping, frothy spit flying in all directions.

Charlotte slowly looked out over the wall, eyes narrowing on the man with Wybert. There *was* something familiar about him, but it was difficult to pinpoint from that distance.

'Can you take him back to my bedchamber, please?' Charlotte asked the guard. 'I need to pack up my things, and then I will follow you.'

The guard looked torn but eventually nodded, wrestling the whining dog along the wall walk.

The moment they were out of sight, Charlotte headed in the opposite direction, towards the keep, fingers dragging along the stone as the man flashed between the merlons. She moved quickly, knowing her guard would return for her as soon as he could. She flew down the steps and headed for the portcullis.

The guard on duty at the gate cast a suspicious look in her direction. 'Can I help you, Your Highness?'

Her eyes were fixed on the two men visible through the latticed grille.

The guard walked out to meet her, blocking her path. 'Where is your guard?'

Charlotte peered around him. At the same time, the man standing with Wybert looked in her direction. Her breath caught in her throat as she recognised him, and she was taken back to the day she had visited him in the tower. He had been restrained and in a cell. She had asked him questions, and he had stared back at her, not answering.

It was the day before his sentence had been carried out. Before he had been hanged.

Except that he was very much alive.

She hid behind the guard as her mind fought to piece things together.

'Are you all right?' the guard asked.

At first she could not reply.

'Your Highness—'

'Yes.' Charlotte blinked to clear her blurring vision. 'I was looking for His Lordship, but I see he is busy.'

She backed up, keeping herself in line with the guard because she was worried the man would see her, *recognise* her. Then everything would unravel in the worst possible way.

'I will let His Lordship know you're looking for him.'

She shook her head. 'No. He is busy. I will speak to him later.' She turned and tried very hard to walk at a sensible pace in the opposite direction.

'I wanted to let you know that your father's attacker was sentenced and hanged overnight.'

Those had been Wybert's exact words.

'He was clearly guilty, and we felt the need to be discreet. I personally oversaw the whole thing.'

If he lied about the execution, what else had he lied

about? He was liaising with the person who had shot an arrow into her father while trying to kill her brother.

While trying to kill my brother.

And now her brother was dead, and there was a good chance that Wybert had something to do with it.

Oh God. She could barely breathe.

Charlotte stopped and looked around, trying to think of what to do next, who to tell, but there was no one. Wybert had completely isolated her. And now her guard would be looking for her, and he would report any and all of her behaviour to him.

Back up the stairwell she went, her body moving and mind barely aware, resulting in the occasional slip of a foot that had her reaching for the wall. Her ankle smashed against the final step at the top, and she swallowed the profanities on the tip of her tongue.

She found her guard waiting with her painting supplies.

'I've been looking for you,' he said.

She began gathering her things. 'I went to check the light further up. I think I shall paint from there tomorrow.'

He appeared to accept her explanation.

As they headed back to her bedchamber, Charlotte glanced at the east wall, to the flag sailing there. Tatum had told her to lower it to half-mast if she was in trouble, but she had no way of doing that. Her guard was not going to let her out of his sight a second time.

Back in her bedchamber, Charlotte paced the length of the room, then stopped suddenly and looked at the window. Walking over to it, she undid the latches and quietly lowered the grille to the ground.

'Stay,' she instructed Sir Miles, who was preparing to follow her.

He lay down with a soft whine.

Charlotte climbed out and awkwardly dragged the grille back into place. Now she just had to make it to the east wall without being spotted.

She ran from shadow to shadow until she finally reached the east wall. Her heart sank when she heard guards chatting up ahead. They had decided to stop a few feet from the flagpole.

She remained pressed against the wall, listening and waiting. The moment the men wandered away, she darted forwards, practically skidding to a stop in front of the flagpole. Her hands shook as she fumbled with the rope, head tipping back as she tried to judge the height.

When she was somewhat confident that it was at the halfway point, she secured it and backed up, looking around to see if anyone had spotted her. Thankfully, there was not a soul in sight. She returned to her room, gently pushing the window grille and wincing when it landed too loudly despite her best efforts. She climbed through before scrambling to put the grille back. When it jammed, she threw her weight against it, then dropped her forehead to the icy bars when it finally slid into place.

Now she just had to hope someone outside the castle noticed it before someone inside did.

'Where did you sneak off to?' came Wybert's voice behind her.

A gasp slipped from her mouth before she could stop

it. She spun around and found him seated in the chair by the fire. He had turned it to face the window.

Charlotte quickly composed herself. 'What are you doing in here?' She looked around the room. 'And where is Sir Miles?'

He leaned forwards, resting his elbows on his knees. 'Your guard told me what happened on the wall. You have lost control of that animal.'

'I have not.'

He nodded towards the window. 'Why are you sneaking around the castle like a rat?'

'I am free to go wherever I please. This is my home.'

His eyebrows lifted. 'Through the window? Without a guard?' He paused. 'Are we keeping secrets now?'

'Not everything is your business.'

'How wrong you are.' He stood. 'You, and everything you do, are entirely my business.'

She took a step towards him. 'I do not appreciate you entering my private quarters without my permission. We are not married yet.' And would hopefully never be once she told her father the truth.

He eyed her coolly for a moment. 'If you are secretive, then you make it impossible for me to trust you. What are we to do without trust?'

He dare lecture me about trust? She could have added to that conversation, but she was already treading on thin ice. 'I want Sir Miles returned to me.'

He shook his head. 'He will be staying in the stables for now.'

That was not going to happen. She would simply get him herself.

Marching over to the door, she tried to pull it open. It was locked. She let go of the handle like it had burned her hand, then turned to him in shock. 'Open the door.'

His expression was almost apologetic. 'I told your father I would take care of you. You leave me with no choice.' He gestured with his head. 'Move back from the door, Charlotte.'

Charlotte's stomach dropped. 'You cannot—'

'And I will be posting a second guard at your window.'

She laughed. 'You cannot be serious. This is not what my father meant when he asked you to take care of me in his absence. When he learns of this—'

'Move away from the door, Charlotte.'

For a moment she just stood there, swinging violently between furious and terrified. Then she slowly stepped back and watched as he walked over to it and said something to the guard. It opened, and he exited with a final glance in her direction.

She flinched when the key turned in the lock, then blinked a number of times before returning to the door. She tried the handle, already knowing it would not open. Slapping the wood, she shouted, 'At least bring me Sir Miles!'

Silence.

'Bring me my dog!'

Silence.

Charlotte swallowed the emotion clawing at her throat. Turning, she saw the second guard flash into view outside the window. She slammed her fist against the door, then slid to the ground.

CHAPTER 37

*T*atum had just finished saddling his mare when Tolly cantered up on horseback with five of his men in tow. He dismounted near Alveye, who was on his way to the mess hall. His expression had Tatum abandoning his horse and wandering over to find out what was going on.

'It's an English carriage,' he heard Tolly say when he got closer.

'What's going on?' Tatum asked.

Alveye brushed a finger down his nose, which meant it was bad news. 'Tolly's men found an overturned carriage twenty miles east of the border.'

'We think it's Lord Elis's carriage,' Tolly added.

Tatum had no attachment to the lord, but the idea of Charlotte losing her only living family member turned his blood cold. 'Anyone found?'

Tolly shook his head. 'Not even the driver.'

'Permission to go to the site?' Tatum asked Alveye.

Tolly raised a hand. 'Before you ride off east, there's something else you should know.'

'Go on.'

'Two of my men passed Dinefwr Castle this afternoon and said one of the flags has been lowered to half-mast.'

A chill settled in Tatum's chest. 'Which wall?'

Tolly's throat bobbed. 'East wall.'

The defender was walking off towards his horse before either of them could get another word out.

'Wait,' Alveye called to him.

'You know what I told her.'

'The wind might have gotten the better of it,' Tolly offered. 'And the English aren't known for their knots.'

'Stop,' Alveye said.

Tatum pulled up and turned to him. 'Don't ask me to ignore her plea for help.'

Alveye raised his hands. 'You want to get us all recalled? You think that will help her?'

'Charlotte's one of the proudest people I know. Something's very wrong if she's asking for help. Add to that the abandoned carriage—'

'I agree, but you're going to let me lead on this because I'm in command. You don't have to dive headfirst into the fire. There are other ways.'

Tatum drew a calming breath.

'I'm going to send Blackmane and Hadewaye to investigate the carriage and find out what became of its occupants.' Alveye crossed his arms. 'Then we're going to find a way to *sneak* into Dinefwr Castle to check on Princess Charlotte.'

Tolly, who had been listening, walked over to them.

'I'd head into Llanddeilo, find out which merchants supply to the castle. There are deliveries going in and out.'

'Until Wybert locked the castle down,' Tatum pointed out.

Tolly shook his head. 'Delivery wagons are still going in. I'll come with you. They'll be more likely to help if I'm there.'

'Good,' Alveye said. 'Make sure he gets safely in and out. I'm going to remain here because I know nothing about it.'

Tatum nodded. 'This conversation never happened.'

The pair set off at a canter towards Llanddeilo with the sun setting before them. The closer they got to that part of the world, the more anxious Tatum grew, imagining all the ways Charlotte could be suffering.

When they arrived, they wandered the town square asking questions. They learned that the butcher was due to deliver meat that evening—the same butcher who had once told Charlotte that she did not belong in Carmarthenshire. They prayed his change of heart midflood had lasted.

Iwan eyed the men with suspicion when he saw them approaching.

'Relax,' Tolly said. 'We're simply here to ask a favour.'

Iwan leaned against his freshly loaded wagon. 'I'm listening.'

Tolly explained their dilemma to him, making it clear that Tatum's only motive for getting inside the walls was to ensure the princess was safe.

'I don't want no trouble with Lord Wybert,' Iwan said. 'I have a house to rebuild.'

Tatum sympathised. 'It's just a quick welfare check. Then we'll be on our way.'

Iwan let out a noisy sigh, head shaking like he was going to say no. 'You're really worried about the princess?'

'Yes,' Tatum said quietly.

Iwan glanced at Tolly, then walked to the front of the wagon, muttering, 'I'm warning you, if I end up in a cell, I'm giving Lord Wybert all the names he wants.'

The men followed the wagon on horseback. It was dark by the time they reached Dinefwr Castle. They stopped and observed the guards pacing leisurely atop the castle walls from the safety of a nearby copse of trees.

'The flag's back to full height,' Iwan pointed out.

That did little to ease Tatum's mind. 'A guard probably noticed and fixed it.'

Tolly looked at him. 'What's your plan once inside? Put on a straw moustache and an English accent and hope no one recognises you?'

'We have to get you inside first,' Iwan pointed out. 'They check the wagons as they enter, you know.'

'What about underneath them?' Tolly asked.

Iwan waved a finger. 'Not just a pretty face, are you?'

'He has many layers,' Tatum agreed. 'I'll ride underneath. If all goes well, I'll be back on board before the wagon's unloaded.'

Tolly frowned. 'And if you're not?'

'I'll figure it out.'

Tolly pinched the bridge of his nose. 'I've got a bad feeling about this. Lord Wybert has close to a hundred men in there.'

'One hundred and four at last count. I've had worse odds.'

'*When?*' Iwan asked, looking bewildered by that proclamation.

'I can't think of the specifics right now...'

'Because you've never fought 104 men solo,' Tolly said. 'Be careful in there. You won't be the only one cleaning up this mess.'

He understood what was at risk. 'I'll be back before you know it.'

Iwan bent and looked underneath his wagon. 'You better not break the reach. I know how heavy your type can be.'

Tatum frowned. 'I'm going to assume you're referring to the amount of muscle we carry.' He disappeared beneath the wagon, wedging himself between the box and the reach.

'You'll be proper muddy by the time we get in there,' Iwan muttered as he climbed back into the driver's seat.

Tatum adjusted the hood of his cloak to cover his head. 'Noted.'

'I'll wait for you here,' Tolly said. 'If you're caught and about to be executed, just lower the flag back to half-mast and I'll see what I can do.'

Tatum rolled his eyes. 'Very funny.'

The wagon lurched forwards.

The journey, while short, was challenging with the strong draft and constant spray of water being kicked up by the horses, but eventually they reached the castle gates. Tatum listened as the portcullis went up and held his breath as the guard inspected the contents of the wagon before finally telling Iwan to go through.

When the wagon came to a stop, Tatum waited for the all clear from Iwan before climbing down and crawling out. He headed straight to the laundry yard where the soldiers' uniforms were normally hung out to dry, relieved to find that had not changed.

The sound of boots echoing off the walls had him pressing himself against the icy stone and covering his face. A guard passed by. As soon as he was gone, Tatum snatched a few uniform items from the clothesline, then dashed into the shadows to change. An English uniform would give him some freedom to move about the castle without drawing too much attention.

After hiding his defender uniform, he put his head down and made his way to Charlotte's quarters, praying that whoever was standing outside her door would not recognise him from his time at Dinefwr.

He rounded the corner of the corridor, eyes narrowing on the young guard on duty. The man stood with one arm resting on the hilt of his sword, gaze occasionally sweeping from side to side. Thankfully, Tatum did not recognise him. He strode forwards with confidence, nodding a greeting at the soldier when he glanced Tatum's way.

'Evening.'

The man looked him up and down. 'Evening.'

'Roberts sent me to relieve you.' He stopped a few feet away, smug in his knowledge of who was giving orders around the castle.

The guard's brow creased. 'I've only been here a few hours.'

'He wants extra eyes on the northwest tower, apparently.'

Nothing like a wild-goose chase to keep him busy for a while.

The guard shook his head and reached inside his cloak. Tatum tensed, worried that the man was going to produce a weapon. Instead, he pulled out a large brass key.

'For when the chambermaid comes,' he explained.

A cold sensation gripped Tatum's spine. Charlotte's door was locked—from the outside. He had definitely made the right call in coming.

He waited until the guard was gone from sight, then a painful minute longer just to be safe, before slipping the key into the lock and turning it. He opened it just wide enough for him to fit through, then locked it behind him.

The room was illuminated only by the dying embers of the fire. Tatum glanced at the bed and found it empty.

'Whatever you are bringing me, I do not want it' came Charlotte's defeated voice. She was seated in the large chair by the fire with her back to the door.

He swallowed. 'It's me.'

She shot up out of the chair and turned to face him, gaze sweeping the length of his red uniform, no doubt a confusing sight. She looked from him to the window. 'There is another guard outside.' Her voice was barely above a whisper.

Tatum retreated to the wall so he would be out of sight

if anyone looked in. Charlotte lowered herself back into the chair, eyes on the fire once more.

'How did you get in?' she asked.

'Delivery wagon.' He walked slowly along the wall until he could see her side profile. 'Did you lower the flag?'

She pressed her eyes closed. 'Yes.'

He had not seen her so void of life since her brother died. 'What happened? Did he hurt you?'

A tear ran down her face. 'How long do we have?'

The fact that she did not answer his question made him nervous. 'A few minutes.'

She nodded. 'Then I shall not waste any time. The bedchamber windows can be removed from the inside. They were designed that way after the fire to ensure that no one would ever be trapped inside a burning room again. That means someone could have come into Oliver's room and killed him that night—and I think someone did.' She glanced briefly in his direction. 'The man supposedly hanged for attacking my father was never hanged. I saw him with Wybert yesterday. Sir Miles saw him too. His reaction was... disturbing.'

'You think he killed your brother?'

'I think he was definitely involved. I need you to find him, find proof, something I can take to my father.'

Tatum dropped his gaze to the floor. 'Charlotte...'

She looked at him. When he lifted his gaze, he saw that her eyes were already filling with tears.

'Is he dead?'

He did not miss the slight crack in her voice. 'I don't know. They found his carriage.'

She closed her eyes and turned back to the fire. 'Oh.' She swallowed a few times. 'He probably did that too. Makes sense. He would have waited until everything was legally changed, and then…'

'Get your cloak. You're coming with me.'

She shook her head. 'Do not worry about me. He still needs me alive. He cannot wipe out an entire family without raising questions. He is smarter than that.' She paused. 'If my father is gone, then all of this is his. There is nothing I can do about that.' She looked at him. 'But he must pay for the things he has done. He must. Can you help me?'

Tatum was working through every possible outcome. If he took her, Wybert would come after them and the defenders. The warden would get involved. England would get involved. She was right. They needed proof in order to properly save her.

'You're getting food? Water?' he asked.

She nodded. 'But no Sir Miles. He is locked in the stables.'

His eyes closed as he realised how isolated she was. 'I'm sorry. I wish I could fetch him for you.'

'Unless he is dead too.'

They were silent for a few breaths. His time was up, and they both knew it.

'I'm coming back for you. I'm going to gather evidence, find out what happened to your father, and then I'm coming to get you.'

She nodded slowly.

'I need you to keep being smart and strong. Can you do that?'

Her gaze went to the window. 'If anything happens to me, make sure he pays for all of it. Tell him I will be waiting for him amid the flames.'

He was not sure he could leave, yet he had no choice. 'Can you do something for me?'

She blinked.

'Can you paint the future you want?' He waited for her to look at him, but she did not. 'The exact life you would choose if you were in control right now, with all its colour.'

No response.

'I'll see you soon,' he assured her.

Her throat bobbed. 'That colour is very unflattering on you, defender.'

'So *don't* keep it for special occasions?'

The weakest of smiles flickered on her face. 'Goodbye.'

Aware that he had stayed much longer than he had intended, he headed for the door, peering out into the corridor before exiting. He locked it behind him and left the key in the lock for the next guard to arrive for duty.

The moon was high in the sky when he stepped out into the night, casting a silvery glow over everything. He quickly made his way back to the laundry yard to retrieve his clothes, tucking them inside his cloak before heading for the wagon.

Iwan glared in his direction when he appeared. 'Cutting it very fine,' he whisper-shouted before climbing up into the driver's seat.

Tatum checked his surroundings before ducking beneath the wagon. His foot had barely left the ground before they rolled forwards.

The gate opened without question this time. No one stopped them or checked anything. They were through and on their way back to Tolly in under a minute.

As the castle fell away behind him, he began to formulate a plan.

Paint the future you want. I'll be out here fighting for it.

CHAPTER 38

Three days after Tatum's visit, there was a knock at Charlotte's door. She did not respond to it because shouting 'Go away' always fell on deaf ears. She was surprised when Wybert entered, looking straight at the piece she was working on.

'That is looking good,' he commented, taking a step towards her. He knew better than to venture too much closer.

She did not have the energy for hate, so she simply stared at him, waiting to see what he wanted.

'Amazing that you can do that from your mind,' he went on.

Charlotte looked back at the painting. She had been working on it solidly since Tatum had visited her. In it, Sir Miles was running across a green lawn ahead of her, tongue out and muzzle free. Charlotte's hair was blowing freely across her face, her skirts twisted around her legs. Dinefwr Castle was in the background. She was safe and happy outside its walls. Then there was the outline of a man she had yet to paint.

'Your guard?' Wybert asked.

'No, not my guard.' She offered no more information than that. Laying her brush down, she turned to him. 'What do you want?'

He looked somewhat uncomfortable. 'I hate to be the bearer of bad news, but your father's carriage has been found abandoned in the east. He is missing.'

This was the part where she was supposed to be surprised, sad. It was terrible news, after all, and her first time hearing it as far as Wybert was aware. But the anger won in that moment.

'Did you kill him too?'

He lowered his brows. 'Why would you ask me such a thing? You know how fond of your father I am.'

She laughed. 'Are you not even a little afraid to be locked in here with me?'

He exhaled in a sort of melancholy way. 'I can only imagine how heavy this news feels. I assure you we are doing everything we ca—'

'Liar. This is all part of your plan, a plan that goes way back. You brought me here to test the waters, to see if people would accept me. You were happy to exploit me. You were happy to exploit my whole family if it was to your advantage.'

'Charlotte—'

'People were wary of Oliver. They thought him cursed.' She swallowed. 'He was your first obstacle, so you promptly removed him.'

She expected him to cut her off again, but he did not.

'You already had my father onside,' she went on, 'so the next part was easy.' She smiled and shook her head. 'But you were not expecting Tatum to be a hurdle, were you? You had to really get on top of that quickly.'

'You were getting attached. I did you a favour.'

'You did *yourself* a favour.' There was venom in her voice. 'I was perfectly happy becoming attached.'

He looked around the room. 'You are jumping to an awful lot of conclusions.'

'If evidence exists, I will find it.'

His expression did not change. 'To be honest, I was not expecting this sort of hysterical reaction given the nature of your relationship with your father.'

'Do not presume to understand my relationship with him.'

He blinked. 'But I do. The absolute betrayal you must have felt when he chose to support me over you, his daughter, knowing our history—'

'I am seconds away from driving a paintbrush through your eye. Are you sure you want to continue?'

Wybert was quiet a moment. 'You know, I think I shall have Sir Miles brought to you. Despite the valid reasons for him being placed in the stable, I can see you require comfort, and I am not the right person to give it to you.'

He was so good, such a manipulator. The man was likely linked to the death of both her brother and father, yet here she was ready to fall down with gratitude because he was offering her something he had been with-holding as some form of sick punishment.

'Would you like that?' he asked.

It was so unsettling to be seething with hate for

someone while simultaneously feeling thankful. 'Yes. I would like that.' What else could she say? She wanted her dog.

'If it will make you happy, then I will do it.'

She did not dare move in case he changed his mind.

He glanced at the door. 'I will find out what happened to your father. I promise you that. Please know I am committed to our plans, no matter what. You will be well taken care of here at Dinefwr... as my wife.'

In the space of a second, her mind went from wanting to press his eyeballs into his head to tears to hysterical laughter, but none of that showed externally. Her face was blank. He actually thought she would still go ahead with the wedding. Charlotte was not waiting to marry him. She was waiting for evidence, waiting for Tatum, waiting to find out what had become of her father. She was there until she no longer had to be. He could keep the castle. She would sooner sleep on the side of the road than under the same roof as him.

He gave her a small smile. 'I shall have the guard fetch Sir Miles.'

She thought she nodded, but she may have just sat there.

A moment later, the door opened, and he was gone.

CHAPTER 39

'We got him,' Blackmane said, jogging up to Alveye and Tatum. The look on his face was the closest he ever came to smiling. 'Found him in Cenarth.'

Tatum's heart began to race. They had been searching for the man for five days, and every lead had brought them to a dead end. 'It's definitely him?'

'Yes. I recognised him immediately, and he definitely recognised me.'

Alveye took hold of Blackmane's shoulder. 'Good work.'

Pure relief flooded Tatum. He could finally get some answers and hopefully take action.

There was still no word on Lord Elis. No body had been recovered. It was likely he had been dumped in water or buried in the forest somewhere.

'Where is he?' Tatum asked.

Blackmane pointed to the south end of the camp. 'In the tent beside Jenkins's. Tolly's questioning him as we speak.'

Tatum was already walking away. 'Did Hadewaye get the information I asked for?'

'He did. He's seeing to the horses and will be along shortly. His name is Joseph Hughes.'

The three men made their way through the camp, the frosty morning air sharp in their lungs. They entered the small tent where Hughes was tied to a chair in the centre of the room. It was him all right. His clothes were ripped and covered in mud. Debris peppered his hair. His lips were bloodied, and one eye was beginning to swell shut. Despite all this, he still managed to present himself with a defiant demeanour, like the one he had displayed in the prison cell at Dinefwr before his supposed execution.

Tatum looked down at Tolly's red knuckles. 'What has he told you?'

'Not enough,' the general replied, stretching out his fingers.

Tatum met the prisoner's determined stare. Hughes was not going to make it easy for them, and they did not have the luxury of time. 'Let's speed things up a little.' He looked over his shoulder at Blackmane. 'Bring Jenkins in.'

The defender did not ask why. He simply nodded, then disappeared.

A few minutes later, he returned with the other prisoner, who was not in the greatest shape. Tatum could not tell whether Hughes recognised the man, but his injuries were enough to make him sit up and pay attention.

Tatum took Jenkins from Blackmane and marched him straight up to Hughes. 'You know this man?'

The prisoner did not respond at first, but when Tatum gave him a shake, he nodded.

'Good. He the one who hired you?'

Jenkins looked down at the ground before answering quietly. 'Yes.'

Hughes's face darkened. 'You weak bastard.'

'He's not weak.' Tatum shoved Jenkins towards Blackmane, and the defender caught him. 'He's just a few days ahead of you.' He took hold of Hughes's giant shoulders. 'You'll be singing facts soon enough.' Then clapped the man's face before straightening. 'Now, we know who you are and most of the things you've done. We know you shot Lord Elis at the market that day, and that Lord Wybert spared your life so he could put you to work for him.' He paused. 'You were involved in Lord Oliver's death somehow—or were at the very least in his bedchamber when he died. You came in through the window.'

Surprise flashed on Hughes's face before he could stop it.

'Then you killed the princess's guards and paid Jenkins and Parry to replace them.' Another pointed pause. 'Now, what about Lord Elis? I'm guessing you have something to do with his disappearance too.'

Hughes stared back at him with those black eyes of his.

The tent flap opened, and Hadewaye entered. 'Sorry, had to take my mare to the blacksmith. Missing shoe.' He looked around. 'What did I miss?'

'Our friend Hughes here was about to provide some information about Lord Elis,' Tatum said.

Hadewaye looked pleased. 'Good. Saves us from lopping off fingers. Messy business, that. We already know you can handle a good beating, so we'll be skipping that.'

Blackmane wandered closer. 'We're all very tired from looking for you, so out with it.'

Hughes responded by spitting in his direction.

Blackmane looked down at the ground. 'That was awfully close to my boot.'

The prisoner did not speak.

'You leave us no choice,' Hadewaye said, reaching inside his cloak and producing a folded piece of parchment.

Tatum shook his head. 'You know you're in trouble when Hadewaye's angry.'

Curiosity settled on Tolly's face. He was as clueless as Hughes as to what was written on it.

Hadewaye carefully unfolded the parchment, then spent a few seconds smoothing it out. Hughes began to shift in his seat, clearly not enjoying the suspense.

'Last chance to answer our questions without the need for this,' Hadewaye said, waving the parchment.

Hughes's eyes narrowed into slits. 'I don't even know what "this" is.'

'We can't always rely on self-preservation in these kinds of exchanges,' Tatum explained, 'so we find other ways.' He gestured to Hadewaye. 'Go ahead.'

The defender cleared his throat. 'We did some research, and it turns out you have a *very* large family. You have a lot of people depending on you. It's no wonder you sold your soul to the devil. Can't say I blame you given the number of sisters on your wife's side whose husbands died during the famine.'

'Must be a full-time job figuring out the distribution of goods you receive from Lord Wybert in exchange for murdering people,' Blackmane said, his stare as cold as the prisoner's. 'I'm surprised you have time to commit atrocities at all.'

Tatum gestured to Hadewaye. 'Continue, please.'

He dropped his gaze to the parchment again. 'Your wife is Gwladus, and you have five children together: Madrun, Robert, Ithel, Mary, and Angharat. You have a brother who lives in Crickhowell, and he got married last year. They've recently had a baby. Both your parents have passed, but your wife's parents are both alive. They have six daughters.' His eyebrows rose at that. '*Six?*'

'That's your plan?' Hughes asked. 'You're going to kill my *wife*? My *children*?'

Tatum brought a hand to his heart. 'Kill them? That seems a little harsh.'

'None of them have committed any crimes,' Hadewaye added. 'Your wife doesn't even know *you* kill people, does she?'

'She thinks you're a messenger,' Blackmane said. 'The best-paid messenger in the kingdom.'

Tatum winced. 'She doesn't sound like the sharpest knife in the drawer, but we won't hold that against her.'

Hughes's mouth flattened into a thin, angry line.

'What we *will* do is keep your secret in exchange for the information we need,' Tatum said. The anger on Hughes's face dissipated, which confirmed to Tatum that he was on the right path. 'She'll be told that you died in an accident while working hard to provide for your family. Your family's honour will remain intact. Your children will grieve you the way children should. They will know nothing of your crimes and dark past. They won't be shunned by their community and rejected by suitors later in life.'

'More importantly,' Alveye said, joining the conversation, 'we'll protect them from any potential fallout that arises from your confession. You have our word.'

Hughes looked between them, saying nothing for the longest time. 'Why should I trust you?' he asked finally.

'Because we're Chadorian defenders,' Alveye said. 'We have a code of honour. If we make a promise, we keep it.'

Hughes stared intensely at him. 'My wife will need some coin to get by. A month's wages while they mourn. A gift from His Lordship, perhaps.'

Tatum's heart was beating fast. He was close to having everything he needed to take Lord Wybert down. 'Done. I'll pay it from my own wages on the condition that you answer every single question honestly and in a timely manner. One lie and the deal's off.'

He could tell the moment Hughes was on board because his shoulders slumped in defeat. The fight had left him. 'All right.' He nodded slowly, accepting his fate. 'I'll answer your questions. What do you want to know?'

They wasted no time in getting started. The four defenders questioned him while Tolly paced the length of the tent, listening. Hughes confirmed all their suspicions, including being present for Oliver's death. He had held Sir Miles back while one of his thugs suffocated Oliver to death before cutting his wrists.

It took all of Tatum's strength not to kill him then and there after hearing that.

They were able to piece together some of the details Tatum had not quite figured out yet. The initial attack on Elis had been a genuine patriotic act, as suspected, but everything after that had been coordinated by Wybert.

'Where's Lord Elis?' was the most pressing question.

'I paid a few men up north to take out the carriage,' Hughes said. 'Haven't seen them since.'

'Why not?' Alveye asked.

'Lord Elis delayed his return a number of times. Then my son got sick, and I had to go home. Paid them half before I left and promised them the rest after it was done.' He paused. 'I got a letter from Lord Wybert a few days ago asking for proof and making threats. Now I'm here.'

'Can you tell us where we can find the men?' Blackmane asked.

Hughes hesitated, then nodded. 'But go easy on them. I may have embellished a few things to get them to agree.'

Alveye and Hadewaye exchanged a look.

'Anything else you can tell us about Lord Wybert that will help our case against him?' Tatum asked.

Hughes looked away when he replied. 'No, nothing.'

Tatum glanced over at Blackmane to see if he had caught the uneasy expression too. A small nod confirmed he had.

'You sure?' Tatum asked. 'Remember our agreement. I'll allow this one correction and this one only.'

Hughes pressed his lips tightly together, like he was holding in a secret. His discomfort was contagious.

Tatum crouched in front of him. 'We can't hold up our

end of this deal if you feed us partial details.' His tone was matter-of-fact rather than aggressive. 'What did he make you do?'

Hughes lifted his gaze. 'It wasn't me.' He licked at the sweat gathering on his top lip. 'I think he did it himself.'

Tolly stopped pacing.

'Did what?' Tatum coaxed. 'What did Lord Wybert do?'

No one moved.

Hughes sniffed. 'The king's brother.'

'King Edward?' Hadewaye asked.

The prisoner nodded. Sweat covered his whole face now. He looked around the tent before saying, 'I think Lord Wybert killed John of Eltham.'

Stunned silence followed.

Lord Wybert was one of the most patriotic men Tatum had ever had the displeasure of knowing. He was in Carmarthenshire *for* England. The earl had been his closest friend for years.

Tatum rose slowly and looked at Alveye. 'We need to get Charlotte out—now.'

CHAPTER 40

'Oh my goodness,' Ita said upon hearing the news. She pressed both hands to her stomach. 'Wybert's a monster, and she's stuck inside that castle with him. One wrong move on her part and she's next.'

'If you could tone it right down, we're trying to stop this one from charging in and getting himself killed,' Blackmane said, gesturing to Tatum.

Ita crinkled her nose. 'Sorry. I'm sure she's fine.'

Tatum swallowed down the giant lump in his throat. He was desperate to keep a level head in order to achieve the best possible outcome.

Alveye crossed his arms. 'We've sent word to Chadora—'

'I'm not waiting,' Tatum said. 'I'm getting her out.'

Alveye sighed. 'We can't invade Dinefwr Castle without the warden's permission.'

'We can't charge in and start killing English soldiers, but we can retrieve the princess if we think she's in danger—which she is.'

'*We* can kill English soldiers,' Ita pointed out. Then, when Tolly looked in her direction, she added, 'With General Blackmane's permission, of course.'

Hadewaye joined the conversation. 'Lord Wybert has proven that he has no problem killing people to get what he wants.'

'Which means you can't go in alone this time,' Alveye said. 'Not now that we know the kind of man we're dealing with.'

'Is there room for two underneath Iwan's wagon?' Ita asked. 'You can do the rescuing and I'll do the killing.'

Tolly cleared his throat.

She sighed. 'With the appropriate permission.'

Blackmane leaned his weight on one foot. 'We'll all go. Defenders will secure the princess, with Ita's help, and then Tolly goes in with the Carmarthen Militia for Wybert. He'll likely flee once he realises what's going on, so you'll need men watching every inch of that wall.'

'No one's going to open that gate for any of us,' Alveye pointed out.

Tatum crossed his arms. 'But they will open for the butcher.'

Ita tutted. 'Poor Iwan. He's going to wish he had never swapped sides.'

'Will he agree to this?' Hadewaye asked. 'There's a different level of risk this time.'

'I'm happy to go speak with him,' Blackmane offered.

Alveye snorted. 'I think you're grossly overestimating your charm. We'll all go, and then we can head straight to Dinefwr.'

'Let me do the talking,' Tatum said. 'Since I've already won his trust.'

Tolly looked around the camp. 'I'll put a unit together and get into position.'

Ita and the defenders went to fetch their horses. A few hours later, they were standing outside Iwan's butcher shop in Llanddeilo with some rare sunshine beaming down on them.

'Absolutely not,' Iwan said. 'We got away with it once because you were discreet. *Five* of you in my wagon is just asking for an arrow in the back.'

Alveye looked at Tatum. 'What was that about having won his trust?'

Tatum followed the butcher as he started to walk away. 'As soon as that gate opens, you're free to leave.'

'With soldiers all along that wall? You think they're just going to let me drive away?'

Tatum looked back at the others. 'As everyone will attest, their accuracy is terrible at that distance.'

Hadewaye dropped his head into his hand.

Iwan stopped and faced him. 'You're going to have to find someone else to be your stooge.'

Blackmane walked over to them. 'It's *your* princess we're saving. You should be happy to help.'

'He's right,' Ita said.

'I have a family to think about,' Iwan replied.

'You want to be on the right side of history, don't you?' Hadewaye asked.

'You lot should ask yourselves why people are hesitant to help. You expect us to protect the princess controlled by an English husband—yes, we know about that—and an English father, both of whom have the protection of an English king.'

Ita interjected at that point. 'Trust us when we say that wedding will not be going ahead, but you do make a valid point.' She looked at the others. 'We brought them a compliant princess instead of a *queen*. Princess Charlotte is at the mercy of men when she should be calling upon her army to control them.'

Iwan wagged a finger. 'Exactly. This kingdom needs a leader, not a pleaser.'

'I think people would welcome her as queen if she was willing to let go of England's hand,' Ita added.

There was a collective silence.

For some reason, it had never occurred to Tatum that Charlotte might outgrow the role she was sent to play. But now was not the time for that conversation. 'The princess may die at the hands of one of these men if we fail to act in time. Can you help us get her to safety or not?'

Iwan released a breath so large it almost blew them all away. 'Fine. I'll get you to the gate. But I'm telling you now'—his finger was wagging again—'I'm going to look as surprised as them guards when you emerge from your hiding place. As far as they're concerned, I had no idea you were in there.'

Tatum's eyes sank shut with relief. 'Thank you.'

~

Ita and the defenders were lying atop carcasses beneath a canvas, ears straining for the sound of the castle guards as the wagon rolled to a stop. The smell had been bearable for the first half of the journey but had become over-whelming by the time they arrived. Tatum heard Iwan's muffled curse as he reined in his restless horse.

'Afternoon,' Iwan called to the guards through the closed gate. 'Meat delivery.'

Tatum's eyes met Ita's when the portcullis began to rise. Nobody moved until it was all the way up and they heard the soldiers walking towards the wagon. Then Tatum gave a small nod, and the pair emerged from their hiding place, bows already loaded and one knee balanced on a pig carcass. They had their arrows pointed at the guards while those popping up behind them covered the wall above.

'Oh my,' Iwan exclaimed with wide eyes, raising his hands. 'Where in heaven's name did you lot come from?'

Hadewaye drew his sword and aimed it at Iwan's neck. 'Stay nice and calm and you may get to leave with your head still attached.'

The castle guards were frozen in defensive stances, looking to one another as they weighed up what to do next.

'Quiet above,' Blackmane said.

'Remember,' Alveye said as he jumped down from the wagon, 'Ita does the shooting.'

'Unless they shoot first,' Tatum replied, climbing down. 'Then it's self-defence.' He kept his bow trained on the guards.

'Tie them up,' Alveye said.

Before they had a chance, one of the men turned and yelled, 'Intrud—'

Two arrows hit him before he got the word out.

One of the arrows belonged to Ita. Alveye looked at Blackmane with regards to the second.

'It slipped,' Blackmane said as he climbed down and headed for the second guard.

The man immediately turned and ran for the gate. Three arrows landed in his back. He fell to the ground and did not move again.

'Unbelievable,' Alveye said, looking around at the others. 'What's the point of a plan if no one sticks to it?'

'I stuck to it,' Hadewaye said.

Tatum rolled his eyes. 'Get your head out of our poor commander's arse, Hadewaye.'

'If one more of you shoots an English soldier for any other reason than self-defence, I'm personally handing you over to the warden,' Alveye said in a deadly serious voice. 'Now put the dead guards in the wagon.'

Iwan's mouth fell open as the bleeding corpses were carried over. 'What am I supposed to do with them?'

Tatum was headed for the gate now. 'You're a butcher. You'll think of something.'

Ita jogged to catch up to him, and Blackmane kicked dirt over the bloodstained earth before following them. Alveye and Hadewaye were to remain at the gate to ensure no one left.

As they were heading inside, they heard shouting atop the wall. The three of them looked up as a group of soldiers disappeared into one of the turrets. The sound of weapons being drawn drifted down to them.

'We'll deal with them in a minute,' Blackmane said. 'We have company ahead.'

Ita shifted her bow up, then turned in a circle, her inexperience showing. 'I can't see them.'

'North wall, three merlons from the left,' Tatum said quietly.

She fired off an arrow but missed, instantly reaching back for another one. Blackmane shot the soldier between the eyes a second later.

Tatum winced. 'If Alveye asks, it was Ita.'

Ita snorted. 'Believable.'

An arrow whistled past Tatum's head, missing by an inch. 'Now seems like an appropriate time to defend oneself,' he remarked.

'Thank goodness,' Ita said.

Blackmane turned, walking backwards. He shot the first soldier who emerged from the turret. Ita helped him with the others as Tatum checked that the path ahead was clear.

'Northwest tower,' Ita said.

Arrows came at them before Blackmane had a chance to shoot. They moved off to the side for cover.

'Top window,' Blackmane said.

Tatum took out the shooter while Blackmane and Ita covered the men on the ground. Guards came from the front now. Tatum signalled, and the three of them formed a triangle, ensuring every view was covered as they forged on.

'Shit,' Tatum said when more men spilled through the chamber's door. He fired off arrows, one after another, while Blackmane and Ita took care of the rear and sides. The castle grounds were soon littered with bodies.

Blackmane pressed himself against the wall beside the door, then disappeared inside. He reappeared a few moments later. 'Clear.'

'Make sure no one gets through this door,' Tatum instructed Ita.

She nodded and reloaded her bow as Tatum and Blackmane headed off down the corridor towards Charlotte's bedchamber. The guard outside her door drew his sword when he spotted them coming. When he recognised their uniform, his hand slackened around the hilt.

Blackmane drew his dagger. 'Last chance to drop your weapon.'

The soldier's hand tightened around it instead, so Blackmane threw the dagger, striking the guard in the throat. The man dropped his sword and clutched his throat with both hands in a vain attempt to save himself. Then he fell to his knees.

Tatum stopped in front of him, patting around his middle in search of the key. He located it just as the guard began to tip, tugging it from his pocket as he slumped to the floor.

Blackmane stood guard while Tatum unlocked the door and entered with a loaded bow. He was surprised to find Sir Miles in the room. The dog barked in warning, the fur on his back bristling, then began wagging his tail when he recognised Tatum.

The defender pointed his arrow at the window, waiting. When the guard appeared, Tatum fired an arrow through the grille, striking him through the chest. He looked around the candlelit room, using his bow to keep Sir Miles at arm's length. Charlotte was standing in the corner, her entire body tense.

'Tell me I am leaving with you this time,' she said.

He nodded in the direction of her wardrobe. 'You're going to need some shoes.'

CHAPTER 41

The relief Charlotte felt when Tatum came through that door was indescribable. She had to remind herself to breathe. Each day, she had felt her sanity slipping a little more, and now she would finally get to step outside her bedchamber and breathe real air. But before she did that, there was something she needed to know.

'Did he do it? Did Wybert kill Oliver?' Deep down, she already knew the answer, but hearing it aloud would justify the rage and contempt consuming her.

Tatum's throat bobbed. There was pain in his eyes. 'Yes. He orchestrated the murder of your brother, your father.' He paused. 'And we have reason to believe he killed John of Eltham too.'

It was funny how one could be prepared to hear something, hold the knowledge in their heart, yet still be shocked when someone said the words. As for the last part... she had not been prepared for that. Prior to coming to Dinefwr, Charlotte had thought Wybert a selfish man but never a dangerous one. Her father had admired his work ethic and dismissed any bad behaviour as the actions of a young man not ready to settle.

'What will happen to him?' she asked.

'He'll be arrested by the Carmarthen Militia, but before that can happen, we need to get you out of here.' He closed the distance between them and took her hand. 'Ready to go?'

She searched his eyes. 'Ready.'

When they exited the room, Blackmane looked at her, then down at Sir Miles. 'Oh good. The dog's coming with us.'

'Good to see you too, defender,' Charlotte said as she passed by him.

Tatum kept a firm hold of her hand as they headed for the exit. Blackmane remained at the rear.

'Thank goodness,' Ita exclaimed when they came into view. 'Are you all right?'

Charlotte was not sure how to answer that.

'You look like you could really do with some sunlight,' Ita said. 'Shall we?'

Charlotte stepped outside and turned her face up to the sky. The air was cold, but her skin greedily soaked up the weak rays.

'Stay in the middle of us and match my pace,' Tatum told her. 'Understand?'

She looked ahead. 'Yes.'

They glimpsed some castle guards while exiting, but none tried to stop them from leaving.

'With me,' Charlotte told Sir Miles when they passed through the gate out into the open. Her heart sped up as she looked back and saw soldiers still watching them from atop the wall. But then she saw the men in green uniforms emerging from the trees outside, their arrows pointed right back at them. With the number of English soldiers already dead inside, she knew they did not stand a chance against the Carmarthen Militia.

'How does it feel?' Ita said. 'Knowing every one of those men is prepared to die on your behalf.'

Charlotte was more grateful than she could put into words. The rush of emotions drowned out the apprehension she felt with Wybert still on the loose. She needed him caught and shackled so she could finally relax.

'Move out!' she heard Tolly shout.

She watched as the soldiers headed for the castle in a circular line that grew smaller until they reached the wall. A second group then marched in through the gate.

Dinefwr Castle looked so majestic with the sun shining on it. Charlotte had never seen it from that angle before. Her eyes were drawn to the solo Carmarthenshire flag rising from its centre. The next residents would inevitably take it down.

'You all right?' Tatum asked.

No. She nodded.

The air grew deathly still as they waited in silence, eyes on the gate.

'Breathe,' Ita reminded her.

She inhaled, not realising how much she needed the oxygen until it filled her lungs.

Another half hour passed before Tolly finally emerged —empty-handed.

Alveye shook his head, visibly annoyed. 'Wait here.' He walked out to speak to him.

Charlotte's chest felt heavy. She could tell by Tolly's demeanour that they had no idea where Wybert was. 'He has to be in there.'

Tatum caught her by the arm when she went to walk off. 'I know this is painful, but you have to let them handle this.'

Ita folded her arms in front of her. 'What if he left before we arrived?'

Charlotte turned in a circle, as though expecting to spot him among the trees. *Where are you?*

'They'll find him,' Tatum assured her.

'If he reaches the border—'

'King Edward will hunt him to the ends of the earth when he learns of what he's done.'

Ita chewed her lip. 'Maybe he's a good hider.'

Charlotte's gaze went to Sir Miles. 'I know a way we can find out.'

Ita and the defenders all looked in her direction.

'Let me go in with Sir Miles.'

Tatum rubbed his forehead. 'Charlotte—'

'He can pick up a scent from twelve miles away,' she said. 'I have seen him do it.'

Tatum and Blackmane exchanged a doubtful look.

'He's either in there or he's not,' Ita said. 'At least let her try.'

Tatum nodded. 'Wait here.' Then he walked off to speak with the others.

He returned a few minutes later, looking from Charlotte to the dog. 'Muzzle on or off?'

Charlotte's lips turned up briefly. 'Off, of course.' She crouched down to unstrap the muzzle. 'You never have to wear this again.'

Sir Miles had a big yawn after it slipped from his head. Charlotte rubbed the spot behind his ears. 'Listen to me.' She waited for him to look at her. 'We need to find Wybert. Can you find the bastard for me?'

The dog closed his mouth and looked around.

'Good boy. Find him. *Go.*'

Sir Miles began sniffing the air, then spent some time walking in circles, inspecting random things. Noting everyone's sceptical faces, Charlotte said, 'It is a process. Do not rush him.'

No sooner had she said the words than Sir Miles took off towards the castle.

'Let's go,' Tatum said.

Blackmane and Ita followed also.

A few minutes later, the four of them were back inside the walls of Dinefwr, where Sir Miles led them in circles for a few minutes.

Ita cleared her throat. 'Is this still part of the process?'

Charlotte said nothing. Just as her own faith was beginning to dwindle, Sir Miles looked in the direction of the kitchen and took off at a trot with his nose a few inches from the ground.

'Here we go,' Charlotte said.

They all followed him.

'Stay close,' Tatum said, coming up beside Charlotte. His gaze moved in all directions.

When they reached the kitchen, Tatum caught Charlotte by the hand and pulled her behind him. 'Remember, he's got nothing to lose at this point.'

The cook, kitchen maid, and a handful of other servants were deep in conversation. They fell silent when they caught sight of Charlotte and the soldiers, then moved closer together when they saw Sir Miles.

'He will not hurt you,' Charlotte said, looking around the room. Wybert was nowhere to be seen.

Blackmane went to check the larder and buttery, shaking his head when he returned. Sir Miles did a lap of the kitchen before exiting.

'Now what?' Ita asked when they were standing outside again.

Sir Miles looked in the direction of the hall, then took off at a run. Even Charlotte was sceptical this time, but they all followed anyway, standing in the middle of the large room and looking around. Sir Miles froze a few times, then began whining.

'There's not even a cupboard to check,' Ita whispered to Blackmane.

The dog ran from corner to corner, sniffing and crying. Everyone waited patiently, most likely as a courtesy to Charlotte.

Defeated, she clicked her fingers and recalled the dog. 'To me.' Sir Miles came and sat at her feet, staring up at her. She rubbed his head. 'Never mind. You are still my good boy.'

As they were filing out of the hall, Charlotte noticed that Sir Miles was not following her. 'Is there anything under this floor?'

Ita thought for a moment, and then her eyes widened.

'The wine cellar. You access it from outside, but it's built beneath the hall.'

Blackmane and Tatum exchanged a glance. Then they all went in search of the cellar door, locating it around the side.

'I need you to wait here with Ita,' Tatum told Charlotte.

Sir Miles was whining and pawing at the timber doors. Wybert was in there. Charlotte was sure of it. She took hold of Sir Miles's collar. 'All right.'

The defenders flung the doors open, and Sir Miles immediately tried to leap inside. It took both Charlotte and Ita to stop him. The cold air drifted up from the black hole, uninviting. Tatum and Blackmane descended the steps, disappearing into the darkness.

'Stay,' Charlotte said, her voice barely carrying.

The dog made a noise that sounded a lot like him protesting before finally sitting. She gripped his collar with both hands, feeling the sharp ends of his fur against her skin.

The clash of metal sounded underground. Charlotte and Ita looked at each other, and then Ita drew her weapon. Tatum shouted something Charlotte could not quite make out before she heard the clatter of a sword skidding along the stone floor. Her breath hitched when a groan echoed up to them, followed by a wail of agony. The sound sent chills down her spine.

Sir Miles began to bark and pull, and Charlotte would have toppled forwards had it not been for Ita's quick action. Dropping her weapon, she caught Charlotte in a hug, keeping her upright. The tap, tap, tap of boots running up the steps towards them had the dog up on his hind legs and baring his teeth. Charlotte did her best to hold him while Ita kept a hold of her.

All of a sudden, she got the urge to let him go. Sir Miles needed to protect her. It was his job. He likely believed he had failed Oliver, and now she was setting him up for failure again. He deserved better.

Her hand went slack, and her fingers slipped from the collar. Then Sir Miles leapt fearlessly into the hole.

Just as she had resigned herself to the possibility of him breaking his neck, Wybert's dirty face appeared from the dark. His eyes widened when he saw the 230-pound dog coming at him. He stood no chance of getting out of the way in time. Sir Miles slammed into him, and the pair tumbled backwards down the stairs.

Charlotte moved to go after him, but Ita blocked her. 'Absolutely not.'

Noises drifted up to them. They had no idea who was hurt and who was not, until they eventually heard Tatum say, 'To me.' Then 'Good boy.'

Charlotte was finally able to exhale. Ita guided her back away from the doors, creating some room for them to exit safely.

A bloodied guard appeared first, pushed up the steps by an equally bloodied Blackmane. Wybert was next, his hands secured behind his back with a belt, a filthy Tatum following him. Sir Miles galloped up last, tongue out to one side and an extra spring in his paws. He was so proud of himself, and Charlotte felt her insides melt. She crouched when he reached her, pressing her head to his.

'Clever boy,' she whispered. 'He would be so, so proud of you.'

'You are going to be in a lot of trouble when King Edward hears of this,' Wybert was saying. 'Look around. It is an absolute massacre.'

Charlotte straightened and glared in his direction.

'He's going to be more shocked when he hears about what *you* did' was Tatum's reply. 'Joseph Hughes really spared no details.' He gave Wybert a shove to get him moving again.

There was a beat of silence before Wybert replied. 'Lies told under torture, no doubt.'

Charlotte watched him for a few strides, then felt her mind buzz—or maybe snap. Swooping down, she snatched up Ita's sword, holding it in a firm grip as she ran at him, with no doubt in her mind that she was going to drive the blade straight through him. Then do it again, and again, and again. Until he was as dead as her brother.

The blade was a mere six inches from the duke's devilish flesh when Tatum realised what was happening. He pushed Wybert to the ground, then somehow managed to both disarm Charlotte and catch her in one motion. She fought to free herself, more than happy to finish the job without the aid of a weapon.

'You killed them!' Charlotte screamed at Wybert, lashing out with her foot. 'They trusted you, and you killed them!'

Sir Miles ran up to Tatum, barking, confused.

All of the anger and grief Charlotte had been keeping a lid on bubbled to the surface like lava. She reached for Tatum's weapon, but he turned so it was out of her reach.

'I am going to cut you from throat to groin and kick your insides across the dirt while you are still alive to watch!'

Some of the colour left Wybert's face when she said that.

Tatum held her in a firm grip while she screamed and kicked and swore. Sir Miles's barking made the whole scene even more chaotic—if that were possible.

'Not like this,' Tatum whispered in her ear.

Ita ran forwards to deal with Wybert while Tatum moved Charlotte away.

'He has to die for what he did,' she said, her heart cracking as the words left her. 'He has to die!'

Tatum kept a firm grip on her, but it was not tight enough to hurt. 'I promise you, he will pay, but it can't be at your hand.'

'My hand is most fitting!'

Tatum buried his face in her shoulder. 'I'm sorry. It's for your own good. A princess doesn't have the luxury of revenge. You must settle for justice.'

She struggled for a few more moments before the anger gave way to tears and her body went limp. 'He has to pay.'

'He will.'

A sob escaped her. 'My beautiful brother.'

Tatum turned her to him and held her in a very different way, like she might break.

'My beautiful Oliver.' Her tears soaked his uniform. 'And my father, who trusted him like family.' She pulled back in order to scream at Wybert, 'Like family!'

Tatum guided her head back to his chest and stroked her hair. 'We have him now. He'll pay for all of it.'

Charlotte's eyes sank shut. The exhaustion of grief shifting inside her was crippling.

The sound of footsteps coming at a run had her lifting her head and blinking to clear her vision. It was Hadewaye, his expression tense.

'What is it?' Tatum called to him.

The defender leaned on his knees to catch his breath. 'You know how there's an army surrounding the castle?'

Tatum glanced at Blackmane, who was just as confused. 'Yes.'

'Well, there's now an army surrounding the army.'

Charlotte stepped out of Tatum's arms, sure she had misheard. 'Which army?'

Hadewaye straightened. 'The English are here.'

CHAPTER 42

here was a breath of silence before Wybert said, 'I guess news of your attack on Dinefwr has travelled.' He looked around at the corpses. 'Wait until they see the mess you made.'

'Be grateful you are not among them,' Charlotte hissed as she passed him on her way to the gate.

'Where are you going?' Tatum called after her.

'To find out why they are here.' She clicked her fingers in Sir Miles's direction. 'To me.'

The dog bounded after her.

'You go ahead,' Ita said to Tatum. 'Make sure she doesn't behead anyone midconversation. I have a feeling Lord Lethal here is going to be rather well behaved.' She gave Wybert's arm a pull to get him walking. 'Let's go.'

Charlotte had calmed down a little by the time she reached the gate, but it was short-lived. Before her was a line of green uniforms facing off against an equally long line of red ones.

'Well, this is an interesting sight,' Tatum said, stopping

next to her. 'It's too risky for you to go out there. They can come speak with you here. At least then we can cover you from the wall.'

Charlotte looked over her shoulder as Blackmane and Ita came into view, prisoners in hand. 'Tie them to the flagpole,' she instructed.

Wybert's eyes followed her as he was led to the pole and tied up. 'Last chance to salvage what remains of your life here.'

She turned away. 'I would sooner burn alive than salvage any life involving you.'

They stood there for around a quarter of an hour before Hadewaye joined them again.

'Is Alveye with Tolly?' Tatum asked, notes of concern in his voice.

Hadewaye nodded. 'He is.'

Some soldiers from the Carmarthen Militia arrived next, positioning themselves along the wall, both atop it and at the base.

'This is not your home to defend,' Wybert said to Charlotte. 'Remember?'

She kept her eyes forwards. 'I suggest you shut your whining mouth, or I will be forced to gag you.'

The next few minutes seemed to stretch on endlessly, the silence excruciating. Then the silence was broken by the sound of boots on gravel—many boots—growing louder and louder.

'What is that?' Charlotte asked.

The defenders' hands went to the hilts of their swords as people emerged from the trees. Not soldiers but plebeians armed with weapons and tools.

'What on earth is going on?' Ita asked.

'Wait here,' Tatum said, heading off in their direction.

Charlotte was not sure who he was talking to, but Blackmane did not wait there. He followed him. The new arrivals stopped to speak with the defenders, and Charlotte no longer knew which direction to look in. There was a lot happening in the scene before her.

'If they are here for Lord Wybert, they will have to get in line,' she said loud enough for him to hear.

The duke did not respond.

Tatum and Blackmane accompanied the group of a hundred or so people, both men and women, right up to the gate of the castle. Tatum instructed them to wait there, then rejoined Charlotte.

'They came on foot from Llanddeilo,' he said. 'They heard the English had crossed the border. They're ready to fight on your behalf.'

The gesture was overwhelming on top of all the other emotions she was feeling. Her gaze settled on Mevanou, who was standing at the front beside Iwan the butcher.

'We thought you might need some help,' the maid called to her.

Iwan raised his butcher's knife in solidarity, and Charlotte's lips turned up. She bowed her head in a gesture of appreciation.

Oliver's voice sounded in Charlotte's head.

'What do you see?'

Her smile grew as she imagined describing the scene to him. *There are two armies and a mismatched array of merchants and farmers, some with makeshift spears and some wielding rakes and sickles. They stand ready to fight with whatever they have in their hands.*

Swallowing, she looked straight ahead once more.

Sir Miles got to his feet, ears pricked forwards and eyes fixed on something in the distance. Charlotte narrowed her eyes as the Carmarthen Militia split apart to let some people through. She immediately recognised Tolly, Alveye, and…

Her lungs stopped.

Her heart slowed.

'Father,' she breathed.

Tatum exhaled through his nose. 'Well, look at that. Back from the dead.'

Wybert shifted, visibly surprised and uncomfortable with this new revelation.

Sir Miles ran out to meet her father, and she heard him say in his usual harsh tone, 'Get down, fleabag,' while pushing the dog away with his boot.

Ita slowly shook her head. 'This day is just getting stranger and stranger.'

He is alive.

Tatum looked at Charlotte. 'You all right?'

She shook her head. 'Not really.' But she *was* smiling.

Theirs was not the kind of relationship that saw them racing into each other's arms. However, she could have sworn she saw her father's eyes well up momentarily. The closer he got, the more facial injuries and bruises she made out. While his stride was confident, he was favouring his left leg. It seemed they had both visited hell.

Elis stopped ten feet away, his expression darkening

when he looked in Wybert's direction. 'I see you beat me to it.'

She ran her eyes over him. 'I thought you were dead.'

He cast a second glare in Wybert's direction. 'So did I for a minute there. Luckily, I was prepared.' His eyes returned to Charlotte. 'I did some digging around upon returning to England. I wanted to make sure I was doing the right thing in leaving my fortune to this man. I was the one insisting you marry him, after all.' He paused, catching his breath. 'Imagine my surprise when I discovered that Lord Wybert's business back in England was failing, that his family's fortune had been squandered, and that he was one trade deal away from financial and social ruin.' He looked at the duke. 'Desperation can make a man do unspeakable things.'

When Charlotte glanced at Wybert, she saw something she had never seen on his face before—shame. Shame in its purest form.

'I had some of my men follow the carriage from a distance, just to be safe,' Elis continued. 'They were able to intervene before the scoundrels could finish the job. We thought it best to leave the carriage in the forest, let him think he had won.' He reached into his pocket and pulled out a letter. 'Then I returned to England for this.'

'What is that?' Charlotte asked.

'A warrant. Signed by the king himself. Lord Wybert will return to England and be tried.'

Charlotte suspected they were talking about different crimes. 'For attempted murder?'

'Among other things' was her father's reply. His disappointment was as thick as grief. He had trusted Wybert.

'Your intentions are now quite clear,' Elis said, looking at the duke. 'You wanted possession of Dinefwr Castle at any cost.'

Wybert adjusted the rope around his wrists. 'You have no proof of that.'

The villagers were edging closer in order to hear better. Charlotte did not object to their eavesdropping. They deserved to know the truth about the man many of them were doing business with.

'I have various letters in my possession.' Elis glanced at Tolly, who was standing off to the side. 'However, I hear the Carmarthen Militia have something even better.'

Wybert was sweating now, and Charlotte bathed in the luxury of his discomfort. When she looked into her father's eyes, she saw the pain of what he had learned. If he did not know all the details of Wybert's crimes before arriving in Carmarthenshire, he certainly knew them now.

Charlotte walked up to her father and hugged him. It was as awkward as she imagined it would be. He stood as rigid as a tree trunk while she held him tightly. Her eyes sank shut. 'I knew Oliver would not leave us by choice.'

A hand landed lightly on her back, patting twice before falling away. Charlotte stepped back, looking to the merchants and farmers.

'I want you to know that Lord Wybert killed my brother, Oliver. He killed a blind man in his bed.' She shook her head as fresh disgust surfaced. 'That is the kind of man he is.' She pressed her lips together in an effort to contain the emotion.

'Murderer!' Iwan shouted, raising his butcher's knife

into the air. 'Hang him!' He marched forwards. 'We'll do it right now. That's how we deal with traitors.'

Her father intervened. 'No. He will be tried in England for his crimes and sentenced accordingly.'

Iwan's feet stilled. 'In *England*?'

There was a ripple of disapproval through the crowd.

'I understand he murdered your son,' said a woman towards the back. 'But he killed *our* prince. His crimes are against *us*. He should be tried and sentenced *here*.'

Charlotte looked straight at Wybert when she said, 'He does not need a trial. He is guilty.'

'Then hang him!' shouted another man. 'This is our kingdom, our rules.'

Wybert gripped the rope and made himself as tall as possible. 'She does not have the authority to order an execution!' He had the audacity to look to her father for support. 'Only the king can sign a death warrant. Tell them.'

Elis dropped his gaze. 'He is right.'

Tatum crossed his arms, glancing from Wybert to the crowd. 'That's true. Only a king can sign a death warrant.'

Wybert practically slumped over with relief.

'Or a queen,' Tatum added. He looked around the crowd, like he was waiting for their reaction to that word. 'A queen could also sign a warrant.'

It took Charlotte a moment to gauge what was happening. She stared out at the villagers, expecting to see confusion or perhaps even laughter, but she saw contemplative curiosity instead.

Ita was grinning madly, clearly in love with the idea. She walked forwards to address the crowd. The

Carmarthen Militia were half listening and half still watching their backs. 'The best protection against an English king is a Welsh queen. I would accept this woman as my queen. Princess Charlotte is strong and hungry for change, like the rest of us. Because she's Welsh.' She paused and looked around. 'You know, if history had gone another way, Prince Oliver would have been *King* Oliver. Lord Wybert would not have been here using this castle for business. Dinefwr would have been a family home, and Prince Oliver would still be alive.' She took another step forwards. 'If history had gone another way, then Princess Charlotte would never have gone to England and had to go through the pain of returning here a stranger.'

Ita walked over to Charlotte and placed an arm around her. 'This woman has opened her home to us during the worst times and funded the army you see before you, making it the strongest it can be. She even agreed to marry this horrid man'—she pointed at Wybert —'in order to remain here as your princess.' Ita gave Charlotte's shoulders a small squeeze. 'But the thing is, she never needed to do that. This was already her home— by birthright. She never needed permission to be here.' She looked to Tolly. 'Do you agree, General?'

Tolly regarded Charlotte for a long moment, then nodded. 'I do.' He dropped down on one knee. 'And I accept you as my queen.'

Elis's eyes grew as wide as plates. His mouth was open as if he were about to speak, but no words came out.

'I accept you as my queen!' Mevanou shouted, dropping down also.

Ita released her hold on Charlotte and moved to stand

in front of her. 'And I most definitely accept you as my queen.' She knelt and bowed her head.

Charlotte watched as the merchants, farmers, peasants, and soldiers in bright green uniforms got down on one knee.

'I accept you as my queen,' they said, one by one.

This continued until the only people standing were the defenders, the English soldiers, who had no idea what was going on, Wybert and his guard cowering beside him, and her father. Charlotte glanced at Tatum, who looked back at her with pure pride.

Ita rose and stepped out of the way. 'Now it's your turn to say something.'

Charlotte could barely find breath, let alone words. She wet her lips and looked around. 'It would be my true honour to uphold peace, justice, and integrity in Carmarthenshire, the kingdom I now call home.'

Out of the corner of her eye, she saw Wybert's face contort. He opened his mouth to say something, to object, but she never heard his words. They were drowned out by a deafening chorus of 'Long live the queen!' that echoed off the wall behind her before drifting up to the heavens.

Tatum bowed before her. 'Your Majesty.' He straightened with the most delicious boyish smile.

She turned back to her father, waiting to see how he would react to this unexpected turn of events.

'King Edward will always be my king,' he said immediately. 'I am loyal to him until my death.'

She nodded. 'I know.'

'But that does not mean I do not respect you as queen

of this kingdom—and as my daughter.' He bowed. 'Your Majesty.'

Tears surfaced, but she blinked them back. This moment was not about her feelings. This moment was about all the people standing before her, praying they had made the right decision in accepting her as their queen. She would serve them the way they deserved and lean into the role with grace and ferocity. And in that moment, they wanted blood.

So she gave it to them.

'My first act as queen will be to sign a death warrant for Lord Wybert for crimes committed against my family and kingdom.'

Tatum stepped closer and caught her eye. 'You sure about this?'

'Yes. Quite sure.'

Ita turned to one of the guards by the gate. 'Someone get the queen some parchment, ink, and a quill.'

The crowd responded with cheering and clapping, but not her father.

'Charlotte,' he said. 'There are procedures even a queen needs to follow.'

She met his gaze with an icy stare. 'He killed your *son*. Where is your anger? Your paternal rage?'

His face reddened. 'King Edward—'

'Has no jurisdiction here.' She waited to see what he would do next.

After a tense moment, his shoulders fell and he stepped aside. 'You are right. This is your kingdom.'

Charlotte felt hopeful that this version of them could prove to be functional.

'Control your daughter!' Wybert said, his voice choked with panic. His face had gone a ghostly white. 'Your loyalty is to King Edward!'

Tatum walked over to him, bringing his face mere inches from the duke's. 'Don't worry. He can tell your king all about it at the same time he tells him who really killed John of Eltham, the king's beloved brother.' He searched Wybert's eyes. 'I would take the hanging if I were you. It'll be much worse if you cross that border —trust me.'

Wybert's mouth went slack. It was clear he had thought that secret properly buried.

A guard exited the castle, clutching the items Ita had requested. He handed Charlotte a sheet of parchment, then offered up the pot of ink with a quill poking out of it.

'Turn around,' Charlotte instructed, using the guard's back like a table. Then, realising she had no idea what to write, she looked to Tatum, who came forwards to help her with the wording.

Once the warrant was written out and signed, she held it up to the crowd. They roared in response. She handed the warrant to Tolly before walking over to the duke. Sir Miles followed. She placed a hand on the dog's head to keep him calm.

'I do hope the hellhound rumours prove true,' Charlotte said, fixing her piercing stare on Wybert. 'I know how you *love* big dogs.'

His face was a blend of sweat and hate. 'I should have killed you and that monstrous dog when I had the chance.'

Her mouth stretched into a devious smile. 'As tempting as it is to let the monstrous dog maul your leg while you gasp for your last breath, I would prefer Sir Miles not get dirty when you inevitably soil yourself in front of this enormous crowd.' She stepped back and clicked her fingers at Sir Miles. 'To me.'

The guards shouted instructions overhead, and a minute later, a rope was thrown down. Tolly stepped up and tied a noose, slipping it over the duke's head.

'Wait!' His pleas landed on deaf ears.

Tatum signalled to the guard atop the wall while looking straight at Wybert. 'Long may she reign.'

The noose snapped closed around the duke's neck as he was hoisted into the air, desperately trying to grip the wall with the soles of his boots in an attempt to delay the inevitable. The crowd was silent now. They watched as his movements grew smaller and smaller, until there was no movement at all. Until he was just a corpse swinging in the breeze.

Charlotte looked heavenward. *It is done, brother. Rest easy now.*

CHAPTER 43

*I*t had been Charlotte's idea to invite her father, Tolly, and the warden to Dinefwr Castle to discuss what was next for Carmarthenshire. The morning they were due to arrive, Tatum watched her closely for signs of distress, but in true Charlotte fashion, she appeared completely unfazed.

'Should I stay in case things go south?' he asked, looking around the new throne room.

She smiled at him. 'No. You should stay because I want you here.'

He brushed a hand down her cheek. It was such a relief to see colour back in them and light in her eyes. 'Being queen *really* suits you. Have I told you that?'

'Yes, but I do not mind the repetition.' She took his hand. 'I still cannot believe they chose me as their queen.'

'They adore you.'

'Even the ugly parts. Imagine that.'

He drew her to him, kissing her forehead. 'There are

no ugly parts. Only honest reactions to a world that can be ugly at times.'

She tipped her face up to him. 'You, defender, sure know how to make a queen feel special.'

He held her gaze, knowing that every day with her was a gift. For the past two weeks, they had lived and loved on borrowed time. Charlotte was the queen of Carmarthenshire. He was a Chadorian defender. Their futures did not align. She had to put the needs of her kingdom first, and he needed to support that any way he could—including getting out of her way when the time came.

'Do you think the warden will still be upset about your involvement in recent events?'

'Are you referring to breaking into Dinefwr Castle, killing more than a hundred English soldiers, aiding the cutting of ties with England, then standing idle while a certain duke was hanged from these very walls?'

She scrunched her nose. 'That was *weeks* ago. I am sure he is over it by now.'

Tatum kissed her to avoid responding.

Her father was first to arrive. Ita, who had accepted the position of the queen's primary personal guard, announced his arrival.

'How does he seem?' Charlotte asked.

Ita released a breath. 'Normal?'

Charlotte looked at Tatum. 'Normal is good.'

'Normal is better than angry,' he agreed with a shrug.

'You can send him in.'

Ita disappeared, and shortly after, Lord Elis entered the room. He stopped six feet away and bowed. 'Your Majesty.'

'Father.' She attempted a pleasant smile. 'How was your journey here?'

'Tolerable.'

Charlotte glanced at Tatum, who avoided eye contact with her in order to keep a straight face. The man was predictable if nothing else.

Elis waited for his daughter to sit down, then eyed Tatum as he headed for the seat on the opposite side.

'Before the others arrive,' Charlotte began, 'I wanted to speak to you about marriage.'

Tatum almost missed his chair when she said this. Elis's shocked face mirrored his own.

'You want to speak about *marriage*?' Elis asked. 'When you have a coronation coming up?'

Charlotte nodded. 'I would like to marry Brock Tatum.'

It took Tatum's brain a moment to recognise his own name. 'You would?'

Elis looked between them. 'You want to marry... a defender?'

'He is not just a defender. He is also one of the bravest, funniest, and most loyal men I know.'

Tatum sat up a little. 'You think I'm funny?'

'Plus, if he were to agree to this,' she continued, 'he can add Royal Consort to that list.'

Elis blinked. '*If* he agrees? The two of you have not discussed it?'

Charlotte glanced at Tatum. 'We are discussing it now.'

Excitement flickered in his chest.

'We both think it is a great idea,' she said, looking to Tatum for confirmation.

He struggled to find words. 'It's possibly the best idea I've ever heard.'

'However, this sort of decision needs the support of everyone involved,' Charlotte went on. 'And as my father, your blessing means'—her voice faded a little—'well, a lot.'

Elis was staring at her like he did not recognise her. After a long silence, he said, 'You would be marrying beneath you.'

She shook her head. 'No. Marrying this man would be my greatest achievement.'

'He is a soldier.'

'He could be a servant and I would love him the same. That said, his father is a baron, so it is not too much of a stretch for a queen.' She cleared her throat. 'Do you have any *valid* objections?'

Tatum's heart felt like it would explode out of his chest. He had spent the past few weeks preparing to let her go while she had spent them preparing for the difficult conversations ahead of her.

'It is more important what your subjects think of your choice,' Elis said.

She nodded. 'While a handful may judge harshly, I think most will be thrilled to learn that their queen is marrying for love instead of political advantage.' She raised a hand before her father could interrupt. 'That is not to say the union is without political advantages. It will strengthen our ties with Chadora.' She paused. 'I do not want an advantageous marriage for display purposes. I want a love story that the whole kingdom can celebrate. And I *know* my subjects want a happy queen.'

Elis shifted in his chair.

Before they could finish the conversation, the door opened and Ita walked in again. 'General Blackmane and the Chadorian warden, Shapur Wright, are waiting outside, Your Majesty.'

The three of them got to their feet.

'You can send them in,' Charlotte said.

The general and the warden entered, Tolly with a casual stride and Shapur with a sense of authority and purpose. His black uniform and crimson-lined cloak always cut an imposing figure, a visual reminder of the power he wielded.

The pair stopped in the middle of the room and bowed. 'Your Majesty,' they said in unison.

She smiled at Tolly before turning her attention to Shapur. 'You must be the infamous warden I have heard so much about.'

Charlotte looked every bit the queen in her green dress made from emerald-hued velvet. The gold embroidery gave it a regal air.

'Shapur Wright, at your service, Your Majesty,' he said, gaze flicking to Tatum. 'Thank you for the invitation.'

'I trust the journey here was uneventful?'

'It was.'

She gestured to the empty chairs before taking her seat. 'You and your men are welcome here anytime. If there is anything I can do to make your visit more comfortable, simply ask.'

'That is very kind of you.' Shapur gave Tatum a thunderous stare as they both took their seats.

'I am incredibly grateful for the assistance your men provided recently under very challenging circumstances,'

Charlotte said. 'Their bravery and loyalty never cease to amaze me.'

'I am afraid I can only vouch for their bravery at this point,' Shapur said.

Charlotte cleared her throat. 'Unfortunately, the matter was time sensitive, and your men did not have the luxury of waiting for orders.'

Shapur sucked his teeth. 'I am not certain they would have followed them anyway.'

An awkward silence followed before Tatum said, 'You should know that Alveye led with confidence. He made a plan, ensured he had our support and that of the Carmarthen Militia, then implemented it with great success.'

'Driving a further wedge between England and Carmarthenshire in the form of a...'

'Queen?' Charlotte offered.

Colour rose up Shapur's neck. 'Forgive me, Your Majesty.'

The door opened and Mevanou wandered in, humming a tune Tatum did not recognise. She hummed it all the way to the table, placing a tray down before looking around.

'I thought you might be hungry,' she said. 'The cheese was made here at Dinefwr Castle. Heaven with some of the fruit paste on top.'

Charlotte closed her eyes momentarily. 'Thank you, Mevanou.' She opened her eyes. 'You can leave it there. Also, do you remember we had that little chat earlier about knocking?'

The maid brought her hand to her chest. 'Sorry. It's

going to take some time to get used to the whole queen thing.'

The new queen pinched the bridge of her nose, and Tatum and Tolly both looked down at their laps.

'I'll leave you with the cheese,' Mevanou said before hustling out the room.

Ita appeared briefly, mouthing 'Sorry' at Charlotte before closing the door.

Charlotte looked awkwardly around the table. 'Cheese, anyone?'

Shapur cleared his throat. 'No, thank you.'

The others shook their heads.

'I'll take some water, though,' Tolly said, leaning forwards to pour it.

Charlotte placed her hands in her lap. 'I was curious, Warden, about your stance on defenders marrying queens.'

Tolly almost spat water across the table. He coughed into his hand to disguise it. 'Excuse me.'

Shapur looked from Charlotte to Tatum. 'A queen?'

'Specifically a Carmarthenshire queen,' Charlotte clarified. 'I am asking how you would feel about the two of us getting married.'

Shapur was staring hard at Tatum. 'Would you be handing in your uniform?'

'I'd rather not.' He leaned forwards. 'Whatever title bestowed on me will never replace the one burned into my soul. I'm a Chadorian defender for life, with or without the uniform, and with or without your blessing. The men I serve with aren't just my comrades—they're my brothers.'

Shapur looked at Charlotte. 'Do you understand, Your Majesty, that every man wearing that uniform reports to *me*, regardless of what other words preface their name?'

She offered him a pleasant smile. 'You think a queen cannot grasp the concept of *kingdom first*? While the Carmarthen Militia would love to claim him as one of ours, green is really not his colour.' She looked to Tolly. 'Do you agree, General?'

He appeared thoroughly uncomfortable. 'Yes.'

'I have no desire to take any part of him that does not belong to me and vice versa. We belong to our respective kingdoms first and foremost.' She looked around the table. 'Before we move on to other things, are there any other objections on this matter?'

The men looked between themselves, then shook their heads.

'In that case,' Charlotte said, turning to Tatum, 'will you marry me?'

Every time he thought he had reached the limits of his capacity to love her, she pushed the boundary out a little further. 'What size dowry are we talking?'

Charlotte laughed, then covered her mouth. Upon seeing the agitation on her father's face, she quickly said, 'He is joking.'

'I am,' Tatum assured him. 'Apologies for the tasteless humour, my lord.'

Shapur exhaled sharply. 'Of all the eligible Chadorian men you could have chosen…'

'She chose well,' Elis said quietly. He smoothed down the front of his tunic. 'My daughter has waited a long time to be happy. For what it is worth, you have my blessing.'

Charlotte stared into her father's eyes as she selected her next words. 'Thank you.' She cleared her throat. 'Right. Moving on to trade.'

The five of them continued through the afternoon, discussing everything from the coronation to the sharing of resources to disaster planning. Tatum contributed ideas when asked directly but otherwise sat back, content watching Charlotte shine in all her brilliance.

When the meeting was over and all the guests had left the room, Tatum took hold of her chair and dragged it to his.

'I cannot believe the warden is *exactly* as bad as you make him out to be,' she said.

Tatum rubbed her arm. 'He's a tough man to love, but we make it work.'

She searched his eyes. 'You seemed as surprised as my father when I brought up marriage. I just assumed you wanted—'

'You assumed correctly. I've always known you're braver than me, but today was proof of it.' He paused. 'I love you, and I've wanted to marry you ever since you gave me that portrait.' He narrowed his eyes. 'I noticed yours wasn't hanging in your room, by the way.'

She tipped her head back in laughter. 'Weirdly, it got damaged in transit.'

'During the two-minute journey from the wall walk to your bedchamber?'

Her nod was enormous. 'What are the chances?'

'Hmm.' He leaned in and kissed her.

Charlotte held his face in both hands. 'I want you to know that I will never put you in a position where you are forced to choose between your kingdom and me. I will love you from afar if I have to, so long as you return to me eventually.'

He kissed her hand, then said, 'That's very kind of you, but I'd prefer to love you up close.'

She was smiling again. 'I cannot wait to marry you. I was prepared to fight the warden for the honour if need be.'

He chuckled. 'I think you would win. Despite no weapons training and being half his size, somehow you would do it.'

'Because I have the best weapon of all.'

'Cruel sentiments that can reduce a man to tears?'

She pinched him playfully. 'I was talking about Sir Miles.'

He combed hair back from her face with his fingers. 'If you really can't wait to marry me, then we'll do it today. A bold young princess once told me it's better to ask for forgiveness than permission.'

A look of surprise settled on her face. 'So you *were* awake that night.' She tutted. 'Where would we go to marry?'

He thought for a moment. 'I'd suggest going into Llanddeilo, but I'm fairly sure you're banned from the church there.'

She shook her head. 'Only from the bell tower.'

He laughed.

'I feel my father has been accommodating enough for one day. Let us not push him.' Charlotte released a contented sigh.

'Are you happy?' he asked.

She nodded. The light that was pouring from her was deliciously blinding.

'Shall we go release Sir Miles from the chamber of torture?' she asked.

'You mean your elaborate new chamber with the house-sized bed he's sleeping in?'

She rose. 'The bed really does not seem that big when he is in it.'

He followed her to the door.

'And that dowry joke could have waited until later,' she said, trying to be serious and failing. 'You need to learn to read the room.'

'Your father liked it.'

'He liked my *reaction* to it. Because he wants me to be happy,' she added in a smug voice.

Tatum wanted her to be happy too. He wanted it more than anything.

He caught her hand, and she stopped halfway out the door, her smile faltering when she saw his expression.

'What is wrong?' she asked.

He stepped closer and wrapped his arms around her, pressing his lips to her hair. 'I just love you.'

She leaned her weight against him, eyes closing. 'I love you too.'

EPILOGUE

*A*s the crown was placed atop Charlotte's head, cheers echoed around the church, spilling out its doors to the crowd gathered outside. The sound made every hair on Charlotte's body stand on end. She looked over to where Tatum and her father stood with their proud expressions. Then her gaze drifted to Tolly and the other defenders. Beside them was Ita, a beaming Isabel, and a teary-eyed Lady Gwenore accompanied by her son. Even Shapur Wright was in attendance, looking far too serious for such an occasion.

Someone had to keep Charlotte humble.

The sun beamed through the church windows as a sceptre and sword were placed in her hands, as though God himself was in attendance. Maybe he was. Tears fell down people's faces as she pledged herself to them.

'Long live Queen Charlotte!' Tatum shouted when the archbishop finally stepped aside.

She rose, the silver accents of her rich velvet gown shimmering with the movement. The crowd responded with deafening cheers, the air thick with excitement. Tolly came forwards to take the sword and sceptre from her, and her father took her hand to escort her from the church. Charlotte looked over her shoulder to make sure Tatum was following. He was exactly where he said he would be. He winked at her.

Outside, she was greeted by waves of cheering peasants, merchants, soldiers, and families of all kinds. The crowd reached all the way to the castle. She rode in the carriage by herself. Her father, Tatum, Ita, and Tolly accompanied her on horseback, two in front and two behind. Charlotte waved at the people lining both sides of the road, revelling in the weight of the crown, a symbol of her people's faith and trust.

The procession made its way to the castle, through the gate, all the way to the courtyard. Tatum dismounted and went to open the carriage door. She took his hand, but instead of letting go and walking off ahead of him, she threaded her fingers through his as they headed for the wall with her father and guards in tow. It was time to address the thousands of people who were gathered out front, some of whom had followed her from the church on foot.

When they reached the top of the steps, she let go of Tatum's hand and turned to her father.

'Thank you,' she said.

'For what?'

She looked around, as though the answer was written somewhere on the wall walk. 'For showing up. For your support.' Her eyes returned to him. 'For caring more than you let on.'

His eyebrows formed a serious line. 'You should be focused on your speech.'

She glanced at Tatum, who gave her a knowing smirk, before heading towards the stone balcony. She hesitated before stepping out onto it, looking out over the crowd. The sight left her slightly winded.

This was her kingdom. These were her people.

She waited for them to settle, but the cheering continued, so she raised one hand to silence them.

'Remember,' her father said behind her, 'you will need to really project your voice.'

She nodded and took a few deep breaths, then began. 'It is such an honour to stand here before you today as your queen.' That was as far as she got before the crowd erupted in cheers again.

'Does she have a short version?' Ita said behind her. 'Or we might be here all afternoon.'

Charlotte raised her hand, and they fell silent again. 'I stand here today because of you, because of the trust you gifted me, which I vow never to break. I swear to you, and before God, that I will dedicate my life to protecting this land and caring for its people.' She took a breath before continuing with renewed vigour. 'Together we will survive this sometimes-harsh existence. Through rain and flood and famine.' She swallowed. 'And death. Even war, if it comes to that. There is no darkness we cannot face as one.'

More cheering rang out around her.

'Today marks a new era where we stand together, united against any force that seeks to harm us! Together, we are invincible!'

The crowd shouted back, 'Long live the queen! Long live the queen! Long live the queen!'

It was a sound she would never forget. No one standing on that wall or in that crowd would forget it either.

A sudden clamour had everyone looking to the north end of the castle. The Carmarthen Militia appeared, marching in perfect formation. Each soldier saluted Charlotte as they passed by. The others stepped forwards to watch also.

'Your army, Your Majesty,' Tolly said proudly.

'I don't think I've ever come across men so capable of killing but *in*capable of marching in time,' Tatum said. 'The drills were painful to watch.'

Tolly chuckled. 'We got there in the end.'

'Well, they are most impressive now,' Charlotte said. She looked at her father. 'What do you think?'

He nodded. 'Impressive, but better in red.'

They continued watching the soldiers until they disappeared behind the south wall.

'Please stay for the celebration,' Charlotte told the crowd. 'There will be food, wine—until it runs out—and dancing, all outside where there is room enough for everyone.'

The outpouring of excitement had Charlotte smiling at the ground as she stepped off the balcony. When she spotted Mevanou, she asked her to go fetch Sir Miles from her bedchamber so he could join in the less formal part of the day. He bounded up to the group as they neared the gate.

'Ready?' Tatum asked, letting go of her hand.

She took hold of it again and met his eyes. 'Let them see.'

The pair walked into the crowd hand in hand, with Sir Miles remaining obediently at Charlotte's side. People did stare, some with complete surprise, some confusion, others with adoring smiles. They kept making their way around the crowd, stopping to talk to people along the way.

It was not long before they ran into Iwan. The butcher was busy loading carcasses onto spits while others prepped fires nearby.

'Looks like this is the place to be,' Charlotte said, stopping behind him.

Iwan turned, a grin splitting his face. 'Your Majesty. Give it a few hours and this whole area will smell like heaven.' He looked down at their joined hands. 'Perhaps you want to book me in for your next big celebration too?'

She shrugged. 'I hear there is an excellent butcher a few villages down. We may enquire there.'

He chuckled as he grabbed a handful of salt and threw it over the meat. 'Likely story.'

Iwan's daughter was nearby, watching them with a sweet smile on her face. 'I hope to marry a soldier one day.'

'Over my dead body,' Iwan said. Then, looking at Tatum, he added, 'No offence.'

Tatum raised a hand. 'None taken.'

Noticing that the smile was gone from his daughter's face, Iwan said, 'Maybe if this soldier of yours shows the same level of commitment this defender has, I'll consider it.'

Her sweet smile returned.

Charlotte spent the next few hours enjoying the music and wine while greeting as many people as she could get through. Isabel came to find her, gushing about her speech before inviting herself to the castle to help with the wedding plans.

'Whatever you need, I know people,' she said. 'Tell me, though, what did your father say when you told him the news?'

Charlotte glanced over to where Elis was speaking to the warden. 'He was surprisingly... fine.'

'Fine is good.'

Charlotte nodded. 'Fine is more than I ever hoped for.'

That made Isabel smile. 'Well, congratulations. It is wonderful to have something so exciting to look forward to. Now, please excuse me. I need to try to locate my son, who has spent the day being passed between family and friends.' She curtsied. 'Enjoy your celebration, Your Majesty.' She flashed a warm smile at Tatum before disappearing.

Charlotte's voice was beginning to tire. Rising up onto her toes, she whispered into Tatum's ear, 'Come inside the castle with me. There is something I want to show you.'

He took her hand once more and led her through the crowd. Once they were inside the gate, Charlotte moved to his side, resting her head on his arm for a moment.

'Tired?' he asked.

'No,' she lied, reaching down to pet Sir Miles's head. 'Grateful.'

His arm went around her. 'So where are we going?'

'My bedchamber.'

'Really?' Tatum perked up at that.

She suppressed a smile. 'Not for anything untoward. I am showing you something.'

'We can always move on to the untoward *after* you show me.'

Charlotte had refused to go back into her bedchamber. There were too many bad memories living in there. No one had questioned why when she had announced that she was moving to the larger rooms beside her father's. She was queen, after all.

When they arrived at her quarters, he entered first and glanced around. 'What am I looking at?'

'Behind the cupboard,' she told him.

He walked over to it. 'Behind?'

She nodded.

Tatum crouched and felt around, eventually pulling out a painting. He stared at it as he rose, then stilled.

'You told me to paint the future I wanted, so I did.'

Tatum went and sat down on the bed, staring at it. 'It's…' He looked up. 'You painted this from your mind?'

She shrugged. 'The vision was so clear.'

He pointed at it. 'Is that a mini-Blackmane in the distance?'

'All the defenders are there if you look closely. Plus Tolly and Ita. Your family is my family.'

He ran a finger over the detailed Sir Miles, then her, reaching back for him. 'The grass is long.'

'From all the sunshine.'

He nodded slowly. 'You're missing your crown.'

Her lips turned up. 'I can add it later when I add my father. I have been waiting to see if this new father-daughter dynamic holds up before putting the effort in.'

Tatum laughed. 'He's definitely trying.'

'He really is.' She pointed to a spot beside the mini-Isabel, who was playfully throwing her young son in the air. 'He will fit there.' She traced her finger down the empty space between the skirt of her dress and his legs. 'And that is where our children will go.'

He looked up, his eyes full of tenderness. 'Will all sixteen children fit in that small space?'

She laughed once, then wrapped her arms around him, whispering, 'I will make them fit.'

He got to his feet and pulled her into one of his famous embraces, the ones that made her feel like she stood no chance of escaping. The ones that made her forget there was ever a time when she was not safe.

Tatum broke away suddenly and returned to the cupboard.

'What are you doing?' she asked.

He crouched, reaching behind the cupboard again and feeling around. 'Aha.'

'Brock—'

'I knew it!'

Sir Miles trotted over to investigate the source of his excitement, sniffing around as Tatum dragged another painting from behind the cupboard and held it in the air triumphantly. 'I knew you kept it!'

He had found the portrait he had painted of her.

'Up on the wall it goes!' he said, heading for the door.

She tried to snatch it from his hands, but he pivoted around her with ease.

'It is not leaving this room!'

Sir Miles began to bark, bounding excitedly in all directions and almost tripping her in the process. Tatum made it out into the corridor, jogging backwards while holding it just out of reach of his pursuer.

'I am the queen!' she laughed, holding on to her crown. 'Hand it over at once!'

He jogged faster. 'Not *my* queen. I'm Chadorian, remember?'

She gave up, slowing to a walk and letting Sir Miles chase him instead.

'Down!' Tatum told the overexcited dog. Then to Charlotte, 'Recall your dog!'

She shook her head, laughing harder. 'Not until you give me that painting.'

Another vision of her future. Messy and chaotic, with blissful moments of reprieve—and more love than she could have ever imagined.

Charlotte picked up speed again. 'Get him, Sir Miles!'

ACKNOWLEDGMENTS

I would like to express my gratitude to the many people who contributed to this book. My biggest thanks goes to my readers. Without you guys, I wouldn't get to do what I love. Next, a huge thank you to my hubby who supports and encourages me even though my writing takes time away from the family. I love you to bits. A big thank you to McKinley, Kristin and the team at Hot Tree Editing for polishing the manuscript into something beautiful. A shout out to my proofreader, Rebecca, for catching everything I missed. A round of applause for Stuart Bache Design for yet another stunning cover. And finally, a huge thank you to my Launch Team for your encouragement, honest reviews, and being the final set of eyes on my work. You guys are amazing.